The Shining Tides

The Shining Tides

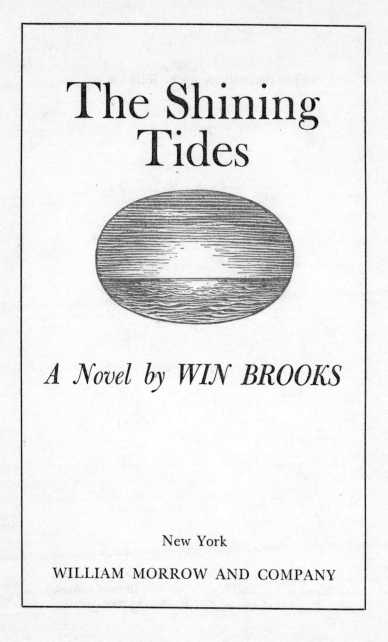

A Novel by WIN BROOKS

New York

WILLIAM MORROW AND COMPANY

The decorations are by John De Pol

This book is for KATH

May

FATHER O'MEARA tasted the day and the day tasted good. Overnight the chill of a tardy spring had vanished from the air and some of it had gone from his old bones. The sweet smell of the river rode a warmth of golden haze, filtered through it, and merged with the pungency of fresh paint.

At his boat station on the estuary Tom Salter lettered a board sign under the priest's critical gaze, using the same white paint which was bright on a score of upturned skiffs and square-stern dories hauled above tide mark beyond an oil drum of rainwater ready for the testing of outboard motors. Salter bent to the job at hand, his girth a distressing handicap, and he breathed heavily.

"I recommend a two weeks' fast for you, Thomas," said the priest.

Salter grunted. He was a short, ruddy man, still powerful despite his years and lack of wind. "I'd survive it," he admitted. "Still I prefer what I have to your lack of it. If you miss a meal you'll throw no shadow. Say the word and I'll recruit a new cook for the rectory."

1

"Rosie will do for the likes of me," said Father O'Meara. This was a theme of which they never tired. The priest's blue eyes twinkled behind steel-rimmed spectacles and his generous ears bobbed, lifting tufts of cottony hair against the black rim of his hat.

Salter smeared a final *T* and a cramped line read:

FREE BOATS AND BAIT

He stood back to appraise his handiwork, brush dripping paint on his turned-down hip boots, and Father O'Meara said, "You made the mistake of starting off too big, Thomas. You end up squeezed and small compared with the beginning. One of life's more common errors."

"There's no error," said the boatman. "I made the *free* big a'purpose. It's got to be the most important word in our language—free this, free that, something-for-nothing."

The priest's laugh was deep and pleasant. Their gaze turned in unison from sign to river, across to the far shore and out to the bay beyond the dunes at the river's mouth. Tide, setting against current, kicked up little ridges of white water. Salter lifted his big nose, like a dog testing the breeze, and sniffed deeply. The priest, leaning heavily on his right foot to ease an arthritic twinge in his left knee, watched him keenly.

"You smell striped bass, Thomas?"

"Nope. Bass are late. Everything's backward. I'm just getting pie rhubarb and there's no asparagus ready." He said this with joyous malice for he well knew a weakness of his old friend.

Father O'Meara knew he was being baited, but he could not prevent his saliva from starting and in spite of himself he said, "I remember Mrs. Salter makes a rhubarb pie with brown sugar."

2

"She does. How else you going to make a rhubarb pie?" Salter glared.

Father O'Meara didn't know. "Rosie makes no pies."

"You don't have to hint. May was going to make one up for you."

"That's kind of her. She'll remember I like it juicy. Thomas, do you ever have cold rhubarb sauce with cream?"

"Can't say's I care for it."

"Some do, some don't. I like it but Rosie can't seem to get the knack of a good rhubarb sauce."

"May'll make you up a batch. Good for what ails you. Might improve your casting."

The priest ignored it and observed, "You're forgetting the important lines for the sign."

"I ain't forgetting; I'm resting up." Salter's heel kicked a hole in the sand and into this he squirted a stream of tobacco juice without splashing the rim.

"You'll not be forgiven if someone slips in there and drowns," said Father O'Meara.

Salter resumed work with the brush and presently the sign read:

FREE BOATS AND BAIT

TILL FIRST STRIPER

IS CAUGHT

They carried the sign to the bait shack and propped it against the wall facing the highway.

"Now the dollar trap is baited," said the priest.

"It will not catch as much as your own."

"Mine is for the work of God and yours is for the stomach of Tom Salter. Some day"—the priest smiled—"I'll catch you as you caught me." He was an avid striped-

3

bass fisherman but not a lucky one, and Salter often expressed to him the hope that he caught more souls than bass. The boatman was not of his faith nor of any religion, holding to an opinion, which he kept to himself in deference to their friendship, that men fishing were as well off as men in churches.

"I made a new surf rod this winter," said the priest. "This year I intend to do more plug casting than bait fishing."

"By all means do that. It will help conserve the bass."

"That's an opinion influenced by your profit on the sale of sea worms."

Salter snorted. "Think what you like, Father, but I've lived on this bay and river sixty-three years without ever sighting a school of plugs being chased by the bass."

"Nevertheless, plugs take the big fish and a plug will last a season while three dozen of your worms, at the same cost, will do but a trip or two."

"You might take up a special collection for bait money."

"I doubt the Archbishop would approve. But that reminds me. Soon the fishermen will be pouring in on Sunday mornings, intent on only one thing and forgetful of the most important. A small sign for the church, alongside your big one for Tom Salter, would be a good turn for God."

"I'm suspicious of it," said Salter. "What kind of sign?"

"Oh, I'll work out the wording. Something like 'Don't miss mass. St. Peter's is just up the road.' Or it could be 'No fishing until you've been to mass.' Something of that nature."

"I don't like it. First you accuse me of being in competition with the Roman Catholic Church and now you'll have me aiding my competitor."

4

"A small sign," prodded Father O'Meara. "One just big enough to ease your conscience as a tempter."

"My conscience is clear, Father. But I'll hang a sign for you."

The priest's laughter startled a gull from the flat. "Thank you, Thomas. Seriously, the parish is in fine shape and we need no come-on for the mass. With the anglers and vacationists coming along, we'll be adding two masses next month. I like to think we may build a schoolhouse soon."

"Build one for young bass fishermen," said Salter.

"It's not a bad idea, though I hold some things to be more important than the how and when and where of taking stripers. . . . How big was that world's record bass, Thomas?"

"You know as well as me. Seventy-three pounds for rod and reel. Two that weighed one hundred twenty-five each in the Carolina nets."

"Perhaps I should get a net. Anyway, I should get along. Rosie will have lunch ready and I'm dreading it. Any news I should know?"

"Manuel Riba is hitting the bottle pretty hard. He's one of yours. Whit Sears was by yesterday on his way to the movies and I doubt he's with us long—his mind is going fast. There's a family moving into that new house up the river beyond Whit's place. Somebody said a professor and his daughter. They might be of your church."

They walked the river edge toward a wooded point where there was a path, worn long years ago by the feet of the fishing priest, leading to the rear door of the rectory. Off the big rock near midstream a school of alewives slapped the surface and Tom Salter sniffed again. All along Cape Cod and as distant as New Jersey and Maine

5

he was known as a remarkable sniffer and an honest man, who, when he said he smelled stripers working up the river, really smelled them.

"With God," said Father O'Meara, moving into the path. He turned to call, "I'm not so fussy about the brown sugar, Thomas."

"Okay, okay, I won't forget the pie."

The priest called again, "I've a hunch, Thomas. A big fish this year—a record fish caught in the river."

Salter didn't answer. He'd dreamed that most of his life and more than once he'd seen the fish. But no one ever caught it.

In the Tavern of the Sun, a restaurant and bar on the main highway of Bournham, adjoining Buzzards Bay village and Wareham, Manuel Riba pushed a dime into the juke box and made two selections at random. He moved to the lunch counter and took a stool in front of the coffee urn so that Maggie Blynn, to serve him, must lean over and partially expose her breasts. Maggie knew why he chose the seat.

They were alone in the place. It was ten-thirty in the morning, an hour at which he liked to come because there was seldom any other customer.

"Where's the big boy?" asked Manuel.

He referred to Nick Constantos, the proprietor. He correctly suspected an intimate relationship between the Greek and his waitress because this was a channel through which his thoughts constantly coursed. The conclusion he derived from his suspicion excited him.

6

"Gone to the bay," said Maggie. "What you having? You eating this early?"

"No," said Manuel. "A whisky and a beer."

She poured whisky and opened a bottle of beer, and his eyes fell on the cut of her blouse as she placed them before him. The noise of the juke box, playing a rhumba, was a background for his thoughts. He downed the whisky.

"You busy tonight, maybe?"

"Sure," she said. She was a well-built blonde, inclined to weight, with good legs. "I'm busy every night, Double-It-Up."

"Don't call me that," he said.

"Okay, baby." She rolled the phrase suggestively and rested the weight of her breasts on the edge of the counter beyond the urn.

His gaze there, he said, "One night you not be busy, maybe."

"Could be," she teased. "You just keep trying. Where you been?"

"Hauled two dozen lobster pots, raked two bushels of quahogs. Did my breakfast dishes."

"My, what a busy little man."

"Good little man." He grinned. He had strong, small, even teeth; he himself was small and strong, thin and wiry despite his alcoholic excesses. "By'n by you know."

"You think so?"

"Sure."

"Pretty sure of yourself, ain't you?"

He grinned and drank another whisky and his beer, his pulse quickening because she showed no resentment over doubletalk she understood. She recognized the symptom and warned, "Take it easy, Double-It-Up."

7

In Bournham and Wareham and all of Bourne, Manuel Riba was known as Double-It-Up Riba, because it was impossible for him to describe any scene or event without exaggerating the details at least twofold, and this characteristic applied to all the commonplaces of his life. Thus, if he said he had raked two bushels of quahogs on a tide, folks knew he had raked only one, or less. If he caught a four-pound tautog it became an eight-pounder and its capture, in the telling, a magnificent achievement. If he told of sighting a flight of thirty-two geese his acquaintances discounted the number by half or suspected a tale out of whole cloth. Some referred to him as a natural-born liar, which was an error, because the twist in his mental processes was not present through inheritance. It had a simple explanation in psychology, born in shame and nurtured by pride during the hungry years of his youth. This was the way of it:

When he was nine, a skinny, olive-hued kid in the fourth grade of Bournham Elementary School, he had as teacher a woman who was also a dietitian, interested in the relation of diet to aptitude and curious as to what foods low in vitamins or calories were contributing factors to scholastic deficiencies. Each member of her class was required to stand and report at morning session the substance of his preceding supper and breakfast while the teacher made notes for later comparison against the quarterly standings of the individual.

Manuel, who lived with his mother in a shack on the river road, was a small eater because there was never much to eat. His supper was often a slice or two of bread without any spread, and his breakfast, more often than not, another slice of bread with, on occasion, a banana. His mother was a quahog mucker who squatted on her

8

broad bottom in the river shallows and explored the mud with stubby fingers for the hard-shell clams. The quahogs she sold, sometimes for more than would buy a fifth of rum, which was her minimum daily requirement. Her purchases for the sustenance of her only child were few and far between. Her husband, or so she called him, had left for parts unknown soon after Manuel's birth, pursued by an empty bottle.

Though he was continually hungry, Manuel had no idea his meals were anything less than normal until in his fourth school year he listened to the reports of his classmates and himself was required to relate the morsels of his meager diet. Then a sense of inferiority came into being swiftly, and with it the defense mechanism of exaggeration was established. Because what he really ate was so pitifully little compared to the meals of his classmates, he embellished the truth with imaginary dishes he came to know only by hearsay. Twice only, in the beginning, he told the truth; it had to do with bread, a banana, and a box of four peanut-butter crackers his mother bought him for a treat by way of smothering a conscience which had roused from long slumber during a forty-eight-hour period of sobriety induced by a heart spasm. Thereafter, in a manner so challengingly vehement that everyone knew he lied, he reported meals at least on a par with those of his classmates. He would tell of eating two eggs and drinking two glasses of milk for breakfast. He had had few eggs and no milk since that of his mother's breast. He would tell of orange juice, which he never had known, and of steak, which he would not have recognized if it had been placed before him, and of desserts he knew only because the other children named them.

His teacher, with good intention and bad result, not

9

understanding the reason for defensive untruth, took open note of this switch from an actual to an imaginary diet and chided him for exaggeration while expressing sympathy for him. So a fierce resentment was born and firmly established. Over the years it grew stronger, extending itself to all his thought processes, lodged deep in the core of his brain.

It never occurred to him, though he dimly recognized some fault in his parent, that any blame for his own misfortunes should be laid to her; and when she died, while he was in the eighth grade, already known for four years' as Double-It-Up, he borrowed money from Father O'Meara and buried her decently though the church would have done it as well or better without cost. He left school to work at such odd jobs as would turn a dollar, and thereafter ate better and lied better. Occasionally he went to mass, but resentment against society and religion was stout within him, and as he matured he became one of Father O'Meara's real problem children and eventually a challenge to the priest's own peace of mind. . . .

On this day of May, Manuel Riba was a well-nourished youth of twenty-four, darkly handsome, with black eyes that sparkled at the sight of good food, a pretty girl, a bottle or a school of fish. He owned a sea sled with an outboard for the shallow waters; he quahogged and clammed and lobstered in the spring and summer and went scallop-dragging during the fall and early winter. He still occupied the river shack, living alone except for the occasions when he enticed a girl of his fancy to share his bed. These were not seldom, but they lasted only a few days because his ardor was of a transitory nature which precluded any permanent relationship.

His present interest was concentrated on Maggie Blynn,

10

who had followed the troops to the vicinity of Camp Edwards during World War II and remained to work for and sleep with Constantos, an arrangement of mutual satisfaction. On the occasions of Manuel's intemperance, which were many and increasing despite the diligence of Father O'Meara, this interest was accentuated.

Maggie had been aware of it for some time and was amused by it as well as, against her better judgment, responsive to it and to his soft-voiced boasting of romantic conquests. Because of his reputation, she discounted Manuel's claims but was not opposed to the development of an affair if it could be accomplished without arousing the suspicions of Constantos, a naturally suspicious man given to outbursts and violences.

Manuel finished another beer and put another dime in the juke box. He could not distinguish tunes, but the rhythm of music set a tempo for his pulses. He returned to the counter and took the seat next away from the urn, and was debating the wisdom of making a pass across it when the door opened and Constantos stood in its frame, big shoulders touching it, carrying a carton of supplies. Nick let the door slam behind him and carried the carton behind the counter.

"Ho!" he exclaimed. "Look who this is here! Little Double-It-Up!"

Manuel said nothing, sipping beer.

"What you been doing, Double-It-Up?" Manuel's sullen glance met Nick's bold eye. Nick, more than any other, taunted him for exaggeration. "Dredging thirty ton of scallops, maybe? Catching all the fish in the bay? No more fish left; all gone! Drinking five bars dry? Sleeping with two dozen girls? I bet! Some fun!"

Manuel wet his lips, wanting another whisky.

11

"Soon the stripers be in," Nick taunted. He was a bass fisherman, too. "Soon you catch the biggest striper in all the world, maybe one hundred pounds! Maybe more! Only trouble, nobody ever see him excep' you!"

Manuel felt the need but anger choked him so he couldn't order.

"You, Maggie," roared Nick, "you be careful that little man. He's big champion. He's got double everything, you hear him tell it."

Maggie giggled and Nick carried his carton out back, rumbling with laughter at his joke.

"Maybe some night, soon, huh?" Manuel whispered.

"Maybe," said Maggie. It was a responsive answer, not entirely freeing her imagination of a grotesque picture Nick's suggestion had conjured up in her mind.

SUN AND a wafer edge of dissolving moon rose a few minutes apart. From a late roost in a scrub oak on Blake Point, Nycti the Quawk, the black-crowned night heron, resented them hoarsely.

Roccus, a great striped bass, swinging a four-fathom curve and following a tide press, passed south of Centerboard Shoal and turned north. From deeper water she moved into nine feet off Bird Island. Spiny and soft-dorsal fins slashed a V-ream in the stipple made by the breeze. Against a submerged granite boulder cored with magnetite, lightning-split from the ledge five hundred years before, she came to rest, tail and pectorals fanning gently, at a meeting of tide and currents.

More than a quarter-century had passed since Roccus

12

first rested beside this boulder during her original migration as a three-year-old in the company of a hungry thousand of her age and sex. To it she annually returned, sometimes with small pods of big fish, more recently as a solitary, in late May or June, when the spawning season of Roccus saxatilis was ended and the eggs were spilled in the milt-chalked Roanoke above Albemarle Sound or, on occasion, in the region of Chesapeake Bay.

This resting place off the southern coast of Massachusetts was her domain until October's northeasters sent her coursing southward. The boulder lie she had found good, and she returned to it as the experienced traveler returns time and again to tavern or hotel where he has found comfort and safety and food to his taste.

This year Roccus was making her earliest journey. For the sixth spring since she had attained a length of sixteen inches, no urge within her belly set her coursing up the Roanoke or the Chesapeake feeders, past the thin tides to the gravel bars where, in other ecstatic Mays, she had reproduced. Instead, on a spangled night when the moon had waned, a counterurge had drawn her into the open Atlantic; and, passing migrating schoolfish too young to spawn, she had turned north and east along a thoroughfare as plainly marked for striped bass by current and tide and pressure, by food and temperature, by the instinct to avoid danger, as any broad, paved highway is posted for the guidance of man. The migrating shoals of small stripers, or rockfish, or rock, had remained in the Barnegat surf when Roccus passed between Sakonnet and Cuttyhunk into Buzzards Bay and into the tides of the Narrow Land where Maushop, giant of Cape Cod legend, still blew the smoke of his pipe down a southwest wind to make the fog.

13

Now the thirty-six-foot beacon on Bird Island caught the first rays of sun, and splintered the dazzling light of new day. The moon paled and Mars and Venus and Jupiter were snuffed out in a sky of azure. Gong buoy 9, better than a mile to the south, winked green at five-second intervals. East, against the sun, the old Wings Neck Light lost color. Roccus grooved her lie. She had come alone, too early, to a latitude of disquiet, troubled strangely, strangely drawn, and here in the merging, changing weights of waters familiar to the nerve ends along her laterals—in the surge of the sucking, thickening tide—she held her place while the light of the dying May moon transfused the direct stream of brilliance of which it was only a reflection.

In an overhang of the same boulder, behind a curtain of rockweed and moss and bladder wrack, on a scour of sand ground from granite by the tides of thousands of years, Homarus the lobster lay partially embedded and concealed, expelling water through twenty pairs of gills, her stalked, compound eyes fixed on the fringe of weed shielding her cave. Her two pairs of antennae rippled with the flow of the weed in the sun's first strike.

Homarus weighed nineteen pounds and was nearly as old as Roccus. Since her final molt as a free-swimming surface larva she had shed shell, esophagus, stomach and intestine seventeen times as her body became too large for the armor encasing it. During her years she had carried more than a million eggs glued to the flexed pocket of her abdomen. She was almost uniformly black with tinges of green at her knuckles and streaks of chitin at the edge of her back shell. She was a cannibal and a glutton, vicious and ugly. In her youth she had made an annual crawl to deep water. During recent years she had strayed little

14

from Bird Island ledge. For her, as for Roccus, the boulder was a familiar lie, the lobster in the hole made by tide scour through the overhang, the bass above the overhang near the holdfast of the weed. Homarus was secure in her knowledge that anything small enough to enter the cavern was prey for her appetite. The aperture was too small for the green snout and jaws of the bass.

Each was aware of the other for hours.

Tide ebbed its extreme. In changing pressure, in degrees of salinity, in varying temperatures, there was conveyed to Roccus the memory of many feeding grounds. Around the boulder's westerly side in slow pouring came drained warmth from shallows over lutaceous bottoms, a peculiar freshness tasting of algae, alewives, larvae and shellfish. This current was the confluence of drainage from Sippican Harbor, the Weweantic and Wareham Rivers, from Beaverdam Creek, Agawam River and Hammett Cove and a score of lesser waters into which anadromous fishes made their way. Around the boulder's easterly side swept an icy current from Cape Cod Bay which plunged with the west-flowing current through Cape Cod Canal. This was underlay for a streak of warmer, less saline water which, on the flood, covered Big Bay and Buttermilk Flats and the Onset mud banks and had been freshened slightly by Red Brook's discharge.

The separate currents ran and slowed, stirred and stilled, and there was a semblance of complete slack, a hushed suspension of motion.

Roccus turned outward from the boulder, and the broad fan of her tail made a roil of water and sand which parted the weed curtain of the overhang and caused Homarus to back deeper into her lodge, waving antennae in anger and snapping her crusher claw. Roccus resumed her lie.

15

The still of the sea was only an illusion; there was no dead calm. End of one tide was but the beginning of a new, and birth of the new tide aroused activity in the sea. Life about the ledge responded. Clams extended their siphons, clearing holes. Crabs settled carapaces deeper. Scallops thrust upward, dropped back like leaves falling through dead air. Sea robins changed lairs, crawling on the first three rays of their pectoral fins, and sculpins settled in the weed on the rocks, awaiting questing green crabs. Soft-finned rock cod moved lazily through caverns; and from countless hiding places the sharp-toothed cunners emerged in schools, nibbling at barnacles and the sand tubes of annelids. The cunners were the bait-stealing curse of bottom fishermen.

New tide awakened hunger in the lobster. Before Roccus' arrival Homarus had dined on a two-pound male of her own kind. Later she had killed a flounder which, by treading her legs, she had buried beneath her as a dog buries a bone for future reference.

Tide also awakened hunger in Roccus. She made a three-quarter leaping turn, a sprung bow of steel, and her tail drove into the overhang. Homarus, nearly dislodged, backed farther into her cave, gripping deeper. The disturbance of Roccus' thrust caused a surface commotion which excited seven herring gulls.

As the tide turned, Anguilla the eel swam to the ledge, surfaced, sucking larvae of a kind she had not tasted for seven years. Anguilla was a thirty-two-inch ripple of macrurous grace, blue-black but showing yellowish-white on her underside in a transformation which would make her a silver eel returned from fresh water to the sea for completion of her catadromous life. She carried within her ovaries, moving down from fresh water, more than

16

ten million eggs which would ripen swiftly when she reached the Sargasso deep. The urge to procreate swept her more relentlessly than any current.

As Anguilla approached Roccus' lie and Homarus' lodge, she deflated her air bladder and sank close to the bottom, moving with slow undulation like a weed torn from anchorage. At the base of the boulder she came to rest, arrowed head near the weed curtain, a third of her elongate body curled beneath her.

Homarus tasted oil from the eel. She withdrew her legs from the sand and buoyed her body and waved her antennae in excitement. She was fond of eels. Stealthily she extended her sharp cutter claw along the sand into the weed fringe.

Roccus saw the eel in the cone of vision of her goldrimmed black left eye. She also tasted the eel's oil.

Anguilla moved an inch nearer the hole, though appearing not to move. Behind the weed Homarus moved an inch nearer Anguilla. Roccus saw the lobster's claw.

Though her superior nostrils sensed danger, Anguilla had no experience with lobsters or striped bass. She moved another inch, questing, tasting, testing. Her head, weaving, swung between the open jaws of Homarus' cutting claw, which snapped like a trap. The cutter slashed embedded linear scales, flesh and bone, its blades meeting between the severed head and body of the eel.

As Anguilla's body reacted in a hoop, Roccus made a violent tail smash against the weed curtain, and the compression dislodged the lobster, overturning her outside the hole. Before Homarus could right herself, Roccus overleaped and bit through her tail, crushing shell and flesh between double-toothed tongue and vomer plate.

In the strengthening of tide, Roccus lay content. She

17

had eaten the tail of Homarus and all of Anguilla. The claws and body of Homarus bumped along the bottom in the quickening pulse of the sea, all but concealed by a cloud of cunners, some already inside the body.

Three days later her body shell, first crimsoned, then paled pink by the sun, was found on Indian Neck by a boy who showed it at home to the amazement of his parents. They had never seen one so large. The boy saved it a few days, but it grew rank and his mother made him bury it in their garden where, in August, it fed a clump of coral phlox envied by all their neighbors.

OUT OF the southern sky, against the afterglow of sun when flashes of the Wings Neck Light grew bolder, a wedge of birds came driving beneath the first sprinkling of stars. They flew in wavering formation, eighteen on the right flank, twenty on the left: Canada geese seeking rest. They were in flight from Texas to Crane Lake in Saskatchewan and since daybreak they had been on the wing. Cutting across Cape Cod, they flew at two thousand feet with a following breeze. As they passed over Bird Island the gander leader sighted the distant sheen of Big Bay and Little Bay, Buttermilk and Great Herring, and the mirrored, shadowed surfaces of Sandy and Long Pond and Gallows and Bloody and Boot, and a score of others. He honked and towered, circling, climbing. Then all the flock began to honk and gabble, their voices like those of beagles chasing rabbits among the constellations.

Nine miles away, coursing a meadow where quail had roaded, a dog fox heard the geese and cocked mangy ears. Saliva drooled from his mouth because once he had tasted gosling in the yard of a farmer. Fear rose in his heart because he had met ganders, to his sorrow. He stood silent, listening, pretending not to listen.

The geese reached peak of tower and the old bird made his choice, which was Little Bay where the eelgrass was thick. Honking ceased, the wedge drove north in silence, losing altitude. The fox did not hear the geese again and was relieved that his appetite would not place a strain upon his fortitude. He wet where the quail had been and went off to hunt a mole.

Until the tide turned, Roccus occupied her boulder lie, at times suspended in the current, at times on the scour outside the empty lodge of Homarus.

Saturn was the evening star. The moon had crossed the meridian with the sun and was invisible from earth; it was dark o' the moon. When the blanket of stars lay close and heavy on the water, shimmering and opalescent, Roccus broke through it with a roll and tail-slap and fell back on her side. The stars scattered, danced, reformed in wavering pattern. The bass slashed the surface, sinuating on her right side, then on her left, leaped half clear. Three yellowish-brown sea lice fell from her shoulder and were promptly devoured by a cunner which an hour later was eaten by a crab which, before morning, was swallowed by a master sculpin.

Nycti the Quawk, belly yearning, flapped from the filth of his roost for a night of hunting in Planting Island Cove. His flight voice was harsh: *quuaawwk, quuaawwk!* Roccus leaped once more in the brief sustention of the tide.

In the kitchen of his barn-red house above Menemsha Creek on the island of Marthas Vineyard, Cal Knight wound nylon thread at the base of a chrome tip on a new boat rod of his own making while his mother, glancing up from her knitting, watched him with a quizzical smile. She had watched his father make similar preparations for the fishing seasons of thirty years.

"The bass will be late this year," she said.

"Seems so. Though there are migrating school fish in the Niantic, they say. They'll be along."

"You plan to base at Onset again?"

"I have the river at Bournham in mind for the early fishing. It's handy for the parties who come from Boston and New York by train. There'll be a half-dozen charter boats in there this summer, I expect. Come late August, I'll likely go swordfishing."

"Unless you run across a record bass." She smiled.

He glanced up from his winding. "I saw a fish last fall that would knock that world's record into a cocked hat."

"So you've said. I heard your father say it more than once. But he never caught it."

She thought, watching him, how much he was like his father—in size; in bold, strong features; in the thick, sandy hair which resented brush and comb; in the deep-set eyes, which were as dark blue and clear as the waters of the bight. War had worked a mystery of changes in him but he remained, in ways other than physical resemblance, the spit and image of Templeton Knight, best bass fisherman and surest swordfish striker in the island fleet.

20

It wasn't true, Mary Knight knew, that a son is always more strongly attracted to his mother. Temp Knight had been a god to his son, really worshiped by a boy who saw in him a better man, by every measure, than any other who walked the earth. Temp Knight had, in fact, been a man who never compromised his self-respect, which is perhaps as true a yardstick as another to measure any man's stature. The self-reliance and boldness and confidence and strength, moral and physical, which he had willed his son had stood Cal Knight well during three years of war, but he had needed them more when, returning from the Pacific, he learned his father had been dead for nearly a year.

Temp Knight had lost his life and his swordfishing vessel off No Mans Land in an October gale while attempting the rescue of a Navy pilot, who had made a forced landing in the restricted area at the edge of Southwest Shoal. Mary Knight had erred in the belief their son should not be notified. There had been a long, tense silence in the house when Cal, arriving unexpectedly, had found it bereft of the parent who had taught him the ways of the sea and showed him the road a man should take ashore. He had kissed his mother and vanished for a week. He was still drunk but the battle was nearly won when he returned.

"I'm sorry and ashamed," he told her. "We'll go along as if he was still here."

And sometimes now, he was so much his father's image, it seemed Temp Knight *was* still there. Cal had scalloped the autumn of his return and during the winter he built lobster traps; but when spring arrived he sold the pots, flew to Nova Scotia and bought a thirty-six-foot Shag Harbor hull still on the ways. In this he installed twin engines and rigged a water-line exhaust. He brought her down alone from the province to the island, a barrel of gas lashed on deck. At one of the island yards he had rigged her for charter: striped bass, tuna, marlin and swords, with outriggers and a fighting chair that was easily removed to make deck space. During the summer, which brought a heavy run of big bass into the Cape area and a heavier run of anglers from many sections of the East, the boat quickly paid for itself. Parties were plentiful and the price of bass was high. Boat fishing was no longer permitted in Cape Cod Canal but there were new waters to be explored. This summer he would have young Bobby Meade along as mate.

As if he had been able to read her thoughts, she asked, "You're sure Bobby will make out all right? He seems so young."

"He's handy," Cal said. "Good head on him. I'll look after him."

He finished the winding, varnished it and carried the rod to the shed workshop. Returning, he said, "Got something to show you." He held a plug the size of a young straight-necked summer squash and of similar shape. It was painted pale blue with streaks of silver and it was equipped with a soft steel diving plane at its thicker end.

His mother smiled, inspecting it. "It looks like the great-granddaddy of plugs," she said. "It's terribly heavy, isn't it?"

"It's teak. I'm going to rig it with 8/0 hooks. Those concaves, carved in diagonal opposition, roll it and dive it at the same time."

"You really think that will take fish, Cal?"

"I think it may take big bass and school tuna. It was an idea Dad had before the war. We never got around to

22

making one up. I tried this one in the creek this morning and the action is terrific. The gangs of hooks may hurt it some but not much. And it will cast a mile and a half."

"You sound like that character on the mainland you were describing last summer—the one who exaggerates so much. What was his name?"

Cal grinned. "Double-It-Up Riba. Well, anyway, I can get it out nearly a hundred yards without trying."

The wall phone rang—a long, two shorts, two longs. He answered and said, "This is Knight. . . . Okay, put him on. . . . Hello, hello, Mr. Fearing. . . . No, not yet, sir. It's a little early and spring is late. I figure we'll have schoolfish in Buzzards Bay in a week's time but few large fish for two or three weeks yet. . . . Sure, we're all getting restless. I'll have *Carey's Chicken* at the river next week and I'll wire you as soon as the fish are in. . . . No, I wouldn't care to do that because I have some other bookings already. But you'll have first choice. . . . Right—I'll let you know."

He hung up and said, "Byron Fearing from New York. One of my best parties last year. Wanted to take a full four-weeks' charter at $270 a week."

"And you said no?"

"Tie me up too much."

She touched his cheek. "Wouldn't give you time enough for your own fishing, you mean."

"Maybe that's it." He grinned.

23

THE NIGHT was articulate with a breeze scuffing the tide and with the distant horn on Cleveland East Ledge and with the high murmuring of wings telling the ancient mystery of migration. Against the stars ducks were on the move, and curlews and sandpipers and purple finches.

Roccus leaped for the sheer joy of leaping, driving upward through two fathoms, cleaving the surface in an arc of silver above a swirl of phosphorescence, falling back on one side, then on the other, then making an overleap in a dive that carried her to the bottom where shadows fled. Wind pricked the bubbles her leaping had made and the phosphorescence, like a shower of sparks from a burning pine tree, trailed and vanished. Her third leap, which was eighty yards from her first, disturbed a goosefish that had risen from the ooze in search of a carelessly napping gull.

The great bass moved in four fathoms past the straining cable of the bell buoy on the western limit of the general anchorage outside Cleveland Ledge Channel on the approach to Cape Cod Canal. Kelp and sea lettuce and rockweed streamed from the cable and a thong of fucoid weed, rising twenty feet from a top-shaped holdfast on the buoy's anchor, swayed and undulated like a cobra risen from a pit to the music of a flute. Roccus brushed the thallus with her shoulder and in water of five fathoms swam beneath a starless overhead—the bottom of a barge anchored with a tug to await the tide serving east before negotiating the canal. Here the water was more saline, thick and uncomfortably cold, numbing the nerve ends along her laterals, and she expelled at a slower rate. In a moment she quickened and rose to a warmer layer, turning southeast with a slant that carried her past Nun buoy 10 on the corner of Southwest Ledge.

Here a school of shrimps newly risen from the mud worked toward Red Brook Harbor, covering a square half-acre like a close-textured carpeting. The shrimps swam with quick jerks of five-fanned tails. Roccus drove along the edge of the school and turned into it, scooping shrimps like a power shovel moving through gravel. Her belly swelled, and when she was surfeited she sank to an old lie by the orange-rusted, barnacle-crusted wreck of a fishing dragger twenty years dead. The splintered hull rested on its side and Roccus lodged beneath the keel. She slept, though her eyes had sight; she expelled slowly, relaxing.

In the moon's absence the darkness pressed close upon the water; the darkness and water were one. North a mile, the fifty-nine-foot beacon on Wings Neck flashed its green warning every six seconds. It was the brightest light in the smother of the night, and it was sighted at a distance of eighteen miles by a golden plover.

The plover had taken wing from the hump of Brazil with two hundred of its kind making a one-hop flight to Nova Scotia on their way to Labrador nesting. Far off the New Jersey coast it had become separated from the flock because of a wing weakened by an old shotgun pellet, and in the evening, becoming confused, it had turned shoreward, seeking rest. The light meant land and the land meant rest; but as it approached the light and the stab of flame grew brighter, the unvarying, hypnotic intermittence drew the bird irresistibly.

As it passed over the waters of the ledge where Roccus rested, the plover tried to swerve from its course, to turn

25

away from the eye of the light and check its dizzy speed. It could do neither. On the ninth green blaze after this passing, its beauty was shattered on the screen of the light and it fell to the rocks, where, within a half-hour, a rat frightened a green crab away from it.

AT DAWN Whitcomb Sears heard the first purple finch of spring, his seventy-fourth. Mr. Sears was spry for his years. He had been born in this house on a knoll overlooking the narrows above the river estuary and he had never been very far from it, nor ever wanted to be. He had married a much younger woman. She and a daughter were part of a past hazy in neighborhood memory. They had, some recalled, vanished together from his life—run away, the story had it. It had been a morsel of lively gossip at the time but over the years it had lost its flavor and few now alluded to it. He had no intimates and those who had known him long suspected that even Mr. Sears had forgotten what had happened. His mind wasn't what it used to be.

This morning, after hearing the finch, he arose, emptied his thundermug out the back door, dressed leisurely and made a sufficient breakfast of a dish of cold cereal and a glass of milk. Then he walked halfway down a path which pitched to the shore at the neck of the narrows. He passed his outhouse, which, having been blown over during the hurricane of 1938, still reposed on its side, half-covered by weed growth. He gazed down-river toward the curve of land hiding Buzzards Bay. His eyes were rheumy but his sight held fair. He could make out the twin spires of the railroad bridge over the canal. He saw a shellduck tacking upwind across the river and followed its flight toward the salt-rusted cedars along the shore.

"Going to be a pretty day," said Mr. Sears. He addressed himself in absence of another. Conversation with himself he found completely satisfactory. He had even disciplined himself not to pay any attention to himself unless he made an important observation. Thus his own talk never bored him. "A pretty day," he repeated aloud. This was an unimportant subject so he ignored his own comment.

His paintless skiff lay upturned above high water under a blanket of salt hay held in place by boards. His eye fell on it and he said, "Got to give you a coat of paint this year."

He had been saying this for many years, but he had not painted the boat and he would never do it again. Yet the topic of the skiff was interesting and he said now, "Why should I paint you when paint is dear?"

When the skiff made no answer he turned his gaze to the oily, quickening rush of water in the narrows. He watched intently, seeking a splash or telltale dimpling of feeding bass. Sighting none he turned back up the path.

"Bass'll be late this year," he said. He had fished the river as a boy with his father, coiling tarred cod line on the steep shelf of beach and hurling a drail into the current, hauling it in swiftly, hand over hand. He had watched his father catch on a tide by this method as many as one hundred and fifty bass, some weighing better than fifty pounds.

"Got to get my bass gear ready," Mr. Sears said. He had not fished for many years but the memory of his fishing was annually rekindled.

27

A young buck rabbit heard him talking to himself and paused during a breakfast on white-lilac bark, cocking his ears, intent. He had long since become accustomed to Mr. Sears' presence and paid more attention to what he said than did the old man himself.

Mr. Sears saw the rabbit.

"Hello there, little fellow," he called. "Bass'll be late. Time to get my gear ready."

The rabbit had heard this every morning for a week. He went back to nibbling.

On the way up the hill Mr. Sears noticed that his out-house had been upended. He regarded the tumbled two-holer with astonishment and dismay.

"My, oh, my!" he exclaimed. "Got to fix that! Must have blowed some during the night!"

So it had, many years before.

As MOON and sun moved toward complete opposition in their tug on the tides, the night tides fell from spring peak, then morning tides diminished, and in intervals of the neaps restlessness grew again in Roccus. She recrossed Cleveland Ledge Channel while a moderate breeze from the east brought rain hissing and bubbling the surface. Roccus rolled to present her scales to the tingling sensation of oxygen-filled water striking with a cold force that was nevertheless warmer than the sea. She swam north of Nun buoy 12 at the edge of Dry Ledge and sank in a kelp bed to rest. The rain ceased but the wind hung east. The moon southed a half-hour before a wan sunset, set two hours after midnight. The tide carried the warming drain of rivers. This was a raw night of spring when Father O'Meara's arthritis gave him plague and no blossoms opened on the apple boughs.

WITH HER father, Evelyn Force walked for the first time along the straw-covered perennial border inside the white picket fence surrounding the house they had built on the river shore. Her thoughts, which should have been on leaving the old brick-end Colonial in Cambridge, or on the new house which she was seeing for the first time, were instead a confusion of reactions centering about Pickman Brown, Jr., to whom she had recently become engaged. She wondered whether she loved him, and, what disturbed her more, why she loved him if she did.

Pickman was inside, superintending the placing of the last of their furniture. Only a few minutes earlier he had engaged in a heated argument with the boss mover over the manner in which a valuable antique cabinet should be carried into the study. Pickman had had his usual arrogant way in his usual obnoxious manner. Cabinet and wallpaper had suffered as a result. So had the girl's disposition.

"Why am I marrying Pickman, Dad?" she asked, as if they had been discussing him.

"Are you? I wonder."

"I thought I was."

"Well, I'll admit I've given it some thought myself and perhaps I can give you the right answers. He's an extrovert, he's inordinately possessive, he's wealthy and he's in love with you. A retiring young woman is naturally attracted to an extrovert. All women want a man to be possessive. Certainly they want him to be successful. And women respond to love—not always with love but with acceptance and a warmth of appreciation for what that love means. Any more questions?" He laughed. "Actually Pickman will probably stand a lot of wear and improve with it. But he could become a boor, and I can't imagine anything worse for you."

The girl said, "I had no idea you read Beatrice Fairfax." She pulled up the hood of her parka against the easterly drizzle and bent to lift wet straw. "You had peonies planted here, Dad?"

"I think it was here. We'll inspect the landscape gardener's plan a little closer."

No reddish bud tips showed.

She liked this house, yet she was sorry to leave the Cambridge home that had been hers during all the years of her father's distinguished service on the Harvard University faculty. The professor had retired a week before, still a comparatively young man, to devote the remainder of his life to three volumes of essays. In the several years before retirement, with it in mind, he had conducted a more-than-casual search for a locale that would meet his somewhat exacting requirements for a new home for himself and his daughter who, though baptized Evelyn, he called Stormy because of the night that her mother had died in giving her birth.

By no means antisocial, Professor Force nevertheless required extended periods of privacy and even solitude for research and creative thought. He had explored the possibilities of northern New England, especially Vermont, and of Connecticut, but his final choice had been a three-acre piece of woodland bordering the Bournham River, and there, according to plans he prepared and specifications he imposed, his new home had been built; an extended Cape Cod, without dormers but with a soundproofed combination library and study occupying an entire open-raftered ell.

Professor Force was a tall, red-haired man with small and distinguished features. He had been completely devoted to one woman and since her death wholly unaware of the existence of an opposite sex, as sex. Indeed, it is doubtful whether he had ever thought of Stormy as feminine until the day of her unexpected betrothal to Brown, although at twenty she was definitely a woman of delightful form and graces, gray-eyed, lithe, with chestnut hair of exceptional fineness and an overall daintiness giving no hint of her remarkable physical strength, though attesting, in curve of high cheekbones and sweep of forehead, in fine-chiseled mouth and chin lines, the strength of character she had inherited.

The girl he called Stormy was as devoted to her father as he had been to her mother. She had left Smith College at the end of her sophomore year to manage his home because this was an exacting duty requiring a quality of affection which no mere housekeeper could bestow. If it had occurred to Professor Force that she made a sacrifice in his behalf he would have accepted it on the grounds of a staunch belief that no woman benefited in the long run from higher education. Actually, it hadn't occurred to him at all.

"The iris is showing tips," the girl said.

"Looks like iris, dear. I'm not sure what's here."

Stormy had had no formal coming-out and never regretted it. She had moved unobtrusively through Junior League and Vincent Club circles, popular enough and sought after, but never really rushed until after her second year at school she had met Brown at a Belmont Country Club dance.

Pickman was eight years her senior, son of the senior partner of Brown, Atkins & Parnell (wool: Boston, London, Melbourne, Rio). At Princeton he had played at football, the javelin, fast cars and women only slightly slower. He held a junior partnership in his father's firm, owned a thirty-six-foot speed cruiser and a sixty-four-foot yawl based on the Eastern at Marblehead, and drove a Cadillac convertible, usually with the top down to allow for general appreciation of his profile. Dowagers of deep-freeze Boston looked on him as a fair catch because of his financial background. The eligible field he had played cautiously, without preference, until he met "the Force brat," as he later called her in a manner of irritating, patronizing affection. Then he had a target and she was it.

Stormy had disliked him at first because of his blatancy. Later she had tried unsuccessfully to analyze her reactions to his aggressive suit. He had kissed her the night of their first dance, driving home from Belmont, and though she resented it as a symbol she had been frightened and dismayed by her own responses. Always thereafter in his presence she was more afraid of herself than of him, aware of a fire within her, newly kindled, which came leaping with his nearness. She had had it in mind the day she agreed to marry him.

"These are lilies of the valley," Stormy said. "Look, Dad, you had my favorites planted." They were brownish spear points in the straw.

He said, "I asked for them. An old man named Mr. Sears just down the road said he would fix up the planting. We can change it later if you wish."

As for Pickman Brown there was no question about his affection for Stormy. He really loved her. The day after they met he wrote finis to an affair involving a pouty dancer. His signature on a five-thousand-dollar check was the agreement. The girl had hoped to do better but was satisfied. And he hadn't had a mistress since.

Now, as the second emptied van moved away from the house and Pickman came grinning above his long stride across the newly greening lawn, Stormy felt an insecurity, a sense of indecision as much related to fear of herself as to the depths of the faults she sensed in him. Yet—she knew—it was well that she was to be married.

"Well, Brat, they're unloaded and away," Pickman said, taking her arm. "The house is reasonably settled, and a good thing I came along to oversee the job. As it was they banged things up something awful. How about it, Doc?"

Professor Force said, "Thank you for your aid, Pickman." He was completely sincere; he wouldn't have had the vaguest idea about handling movers and Pickman had done the job.

"Come on, let's get out of here for lunch. I'm starved. We can take *Tiderunner* down-river or drive down, doesn't matter."

"Let's stay awhile," Stormy said. "Let's walk around. I want to get used to the house." He had given her no time with her Cambridge memories; she wanted time here.

"Come on, Brat! I've got a hollow only a steak can fill."

"No," she said, "I want to stay and explore a little while. Why don't you take the boat down to Bournham and Dad and I'll follow later?"

He said, in the tone of a small boy denied a lollipop, "Okay, we'll all stay." Next minute he was noisily enthusiastic. "Hey, Brat, listen to this. We're going to get in some hot striped-bass fishing this summer. Here's the spot and I'm the man to show you. Big fish come upriver and a sea worm is the way to take 'em. I can be here often. Fast run down and through the canal. Then it's just around the corner. How does that fishing sound?"

Stormy said it sounded interesting. But it didn't. She wished he would leave her with her thoughts and give her an opportunity to assemble them.

"Say, Brat, I'm starving. What say we go?"

She was suddenly conscious of his hand, the touch of the back of his hand against her breast.

"All right, Pickman. Let's go, Dad. Are you hungry?"

"Only mildly so," said the professor.

FROM DRY LEDGE, Roccus drove northwest again seeking warmth. Alewives were in abundance but her appetite was held in check by enervating cold. In the rivers a few bass which had wintered over began to lose sluggishness.

On a morning ebb there was a definite change of pressure and the wind backed into the northeast. Roccus swam to the sandy shoal between Warren Point and Long Beach Point, lay finning in three feet of water. Even the hermit crabs had moved off the shoal in advance of the storm. The wind made up and the surface ran angrily in lifts, sulkily in hollows, and Roccus gave herself to the conflicting movement of the water, warmed by water thinned by rain. Half-buoyant, she was vibrant with storm, knowing it with all her body, comforted by its warmth; she was of the storm as well as of the sea. Wind pushed against the tide, tide pushed the surface; the surface waters ran

34

counter to the movement of the tide. Roccus lent herself to the opposing actions and in the turbulence maintained her lie without effort, now feeling the scrape of sand against belly and anal fins and tail, now delighting in the lash of raindrops along her dorsal.

By slack of ebb the wind was a half-gale and seas ran more regularly and higher over milky sands. Roccus dropped back into deeper water. The first northeaster of the reluctant spring gathered force from a thick, gray ceiling of clouds.

WHEN THE brass knocker rapped twice, Clifton Hartwell was seated before the open fire in the second-floor study of his mansion on the rise of hill overlooking Buzzards Bay. He had finished an excellent dinner of sea clam chowder, double-kidney lamb chop (no potato), two slices of hothouse tomato, imported endive, ripe Camembert and black coffee. He was enjoying a second cup and puffing a cigar when he heard the first summons and presently a quick, impatient knocking that bespoke the arrival of a caller lacking in proper diffidence on the threshold of a Colonial grandson. Hartwell frowned, listening. He heard Mrs. Grace, his housekeeper, open the door and he heard voices. Then Mrs. Grace's step on the carpeted stair. Her drawn, angular face, wearing an expression of apology, appeared in the doorway.

"Mr. Webb Everly is here, Mr. Hartwell."

"What does he want?"

"He said it was a matter of important business."

"You know I conduct my business at the bank."

35

"I'm sorry. He said it was urgent and that he could not call at the bank tomorrow."

Hartwell put down his cup. "Have him up, then."

Webb Everly was a lean, dour man of small stature with a thin nose under round eyes and peaked, graying brows. He was skipper of a seiner mortgaged through the bank of which Hartwell was president. Entering the study he still wore a gray woolen cap which, when he faced the banker, he did not trouble to remove.

"Sit down, Everly. I thought you were off Cape May for mackerel."

"So we were. We ran three trips of fish into New York. Mackerel ain't plentiful yet but I guess they will be. Usually are."

"What brings you back so early?"

"A plan I've had a long time. Wanted to do it last year but let the chance slip by. This year I'm going through with it."

"Don't tell me you want to convert to drag."

Everly yanked the visor of his cap. "Drag hell and do as well," he said. "The Portuguese and wops have swept the bay floor clean as a billiard table even in closed areas."

"What is it then?"

Everly glanced around, arose and pulled the door of the study to as if about to impart a plot for murder.

"Striped bass," he said, resuming his chair.

Hartwell dipped the butt of his cigar in the lukewarm coffee. He said nothing and his failure to respond goaded the skipper.

"The price of bass ranged from eighteen to thirty-five cents a pound last year, round fish, New York market. It will be as good or better this year. There's a fortune in it. And I'm for it."

"How do you mean? Charter to sport fishermen and market their catch? I don't see how you'd expect much from that."

The banker's deliberate misunderstanding provoked the other's obvious discomfort and provided Hartwell with secret amusement.

"Rod and reel fishing? Do I look crazy?"

"If you by any chance mean seining, you know it's illegal."

Everly's yellow-toothed grin was twisted. "I ain't never heard it's illegal and there's plenty more hasn't."

"Then you hear it now. Massachusetts law prohibits seining stripers and the sportsmen are hot over last year's violations."

"Nothing's illegal you don't get caught at," said Everly.

"That's a false premise that has filled our jails."

"Well, you know what I mean."

"Just what *do* you mean? Why do you come to me?"

"I know water alive with striped bass from June to September, bass constantly there for the smart taking, a steady movement of fish, and many big ones. Every bass entering Buzzards Bay spends a lay-over in the area."

"Where?"

"Moving within an eight-mile half-circle of your front porch. Fish never bothered in the darkness."

"But why come to me?"

"Because I need money. I need a seine—mackerel seine won't do—and I need a plane spotting the location of the schools before dark. I got the pilot, one of my own crew."

"How much money altogether?"

"Seven thousand dollars will cover it."

"Why not drop in at the bank tomorrow?"

"You want to discuss this at the bank?"

37

"No. I don't particularly want to discuss it anywhere."

"Oh, yes, you do. You ain't never fooled me, Hartwell. It's your money I'm talking about, not bank money. There's a fortune here for easy taking and no risk. You can have in if you want to."

The banker studied his dead cigar. "You've got to be a better salesman than you've been so far."

Everly slapped a chart from his pocket, unfolding it. He laid it on the braided rug and, kneeling, ran a short, stubby forefinger across its surface. He said, "I know that water like this," and turned his palm upward. "I can work it in the dark without lights better than any other skipper can work it in daylight. I know a feeding ground here, a hole here, a blind creek there where, on the night tides, the fish move in close following the feed. I can work the net with three other men, the three best of my present crew and the air spotter, and I can take striped bass in quantity every night between the first of June and late September that the weather's anywhere near decent. I can pay for seine and plane in damn few sets."

Hartwell said, "You've still got to talk better. How are you going to dispose of fish illegally taken?"

Everly grinned. He knew he was making progress. He knew, to a limited extent, the man with whom he dealt.

"There's plenty shippers to handle them. I know two who do."

"Sometimes under conditions like that a product will not bring its fair market value," Hartwell mused. "A sort of blackmail comes into being with a black market. And what about the marine fisheries patrol boats?"

Everly laughed. "There's no blackmail. And the marine wardens are more concerned with clammers digging in contaminated areas. Besides, the marine division has only one hull which has a bad engine. There's no way to enforce the law, and the wardens are snake-belly low."

"If I were to put in seven thousand dollars . . ."

"A sixth share of the profits plus six percent. In a thing like this it would have to be share-and-share-alike or there's a chance of hard feeling and loose talk."

"I don't think I heard you. What was it you said?"

"A sixth share of . . ." Everly stopped, realizing that Hartwell *had* heard. "What do you want? You're talking for yourself, now, not the bank."

"A third share in cash every week, delivered here at my home."

Everly folded the chart, his tanned cheeks drained by anger. "To hell with it. I'll get it elsewhere."

"No."

"What do you mean, no?" the skipper demanded.

"I mean no. You'll get it from me on my terms."

"I can raise it somewhere else on better terms."

The banker lit a fresh cigar. "You might at that. But think it over. Would it be wise? Would it be smart, as you say, to go elsewhere for funds to back a proceeding of this kind after telling others about it, causing—you used the term—hard feelings?"

Everly said thinly, "You mean someone might give information?"

Hartwell laughed. "Of course not. Of course I mean nothing of the kind. But after all, the bank does have an interest in your vessel, a sizable interest, and I don't think the bank—strictly as a bank, mind you—would care to undertake the risk involved in your proposal to me."

Everly said, "A while back you were speaking about blackmail."

"That's a harsh word to use in this case. You come to

39

me for something you need. I offer to provide it on fair terms. Unfortunately you have to take it on my terms if you want it at all."

"Then let's forget the whole goddamned thing and I'll go back mackerel fishing."

"That's satisfactory to me and I'm sure it will be to the bank."

The skipper started for the door but he had no intention of opening it. He turned when he reached it, Hartwell not having spoken again; he walked back to the center of the room. "A third share is a hard bite with you taking none of the risk," he said.

"But there isn't any risk," said Hartwell. "You've just been telling me that."

Everly rubbed his right knuckles on his left palm. "Okay. You win. Write the check."

"There'll be no checks in this transaction one way or another. Keep that in mind. Return here tomorrow night and I'll give you cash on a note on a personal loan. Now, before you go—and don't go as angry as you look—let's have a drink on it."

The banker poured liberal brandies. "Here's to fishing," he said.

The drink was hot in Everly's throat and stomach but not as hot as the injustice burning him. He said, gasping a little, "I wish to Christ my ancestors came over on the *Mayflower* so my mother could have raised me to be a banker."

OUTSIDE THE estuary, on a bottom of gravel and small boulders, Roccus drew comfort from the warmth beaten into the sea by the rain. Across brown marshes flanking the river the rain sheeted and fed the tide in countless thousands of rivulets draining thinly over asphalt and mud and grass roots into potholes. The sky fed the earth and the warming land fed the sea of the clouds' abundance; the sea sucked the warming life from the earth and fed the fish in her only need.

Against the current of the river and the drain of the tide, the rushing, murmurous winds pushed a thickening line of thatch grass, sea spear, spike grasses and fox, up-rooted kelp and sea lettuce, Irish moss torn from boulders, rockweed torn from mussel beds. These formed a mile-long swath, five to twenty feet wide, where wind and tide opposed each other in greatest force. In this wavering demarcation, shifting constantly, life in microscopic form, most of it crustacean, was concentrated in the greatest warmth of surface water. Under the weed many fish assembled, attracted by food and warmth: alewives and lesser herring, cunners and small codfish, the first of the tautog come to spawn, fat as cows nearing their time.

Herring gulls circled aimlessly; the quick terns dropped over the drumlins; waterfowl took refuge in the moors or rode outside the surf line in rafts. A few heron stalked the shallows and a few robins hopped the untilled fields, scanning last year's ridges like proofreaders scanning the lines of manuscript. Quail, pheasant and migrating wood-cock lay close in cover.

Earth drank deep. Green tips showed on the wiry bristle of the Scotch broom, the thorny branches of the wild rose glistened, arbutus perfumed the brown blanket of pine needles and the leaves of the scrub oak. Elms beat their arms, quickening circulation, and conifers shed new cones. Here and there a live branch gave way before the assault of wind. Ground phlox, violets and anemone emerged from the sodden earth.

Man kept shelter as best he might. The movies were scantily attended, taverns lacked patronage, lodge rooms were thinly occupied. Some men argued with their wives and some played cribbage with them. Some overhauled their fishing tackle, dreaming of record fish.

In the lighter, warmer water, disrupting the regimen of opposing forces, Roccus leaped once, scattering algae and plankton. Night was a torrent of elements shriving the land.

IN THE rectory of St. Peter's, from which, except in the months of heavy foliage, he had a vista of the river, Father O'Meara adjusted the spectacles on his hairy ears and read for the third time the letter signed with a strong, bold hand. For his humble soul there was inspirational satisfaction in his superior's salutation, "My dear old friend," and in the text there was substance to assuage the thirst of the lean years of labor in a vineyard whose harvest had often produced only bitter wine for the palate of a man of grace:

> There will be made in the late autumn a number of changes long under consideration in the archdiocese. In

Worcester, where I have in mind you were born and attended Holy Cross, there will be another permanent pastorate created and it occurred to me you might care to
undertake the work of God in this broadened field. Yet
I must also consider the many invaluable associations you
have made over the long years in your present post. So
this is not an assignment. I leave you free to make your
decision after consulting God and conscience. But in order that the schedule of changes may be worked out most
efficiently, I request your decision in hand by the end of
September.

There was more in the same kindly vein, and Father
O'Meara, who had been sent to Bournham by a cardinal
whose displeasure he had evoked many years before, removed his specs, brushed at his right eye with a swollen
knuckle and pounded his rubber-tipped cane on the floor.

"Rosie!" he shouted. "Rosie Carmody! Where are you?"

"I'm here," she said quietly. "I've been here in the
doorway five minutes gone trying to tell you supper is
ready. Father Simpson is off to Barnstable and you'll be
eating alone."

"I know," he said. "Rosie, would you wish to be housekeeper in the rectory of a permanent pastor in Worcester?"

"I would not," she said.

"Myself, that is," he said.

"I would not," said she.

"Your pay would perhaps be a little better."

"The pay? Who cares about pay?" She was a tall, angular woman with hair as white as his own and she had
been housekeeper at the rectory of St. Peter's for more
than twenty years.

"I would not have thought there was that to hold you
here if old Father O'Meara went away."

"You've been transferred?"

43

"I've been offered," he said. "The choice is mine."

"Then you'll stay here," she said matter-of-factly.

"Why do you say that? Worcester is my home. You know my sister is there. You know the advantages that accrue with a permanent pastorate. And I guess you know my age."

"And I know there are no striped bass in Worcester," said Rosie Carmody.

Her words hit him a staggering blow. The thought had not occurred to him. He had fished in his youth in the streams and ponds near home, but he had never wet a line in fresh water after catching his first striped bass. There were no stripers in Lake Quinsigamond! He thumped his cane to hide his agitation. This was nothing to show.

"The shame on you," he said. "Is my pleasure to be considered where there is need for my work in the name of the Holy Father?"

"So far as I'm concerned it is and will be."

"Have done," he ordered. "What's for the table?"

"A bit of this and that," she said.

"A bit of this and that," echoed the priest. "The menu does not vary an iota."

"The fish chowder warmed from last night. It's always better the second day. Saltines. And—" she paused to give full weight to the announcement—"fresh asparagus on toast."

"All right," he responded automatically. "Serve it out; I'll be right in. But wait— What's that you said?"

"Asparagus," she replied, relishing his retarded reaction. "Fresh asparagus on toast."

Of the belly, except for rhubarb pie and sauce, he had no other appetite. He had always been greedy for work in promoting respect for God among mankind, but his earthly needs were few and his operating budget, for the size of the parish, was the smallest in the archdiocese.

So now he asked sternly, "Where did you get the asparagus?"

"At the First National. I asked Tom Salter but his isn't ready. This is California grass but it's fresh."

"You asked Tom Salter for asparagus?" he demanded.

"Why not? He said you asked him for a rhubarb pie."

He was used to her angled assaults. "What did this asparagus cost us?"

"It was cheap," she said.

"The price, Rosie Carmody?"

"Seventy-nine cents. A dollar and a quarter ten days ago. Ninety-five cents last Wednesday. If you want someone else to do the shopping, say so, but don't sit there all night talking about the price or it will be cooked too long and no good at all."

He rose from the leather chair. "Have it on or it will be as tasteless as a shoe lacing. Did you cook it all?"

"I did not. I've half of it standing in water for tomorrow, freshening."

"Cook the half for yourself or I'll eat none. Hear me now."

"You'll mind I hate the stuff. So does Father Simpson. Grass is for animals." She liked it well enough, and later, when it was cheaper as native grass became abundant, she would eat her share.

Seated alone in the candlelight at the old refectory table spread with a linen his cousin Agnes had sent from Ireland a dozen years before, the old priest paid scant attention to the warmed-over chowder of a haddock donated by a parishioner. However, he addressed himself

45

with dispatch and robust appreciation to the asparagus, which, despite his fears, was not so overdone as to be flavorless. And for once Rosie Carmody had not spared the butter. The delicacy answered a craving of his belly juices as a steak or a lobster or an alcoholic drink will do for other men.

He was engaged with his second helping, his half-finished chowder growing cold, when the doorbell sounded and he heard Rosie Carmody, mumbling to herself, respond to it. Fearing an interruption of an emergency nature he concentrated on the butter-sogged tips of the grass, so that when the housekeeper appeared he was prepared for whatever quick action might be required. On his dish nothing remained except the butt ends, which ordinarily, his upper plate being loose, he would gum at leisure in Rosie's absence from the room.

"It's Chief Maddox from the Coast Guard Station," Rosie announced. Her disdainful sniff was audible. "He can wait."

"No," said Father O'Meara, rising. "I'll join him now." He felt a twinge of conscience for appetite satiated. There was hunger among children the world over. If he could have fed them by starving himself he would have starved happily. "Serve us tea and mind you make it strong."

"Have they no tea in the Coast Guard?"

The priest paused. "You'll not be meaning it."

"Maybe not. But he's a bold one and the likes of him without respect. I'll not be telling you what he just said."

"You will," said the priest.

"He said if I were ten years younger he'd be taking me to the dance this night."

Father O'Meara laughed. "So he might."

"If I were ten years younger I wouldn't go with him."

46

Chief Boatswain's Mate Jeffrey Maddox drank his tea clear, as hot as he could noisily sip it. He was a powerful, blocky man giving somehow the impression of a granite statue done by a sculptor who had failed his inspiration. His black hair was trimmed short. His forehead bulged above nearly browless blue eyes of a beguiling innocence which challenged the fact that he had denied the body none of its desires. His nose had been broken more than once and looked it. His muscular, short legs bulged the trousers of his uniform.

A man without inhibitions, Maddox had a vast understanding of human nature, much of it gained during thirty years in Coast Guard service. He had fought in two wars, the first at the age of sixteen because at that age he had already matured and was a good liar in a good cause. No religion had held him, no particular doctrine or theology attracted him, yet he possessed an affectionate and respectful regard for any priest, minister or rabbi who demonstrated, over and beyond generalities with which Maddox had no patience, the ability to deal successfully with any problem of human relationship which Maddox could not solve. Between Maddox and Father O'Meara there had been for years a relationship somewhat akin to that which existed between the priest and Tom Salter, except that Maddox never pulled a punch in deference to the Roman collar. He and Father O'Meara understood each other completely and maintained, each for the other, a mutual respect.

The tea was strong. Father O'Meara, sipping, led off. "You'll have come to tell me the station lookout has sighted striped bass in the surf."

"Not yet, Father, but any day soon." Maddox's wide mouth grinned. "I can see you now, that day you were

47

on the way to bless the scallop draggers last year and you saw the bass in the surf at Rocky, your cassock—is it?—flying in the wind and wet by the lick of the waves, running along with your borrowed rod and shouting something not out of the mass. Got a fish or two, I remember. It would have made a picture for the Pope!"

"So," said Father O'Meara. He recognized in this approach a challenge on an issue still to be raised. Maddox would not have mentioned the incident except to put the priest on the defensive.

"Your tea—a bit hottening will help it."

"I've enough, and thanks. I don't come to drink your tea, as you know."

"I know. Why do you come?"

"Manuel Riba."

"Ah, what now?"

"Just more of the same. Drunk again."

"In itself, to be drunk . . ."

"The sin is the loss of his dignity." Maddox pounced. "As a sin I'm not concerned with it. But I won't like it when he kills someone, perhaps himself."

"What makes you say that?"

"I've watched that kid grow up from a river brat starved for food and affection, the butt of a cruel joke that has become almost a legend on the Cape, to a man nearly completely consumed by a hatred of all society so strong that a complete tragedy is almost unavoidable. The booze he has tried to quench that flame with has merely fed it. He used to hang around the station in the days when that no-good bitch of a mother of his was still alive, and I could see it shaping then. What little I could do to help him, I did. Later, I thought you might be the one, but it doesn't seem the Church has done any better than I "

48

"Don't put the blame on the Church, Maddox. I'll take it. Where do I fail this man?"

"In the way we all fail him." Maddox was intense. "By withholding sufficient kindness. Except for you and me, I doubt he ever heard a kind word in his life—a word from someone actually interested in his welfare. I can't act as his guardian because I haven't the time; we're undermanned at the station as it is. But I do think it's your job. That *is* your job, isn't it—the rescue of wrecked souls?"

"If it please God."

"Why wouldn't it please Him?"

"I will say more prayers for him."

"I have no faith in them. Nor has he."

"I will spend more time with him."

"That will help. Leave some of your hypocrites to their own fate for a while and give more attention to a kid who thinks the whole world's against him—as maybe it is."

Father O'Meara felt no resentment. "What do you think he needs most, Maddox?"

"Someone to love him. Nobody ever loved him. His life has been a constant search for affection and all he ever found was ridicule. He needs a woman to love him." He grinned boldly but the priest was not discomforted.

"It could very well be that a good wife would help."

"I didn't necessarily mean a wife or a good wife, or even a good woman. A woman who would love him, Father. It would be okay if she were a good woman of beauty and gentleness and understanding. You might pray for that, though I think he'd settle for less. His search for what he needs, without knowing what that need is, has sent him after every trollop in the community. Right now he's after that waitress of Nick the Greek's and someone's likely to end up with a knife in his back."

49

"Where is he drunk now?"

"In his shack on the river road."

"We will go to him. Wait till I fetch my coat. The storm is bad for my old bones. Father Simpson has our car; have you yours?"

"Mine's outside."

Manuel Riba sat at his kitchen table with his face on his arm so that the light, when Maddox touched a match to the lamp, etched the dark profile dirty with beard and found an auburn tint in the thick, curly hair. His eyes were closed and Maddox touched him heavily on the shoulder.

"Wake up, Manuel, I've brought a visitor."

There was still a boyish appeal in the face Riba raised to the light.

"How are you, Manuel?" asked the priest.

"Drunk, Father, drunk. What brings *you* here?"

"We were just passing. Will you be wanting anything?"

"No. Yes, another drink—the jug is empty."

"Later it might be supplied. Have you eaten?"

"Two steaks at the Tavern of the Sun. No, Father, I didn't eat. There's not room for whisky and food. When was it I took the pledge, Father?"

"About a month ago, after your last confession. No matter. We'll try again."

Manuel shook his head, though not in negation.

"What troubles you, son?" asked the priest.

"Nothing. I just got drunk." He stood suddenly, holding to the table. "Tell me, Father, do the people laugh at you when you tell them about God?"

"No."

"Yet they never saw God."

"In the old days they saw Christ in His image."

50

Manuel sat and placed his head on his arm again.

"They wouldn't laugh at you. But I'm a lying bum and everyone laughs. That's why I get drunk. Because after I'm drunk I almost forget them laughing."

"You're no bum," said Maddox, "but you will be if you keep on."

"No," said the priest, "you will never be a bum."

Manuel said in the tone of a small boy, "Everybody makes fun of me. That's because I used to lie about things. Now I try not to lie but they still make the fun."

"After a while they won't laugh any more," said the priest. "You just keep trying. I was thinking; maybe if you came to work at the rectory for a while it would help us both. Father Simpson complains about the furnace and there's work to be done around the grounds. In that way you wouldn't be alone so much."

"I don't think I could do it," Manuel said.

"Do you like asparagus?"

"When I'm hungry, Father."

"It tastes like spring. Get his coat," said Father O'Meara to Maddox. "We'll go to the rectory and Rosie Carmody will give him some asparagus on toast and tea, and maybe, if she will let me, I will give him one drink to help against the sickness."

THE STORM ended at daybreak. Roccus fed from a school of herring which had dropped down the river. . . . The moon southed two hours after sunset, bursting through the rack, and the shifting wind quieted the seas. Wives remarked to their husbands that it would be good to go to the movies, to get out again and away from the children for an hour or two.

IN HER big bed in the downstairs bedroom of the house in the dunes beyond the Coast Guard Station, Clystie Harrow slept late and dreamed of a cottage in Kilmessan Village near the hill of Tara, County Meath, in the province of Leinster, across the sea.

She roused once while the light was still small and heard from the kitchen the sounds Myra made preparing the breakfast, heard Donald's piping voice denying appetite and expressing eagerness to be off on the picnic to Rocky Point. Thereafter she slept fitfully, unaware of the departure of her son, and dreamed of shifting dunes cut by the wind, of dobbies riding stolen colts, and of the mythical small folks of the land she had left behind. Then the scene shifted and was ugly and there were flames in the black sky, towering, and the roar of engines diving. There was pain like a knife thrust, and a twisting force within her and a guttural laugh that mocked. There was a sound of shots, three shots spaced by trigger-pull.

The shots sounded again and she awakened because there were more than three and more than three were too many. The sound was of someone knocking. She sat up and called, "Who's there? Who is it?"

"It's Jeff Maddox," a voice sounded distantly.

"Wait," she called. "I'll be right there."

She pulled on a robe and went out through the kitchen and unlatched the heavy door. Maddox, out of uniform in old flannels, stood in the burst of sunshine.

"Good morning, Chief," she said.

"It's near noon of a fine day. There was a letter for you.

So I fetched it over. It was just an excuse to see you, though."

During the few weeks of her residence here, she had found his frankness disconcerting but attractive; she interested him because she was beautiful and he didn't understand her, and he had told her so at their second meeting on the beach after her return home—or as close to home as she had dared to come.

Now she said, "I doubt you ever need an excuse. Where's the letter?"

"In my pocket. We're told never to deliver a letter at the door."

"Come in, then." She smiled. "Sit in the kitchen while I do my hair. Or better still, make the fire and heat some water for coffee."

She returned to the bedroom to brush the black hair which fell to her shoulders, shining. They talked back and forth through the thin partition.

"Where's the lad this morning?"

"On a picnic with Myra. I'll be joining them."

"A picnic is good for a boy, though I can't imagine enjoying one with the old crone. With you, now, it would be different."

"With me there would be none for you," she said. "Are the striped bass in?"

"No. What do you know of stripers?"

"I told you I lived near here as a girl."

"But I don't believe you because, if you had, I would remember you. I never forget a pretty girl."

"The blarney is Irish but your face and name are not."

"I'm a dour Scot," called Maddox.

She rejoined him in the kitchen, freshened, and made the coffee strong. The letter was propped against the

53

sugar bowl; she made no move to open it and he did not mention it. The thought occurred to him that it might be from her husband. She had never mentioned a husband but the boy was hers.

"This is a fine place to bring up a boy," he said. "The likes of the Cape folks you will not find in many places."

"I know," she said. "I've been many places."

"He's old enough for school."

"Yes, but I'll not start him until the fall, until he gets accustomed. His life has been a little different from most. He was born in France and has lived most of the time in Ireland."

"Yet your home is here. And that would have been during the war when he was born in France."

"You could leave it, or go on prodding, or go back to the station."

"I'll leave it. Do you know Father O'Meara?"

"The pastor at St. Peter's? I know *of* him."

"He has relatives in the old country; perhaps you would know some. I could bring him out some day. He's a grand old man."

"I wouldn't know his relatives," she said. "Why don't you go now?"

He rose promptly, smiling. "Perhaps we could go to the movies tonight."

"I don't like them. I never go."

"Bass fishing some day, then?"

"Perhaps. Some day."

"We would take the boy."

"He would like it."

"You would like it, too. Thank you for the coffee."

The letter, as she had hoped, was from her old agent, Felkstrom, in New York. He wrote:

Frankly, not too many who count remember what you did in pictures, and those who do remember you mention unfavorably how you just walked out on your Galaxy agreement and vanished, with never any explanation. The movies aren't what they were; the whole setup has changed.

I don't think we can do any business unless you come to New York and perhaps go on to Hollywood for a renewal of contacts but I'll continue to make inquiry and keep you posted. Should you change your mind about coming, wire me.

She rested for a quarter-hour, staring across the years. Then she tied a narrow ribbon of yellow in her hair and went across the dunes toward the point, where her son would be enjoying his picnic.

ON A NIGHT brilliant with stars, from the black tide newly astir with hungry life into the cool quiet of high-pressure atmosphere above her natural element, Roccus leaped. She fell back on her right side and swam in a tight circle and leaped again. Her ream tossed stars and phosphorescence. She headed into the river.

AT FIVE MINUTES before four o'clock, Judge Leander Wickett shrugged his slim shoulders to gather his black robe and strode purposely from bench to private chambers while a court officer intoned adjournment until ten o'clock of the next day.

His Honor had put in a somewhat boring day as presiding justice over the first criminal session of Suffolk County Superior Court sitting in Boston. The case was one involving a charge of assault with intent to kill by a defendant named Anthony Barta, who had attempted to blow off the head of a South End neighbor, one Harrish Bardinian, during an altercation over the division of loot from a pawnshop holdup. There were involved no fine points of law interpretation such as His Honor was justly noted for handing down, and there was little or nothing about the case to interest the jurist whose rulings and decisions and charges over a period of many years had been held by bench and bar alike to be models of judicial wisdom. Yet there was one thing unusual about the case and, having it in mind now, Judge Wickett sent his secretary for the court clerk, Will Effin.

"Who is Number Three on the jury, Will? A short, dark man wearing glasses."

"Man named Harbor. Lives in Revere. Sat as a juror two years ago. Something wrong, Your Honor?"

It was an indication of Judge Wickett's stature that the veteran Effin never addressed him as "Judge."

"I'm not sure. Just my overcareful self, I guess. But I thought this afternoon I caught a glance from him to the defendant which seemed to convey a message. I would not want an injustice done."

"Shall I notify the D.A.'s office?" Will Effin knew—every officer in the courthouse knew—that when Judge Wickett even vaguely suspected something amiss about any situation the chances were a thousand to one that there *was* something wrong. His Honor had a keen perception coupled with the integrity which long ago had lifted him above the level of political criticism.

"Perhaps you should," he said.

His gaze wandered out across the city rooftops to the harbor, a white-chalked slate. A distant sail reminded him of something and he rang for his secretary.

"A letter to Eben Snow, Snow Boatyard, Bournham. Dear Eben: I will be grateful if you will make a special effort to have the *Coralee* in the water early this year. If I can avoid a special sitting I intend to spend a long vacation at Skipper's Knoll. She certainly needs a scrape-down varnish job and I think you mentioned something about a new strake. Sue and Andrew are both well. Give my very kindest regards to your charming wife and, when you see him, to our mutual friend, Father O'Meara."

Effin returned with the assistant district attorney prosecuting the Barta case, young Arthur Degan, visibly perturbed and frowning.

"Effin informs me you have reason to suspect a juror, Your Honor."

"Little enough reason, Degan. Sit down. What check did your officers make on the panel?"

"A routine one. There was nothing on the docket that seemed to require special vigilance."

"Every case in Suffolk County requires special vigilance," Judge Wickett said with a dry, friendly smile. "For my own peace of mind have a check made on Number Three."

"We'll put two men on it tonight, Your Honor."

Minutes later, closeted with the district attorney, Degan protested, "But all he says he noticed was a little glance. What the hell kind of a basis is that for suspicion?"

The D.A. grimaced. "I'll bet you two to one we discover something and he mistrials."

"You're on for a buck," said his aide.

"And to your sorrow. You will live to learn that those pale Wickett eyes see all, know all and never are in error."

The Judge walked down Beacon Street to his home, where his daughter, Sue, and his grandson would be waiting. He noted with pleasure that despite the recent storm the magnolias had not suffered. Daffodils were gold behind the iron fences, the tulips blossomed.

Next day the district attorney said to Degan, "Want to pay me now or later?"

"Why? What turned up?"

"Juror Number Three is married to a cousin of the defendant's wife. Go in and tell the Judge and he'll mistrial and you can start all over again." He laid a fatherly hand on a suddenly sagging shoulder. "Don't feel badly about it. That's the best mind on the bench today and perhaps in all the history of the Commonwealth. Certainly it's the most honest. If there is any justice at all in politics, he's going to the Supreme Court."

So THE May was gone. The backward spring leaped to keep abreast of the sun's orbit. Anglers sandpapered rods, wound guides and tips, varnished with their fingers, cut sticks of glass, Burma, Calcutta cane; cleaned reels, tested old lines of nylon and linen and discarded them; applied emery to dulled metal squids; replaced rusted hooks in favorite plugs; built herring cars; wired squid rigs for bottom fishing; cast lead for surf weights; filed gaff hooks; counted eelskin rigs; stood hypnotized before tackle displays, mobbed tackle counters; made phone calls to charter boatmen.

The bass were in!

Gilligan wrote in the *New York Herald Tribune* that a few were being taken in the New Jersey surf. Ray Camp in the *New York Times* said they were off Shinnecock Inlet. Trullinger and Hurley and Brawley sent word to the *World-Telegram,* the *Mirror* and the *Journal* that they were knee-deep in them in the Sound. In the *Boston Herald* Henry Moore wrote that there were bright fish in Buzzards Bay. Earl Banner in the *Boston Globe* said he had reports they were in the Weweantic River but he wanted to be shown. Dark Montreal in the *Boston Advertiser* outlined the Cape Cod Canal Derby, and Cliff Davis in the *Post* wrote of the Marthas Vineyard striped-bass tournament.

The bass were in and it was time for fishing!

There were at least four good months ahead. The sea, which gave earth life and might some day reclaim it, traced pattern and plot in the shining tides. The net was of greater strength and wider sweep than any Roccus had avoided. Roccus and the shining tides were one. She cleaved upriver.

June

"MIND THAT PIE, Tom. You'll break the crust carrying it like that."

"I won't do no such thing," Tom Salter called back to his wife. Even as he said he wouldn't, he did it. Under the waxed paper he felt the edge of crust crumble beneath his thumb. He glanced quickly over his shoulder to determine whether she'd noticed; she stood watching apprehensively from the doorway.

"I won't do nothing of the kind," he called. She closed the door.

Tom was headed for St. Peter's rectory. The rhubarb pie for Father O'Meara he gripped in his wide left hand, and balanced on his right palm he carried a bowl of rhubarb sauce as pearly pink as sunrise. Plate and bowl were still warm. His stride, in his paint-stained boots, was habitually awkward. He walked along the sand by the river's edge, and after a few steps he walked in the river. He couldn't stay out of the water any more than a small boy could.

May had made two pies and a batch of sauce that

morning. Rhubarb had grown five or six inches since the storm, he figured. His thumb crushed another edge of crust. Father O'Meara wouldn't mind. At his boat station by the newly rigged float he rested a few minutes, appraising his skiffs and dories. These had been hauled up during the northeaster, but yesterday he had dragged them down again, anchoring some off and securing some to the float. They shone in the after-storm brightness of the sun. If the warmth stayed, as it promised, the bass would soon be in.

He set pie and sauce on the thwart of a dory and gazed upriver past the tiny island to an old gunning-stand cover where the current pitched in a bubbling dog's-leg with the bend of the riverbed. He sniffed. He smelled the fresh tide smell and the new salt on marshes beginning to ripen. He smelled alewives and white perch moving up to spawn. He didn't smell any stripers. Yesterday there had been two fishermen but no strikes from bass. He could have told them before they went out that there would be no bass that day. This day was different; he wasn't sure. He sniffed again. He could not have described the distinguishing characteristics of the scent of stripers but in his nostrils it was unmistakable; and now it was in his nostrils. Bass *were* in! There were bass in the river! He picked up the pie and sauce and moved quickly along the tide lip toward the wooded point, waddling like a duck.

Father O'Meara came down the path.

"Bass are in!" Tom shouted. "I can smell 'em!"

"I believe you," said the priest. "I can't smell them but there's a pleasant perfume in the air. It smells like a warm rhubarb pie."

"May made one up, and some sauce."

"God forgive my belly hankering," said the priest, "and

61

His blessing on your good wife. Come up to the rectory."

"Wait," said Tom. He turned to face the river again; he never turned from it without a lingering glance. Now, balancing pie and sauce, he focused his attention, suddenly alerted, on a riffle-ruff on the near side of the big rock in midstream.

"There's fish under them alewives, Father," he announced. "See that flurry of water—bass herding 'em."

"I see it." Tom's excitement had communicated itself to the priest. They gazed intently at the slapping of the harried alewives, and suddenly, in the center of the school, a silvery-green shape bulged the surface. The smash of Roccus' tail threw water a dozen feet. Tom Salter's jaw dropped and weakness drained his limbs. The balanced bowl of sauce began an outside loop. He lunged with both hands in an effort to save it. Pie and sauce fell in the river at his feet.

"You see that, Father?" He was shouting.

"I did, Thomas, I did. I also saw what you did with my pie and sauce."

"To hell with the pie and sauce! There's the biggest damn bass ever I see."

"It was big," Father O'Meara agreed.

"You rigged up? You got your rod rigged?"

"I've been rigged a week." Tom's excitement made contact with an end of the wire that would be alive in the priest until the dynamo itself was dead.

"Fetch it then and let's get going. That's a bass would go a hundred pounds!"

"I doubt that was a bass, Thomas. Too big. It may have been a shark."

"Damn it, Father, don't argue with me. I know a bass break when I see it. Get your rod."

Father O'Meara went swiftly up the path for his gear. Tom Salter, waiting impatiently, noticed the tide was washing sodden crusts upriver. He scraped them out with his boot and buried in sand what he could salvage of the disaster and spat tobacco juice on the little mound.

When Father O'Meara reappeared he had his boat rod rigged with nylon leader and a silver spinner, but some of his excitement had drained away. He doubted what he had seen.

They trolled for an hour, changing spinners and sea-worms, finally resorting to a blooper of an eelskin, but had no strikes. Once in the eddy near the gunning stand Roccus glimpsed the eelskin and turned lazily toward it and followed it a little distance merely out of curiosity.

The priest said, "You actually threw that bowl of sauce but you should have saved the pie." His belly's loss was his humor's gain; he would rag Salter unmercifully about this for months to come.

"You'll have to make off to May you et 'em," Salter said.

"You mean you're asking me to practice a deceit?"

"You can say they were wonderful, can't you? That's no lie."

"I couldn't be a party to it," said the priest.

"You could, though. There's another pie to home. I'll smuggle you a half and make off I et it."

"In that case," decided Father O'Meara, "I will pay my respects to Mrs. Salter and to the merits of her baking. I will be able to do it in good conscience. But a full half, mind you, Thomas."

With the night drain of the river Roccus dropped back to the bay, restless. She had fed for three days and would fast for two. She swam across-bay through the turbulence about Stony Point Dike and with the first of the incoming tide let herself be carried into the mouth of Cape Cod Canal. She rested in a backwater by a wooden dolphin east of the Socony Oil dock near the railroad bridge and twice worked against the current to swim under the dock. Hidden on the bottom there, secured to the dock piling by a line, was a big lobster pot which Manuel Riba had baited and set in violation of the canal regulations imposed by the Corps of Engineers. Riba felt a strong satisfaction in this defiance of the United States Army. And it was a good spot for lobsters.

Voices were a jumbled overtone for juke box music in the Tavern of the Sun. Waves of sound—a jumble of talk, a shout, a girl's laugh—stirred the smoke haze, eddied it, tinkled one sensitive glass on the shelf behind the bar.

Manuel Riba stood a moment in the doorway, gulping the stale air, glancing around the square room. Manuel had not taken the job Father O'Meara had offered at the rectory, but he had taken the pledge again and he was cold-sober now.

The Tavern of the Sun did most of its business after the sun went down. With all nine booths occupied, it was crowded with the kind it nightly attracted, some to eat and linger and drink and visit, some who had wandered in after eating their suppers elsewhere, to drink until closing time.

Big Nick was behind the bar, sweating profusely as he did even in midwinter. It was a standing joke among his regular customers that he once beat a rap before the State Alcoholic Beverages Commission, which had accused him of watering drinks, by proving the dilution to be the saline excretion of his own fat body. The heavy flesh beneath the wet shoulders of his shirt shimmied above a shaker and felt the draft of cool air from the open door. Then he saw Riba standing there.

"You, Double-It-Up! Shut the door from one side or the other!" he shouted. "Goddam, you live in a barn, that's right."

Manuel smiled thinly, but he was glad of Nick's attention and the announcement of his arrival. For once in his life he was glad he had been called Double-It-Up. Because he had a plan. His plan was patterned along the lines of general advice Father O'Meara and Chief Maddox had given.

He shut the door from the inside. His eyes followed the movements of Maggie Blynn, who, back to him, wiped a tabletop preparatory to serving a party of four. She had good ankles and wide hips of promise. Before he advanced across the room he waited for her to turn from the table, because he wanted to observe the profile of her heavy breasts above the small curve that flowed outward to the hips. She gave him a quick smile and he felt a thickening in his throat. He walked across the room to select his company.

Manuel had been able to plot a sensation by the grace of whoever watches over the fate of lobsters, and this night, for the good of his soul, he needed an intimate and attentive audience prepared to disparage his every statement. As a condition of his plotting this was not difficult

65

to attain, though Stud Benton, who waved at him, was too prone to accept Manuel's exaggerated claims with morose silence rather than challenge. He ignored Stud, and his glance searched for someone more likely to taunt him. When he saw Lyman Conway beckon from a corner booth he didn't hesitate. He knew, and the knowledge was bitter, that Lyman wanted his company only to poke fun at him.

Lyman Conway sat with his brother, Phil, also a Wareham boatyard worker, and a black-haired, thin girl he had seen in their company before. The girl had been around. Manuel had decided long ago she was too thin regardless of recommendations to the contrary.

He took the seat beside Lyman, opposite Phil, the girl against the wall diagonally across. Maggie came to serve him and as she wiped the table he reached over to pat her hand.

"How's it go, baby?"

"Good. With you?"

"Twice as good as with anyone else," Lyman Conway interjected, laughing.

Manuel ordered drinks all around, ale for Lyman, whisky for Phil and the girl, a coke for himself. "Have yourself a drink on me, Maggie."

"I can't while the joint's open. But thanks." She smiled.

"Why not?"

"Nick won't let me."

The thin girl stirred in the corner. "Who the hell is the Greek to say if you can or you can't?"

"Maybe later," Manuel suggested. "Maybe—after—we can go somewhere."

"I can't tonight," she said, moving away.

Well, he thought, you might even tonight after you see

66

what happens. Manuel Riba was going to establish himself in contest with his detractors.

The thin girl said, "If you're after Maggie remember the Greek carries a banana knife." Something about it struck her as a top joke. She repeated it and laughed shrilly. Phil's hand went to her leg to calm her.

Lyman Conway, hunting laughs, asked, "How's fishing, Double-It-Up?"

"Good," Manuel said. "Getting my share. Cherrystone kind of scarce but plenty littleneck. Lobster starting to move."

"My God, you ain't going to talk fishing!" The thin girl took her head from the wall. They ignored her and Lyman winked. She sat back in the corner, sullen, unresponsive to Phil's hand.

"I see a big flight of brant today," Manuel said. He knew Lyman to be a gunner and thought to arouse him. "I ran out to Abiel's ledge to haul pots and thirty, forty brant came over."

Lyman pitched into it. "Thirty, forty brant, my ass! There ain't thirty brant using the bay. Weren't all last season."

"Shag likely." Phil laughed.

The thin girl dropped pink lids over gray eyes.

"They were brant," Manuel insisted. "Most as big as geese."

"Hey, Nick!" Lyman's voice was loud above the juke box sound. "Double-It-Up see thirty, forty brant today!"

Nick, stirring a Martini, roared laughter. "Ho, that little Double-It-Up taking a shot in the arm. He got double everything, I say!"

There was laughter from the other booths at Nick's sally. Maggie served the drinks, Manuel's eyes on her

67

bosom. For the little time it took her to down her whisky, the thin girl lost her sullen boredom. Her eyes were beginning to pucker.

"I run in from Abiel's in twenty minutes," Manuel said casually.

"In what jet plane?" Lyman Conway demanded, grinning.

"That's right," said Manuel. "Twenty minutes. Had my sixteen horse on, wide-open."

"Twenty minutes, my ass!" Phil said.

"Mine, too," said the thin girl. "Take your hand off it."

"Hey, Nick! Manuel came in from Abiel's in twenty minutes," Lyman called.

"Woosh!" Nick shouted. "That little Double-It-Up got speed to burn. He fast with everything but a buck. You watch out for your girl."

For once this was good for Manuel to hear. He sipped his coke and showed no resentment. He waited a minute and asked casually, "You boys taking any lobster?" It was the build-up question for the jackpot.

The answer was as he hoped. "We'll stick to the boatyard," Phil said. "Lobsters ain't moving any yet. Few shorts, maybe."

"I got a big one today," Manuel said, raising his voice.

The thin girl said, "Oh, for God's sake, let me outa here!" She stood in the corner awkwardly, a hand on her cheek. Manuel silently cursed the interruption; he felt like slapping her down.

"Where you going?" Lyman asked. "Sit quiet."

Her lips twisted. "You want me to do it here or in the ladies' room?"

Phil chuckled. "I vote the ladies' room. You, Lyme?"

"Here's okay with me."

68

"Let her do it where she wants," Manuel voted and Phil stood to let her out; and Lyman said, "Manuel just wants to get on with his story."

"No story," Manuel protested. "I caught a big lobster today. Eleven and a quarter pounds. In one of my pots on Abiel's."

Lyman's eyes showed double crow's-feet. "I'll weigh eleven pounds of fist on your beak," he threatened. Then the humor of the claim hit him and his voice boomed again. "Hey, Nick! Manuel caught an eleven-pound lobster today!"

Nick stopped mixing and his voice sent the smoke swirling. "Jesus Christ, what you know about that! Everything big for little Double-It-Up. Me, I think maybe he catch one little short lobster and throw him back, huh? Maybe we call him Triple-It-Up? What you say there, Triple-It-Up?"

"I said I caught a lobster weighed eleven and a quarter pounds," Manuel shouted. "Anybody says I didn't is a dirty liar."

He glanced to another booth to make sure Maggie heard. She heard. All the room heard.

Nick stopped laughing. He called, "That so? I say you didn't and I ain't a liar. You maybe catch one little short. You a big—what you call it?—hot air, Double-It-Up! Everybody knows you full of—what you call it?—you say it."

"Bull," said the thin girl, returning to the table.

Laughter rocked the room. Manuel walked to the door and strolled into the night, and the laughter followed him. They thought he was fleeing it. They thought he was afraid of the big Greek.

From behind a shrub by the side entrance where he

69

had cached it, he quickly retrieved a burlap bag, slung it over his shoulder and re-entered the Tavern of the Sun. Laughter still held command of the room. He took the crocus sack by the bottom corners and on the floor noisily dumped its contents: a huge lobster, black and ugly. The laughter ceased and people stood to stare. The lobster flopped on the linoleum, scraped backwards, waving its slasher claw, which had come unpegged. The patrons gathered close.

Manuel said to Nick, "You got a scale. Weigh it."

Nick said nothing and made no move, but Stud Benton gingerly lifted the brute and tossed it into a basket scale. The hand swung, swayed and stopped. Stud announced, "Eleven and *three*-quarters, by God." Manuel, planning this triumph, had deliberately understated.

It was up to Nick and he knew it. He said, "What you know from that?" The answer came to him and he grinned. "Where you buy that big lobster, Double-It-Up?"

Manuel hadn't figured on that question in his scheming. The general laughter that followed it turned sweet victory, almost within grasp, into the most bitter defeat he could conceive. He looked up at Nick and spat in his face.

Nick reached out a huge hand to grasp Manuel's shirt front and lifted him from the floor; Manuel felt the blood course down his dangling legs, felt the binding of his shirt, felt Nick's hot breath. Nick cocked his arm ready to throw him across the room. Then Maggie's voice whipped out, "Put him down, Nick! You had it coming."

Nick set him down. "I'll kill the little lying bastard," he said. Then he grinned. "Okay. Drinks on me, on the house. But where you buy that lobster, huh?"

Manuel didn't wait for his drink on the house. He wanted a whole bottle and there was a package store

70

still open. He slid the lobster back into the sack and left the laughter behind him; that is, he left those who laughed. Their laughter went with him. They all believed he had bought the lobster. Actually, he'd caught it, not on Abiel's but in the pot in the canal under the oil dock.

Outside the Tavern of the Sun, the thin shadow was the thin, dark-haired girl, weaving slightly. She said, "I think you caught it, Manuel. I know you did."

She swayed close and Manuel put an arm around her. She was skinnier than he'd thought but it didn't matter. His hand searched roughly and she was flatter than he'd thought, but that didn't matter.

"Let's cook the lobster, kid," he said. . . .

In the apartment above the Tavern of the Sun, Big Nick said to Maggie, "What you butt in for when I'm going to flatten that Double-It-Up?"

"I didn't want you to get into trouble," she said.

He was suspicious but he couldn't see her face in the dark.

"Oh, yeah?"

"Yeah," she said. "Nick, come here."

BOBBY MEADE steered a twenty-five-degree course through the platinum haze, holding the bow of *Carey's Chicken* in line with the first left-hand buoy marking the Hog Island channel approach to Cape Cod Canal. Both engines were revved to twenty-one hundred and the slipstream was wet, pouring past the spray shield. He and Cal were taking her over from the Vineyard to the base on the river for the first of the fishing.

Cal Knight lay on his back, an ear close to the panel opening of the port engine housing; his eyes were closed under a frown of concentrated listening. If there was a fault in the engine the skipper'd find it, Bobby thought.

Hooking on as Cal's mate had taken a deal of doing. Not that Cal, who was his second cousin, didn't want him, knowing him able, but his ma, and Cal too, had needed convincing that three years of high school were enough for a boy not planning college, and that this particular boy could quit before the end of his third year as well off as ever he'd be.

"Your pa always said you can't learn navigation without you know your arithmetic," his ma had warned, using the strongest argument she could muster.

But he had the need to earn some money. "Pa would figure I should. I'll make more working for Cal than I can off the Vineyard on somebody else's boat."

"You'll spend, boarding places and such like."

"I'll sleep aboard and mostly eat aboard. And Cal will pay me ten dollars every day he has a charter."

"On days he doesn't you won't earn."

"He will most every day 'cept in foul weather. All the best fishermen want Cal. We'll maybe go for tuna and make a lot of money."

"I don't care; you're too young."

"I'm seventeen!" He'd sounded as if seventeen were mighty close to man's expectancy. "Besides, I'm big enough."

He was, too: tall enough, at any rate, tall like his pa had been but skinny as the pole of a boathook. He had a knowledge of boats and fishing gained from his pa, who had always been a good earner, though with him it was easy come, easy go. It was Cal, in the conclusive argument, who'd won his ma over. "I'll look after him and Father O'Meara'll see that he gets to mass. Holds an early mass for the boatmen and anglers." It was Cal who'd . . .

"Mind your helm!" Cal said.

Bobby started from daydreaming and noticed he was three points off course. Cal still lay with eyes closed, listening. The boy turned the wheel gently.

"Hey, Cal."

"Yuh?"

"How'd you know I was off course?"

"Wave slap changed on the bow."

"How can you hear the slap above the motor?"

"Pick a fiddle out of an orchestra, can't you?"

"You find the trouble?"

"Carburetor adjustment. Doesn't amount to anything." Cal slammed the panel back into the housing box and secured it and came standing without touching his hands to the deck. "I'll take her now. Bad water here for you to learn." He took the wheel.

"You sore, Cal?"

"Nope."

"I shouldn't have let her fall off like that."

"You shouldn't have."

"Nothing happened that time, but next time it could."

"That's right. Now you've said it all yourself without my having to say it. No next-times. We set a course, we hold it. Right?"

"Right, Cal."

"Fetch one of the glass rods and rig a plug. Get that big hooper-dooper I made. Might's well wet a line."

Bobby fetched a rod from the cabin ceiling and snapped the big teak plug to the leader. Cal throttled down to four hundred, to three hundred, to two-fifty, and Bobby let the plug go astern, thumbing a free spool. "Boy, what action!" the boy said.

"Let out a couple hundred feet, get it deep. Any fish around here, they'll be deep. Tell you something."

"Yuh?"

"Throw your reel in gear and loosen the star drag. Strip your line off against the drag. Know why?"

"Guess so. Fish hits when I'm free spooling I maybe get a backlash or a burned thumb."

"And if you don't and you throw into gear with the drag set up, you break off. So you knew half it anyway." He grinned. "Guess I can't teach you much, mate."

Cal swung right rudder to a forty-degree course, leaving Abiel's close to port for the run along Stony Point Dike toward the canal proper. They bucked an outgoing tide with the rips strongly made. Revved down they had barely steerage way. There was little traffic. A tanker was standing down past Mashnee, riding light, and a dragger, loaded to the gunwales, passed them with her Diesels pounding, Boston-bound. There were a few small craft distant and one closing rapidly on their starboard bow.

Cal said, "That's a fast job, Bobby. Coming up."

The approaching cruiser's bow was a brown dot in a ten-foot V-fountain of spray. She passed a hundred feet distant at not less than thirty knots, a low, three-quarter-decked mahogany hull built for speed and some weather. The big man at her wheel kept his eyes ahead but the girl beside him, her hair streaming, waved. Cal waved back and Bobby pumped the rod and cranked the reel to give an imitation of handling a fish. The sucked-down stern of the boat showed the bronze letters, *Tiderunner*, and beneath them, *Marblehead*.

Bobby stripped line, and the action of the plug was in

every fiber of the line and rod and in the nerves of his hands. Then he felt shock up his arms to his shoulders.

"Call!"

WHEN THE tide ebbed with the west-flow of colder water through the canal, Roccus in mid-channel dropped back with it under the railroad bridge, past State Pier, through the straits between Hog Neck and Hog Island into the warmer waters of Buzzards Bay. She swam onto the shoal at Cedar Island Point and in three fathoms there hunted food, finding little except a few of the first of the hump-backed scup. These, in the adult growth, had dorsal fins too sharp to be relished. Some of the smaller ones she swallowed. She pursued and lost a small school of sand launce. She rooted for them but could not find where they had buried themselves.

With the wash of *Tiderunner*'s wake over the shoal she swam into deeper water, not alarmed but wary, and within the cone of vision of her right eye detected an active, elongated shadow, something like a whiting, swimming in jerks as if wounded, and fluttering from one side to the other. She closed on its strangeness and followed leisurely until the object leaped away from her. She accelerated and swam abreast of it, but it jerked away swiftly. She swam beneath it and bunted it gently with her head. In her years Roccus had encountered many kinds of artificial lures, and a few, when they had proved sufficiently tantalizing in action and the conditions of light or approach were such as to obscure leader and line, she had struck. Decision and action in this case were simultaneous. She swirled and took the hooper-dooper head-on just as it jerked again. Two of the gang of head hooks embedded themselves in her upper lip.

"Cal!"

Cal heeded. "You hung on bottom, Bobby?"

"On fish!" Bobby grunted. The rod arced and the line hissed against the light drag, and hissed cutting the surface.

"Good boy!" He revved the port motor, turned right rudder to keep the line from the hull. "Take him easy. Bass?"

"Yuh. Big one, Cal."

"They all feel big first-out in the spring."

Bobby held the rod tip fairly high and kept the reel cranking, but the line still payed out.

"You best tighten up a little on that drag."

"That's what I was going to tell you," Bobby grunted. "I'm buttoned down tight already."

"Oh." Could be a big fish at that, Cal thought, though it was awful early. He gunned the motors and began to follow the fish across-channel. Bobby picked up some line. The fish dogged deep and the rod butt, jumping alive, bruised his groin. "Get me a belt, Cal."

Cal reached into the cabin for a leather bib and buckled it on the boy and helped set the butt in the pocket, feeling as he did so the springy surge of power away out at the end of the line. The fish *was* big. Twenty minutes passed. The battle had taken them across the channel to the south end of Mashnee, a boulder-strewn bottom.

76

"That rod'll stand all you can give it and the line is new. Your fish is well hooked or you'd have lost him long ago. Better go to work, son."

The young mate lowered the rod tip, reeling; pumped, lowered reeling; pumped again, repeated.

"Gets in those boulders, he'll cut off, Bobby."

"Know it. Moved him some. This can't be no bass."

"It's bass," Cal said. "Nothing else acts like that. Give it to him."

Bobby gained fifty feet, lost it; gained sixty, lost fifty. Ten minutes later after a series of short runs the fish had only a hundred feet of line.

"Coming up!" Bobby yelled in triumph.

Off the stern Roccus surfaced in a great shower of foam and Bobby called on the Mother of God to witness the sight. Cal kicked into slow reverse and said quietly, "Don't give him slack. Ease off a little on your drag and watch out. He just came up to look around; he's going to move sudden."

Roccus sinuated, swirled and sounded, and all the line so laboriously won was lost before the boat could be brought on a following course.

"He ain't even winded," Cal said.

"Cal."

"Yuh."

"You take him."

"If you don't want him I'll cut him off."

"But you saw him."

"Yuh, and how!"

"How big, Cal?"

"Oh, maybe thirty, forty pounds." He knew it was wiser not to say how big.

The fish lunged and the line sang.

77

"I saw him, too."

"How big you think?"

"Bigger than any bass I ever saw."

"That so? Well, watch your rod tip."

No kidding him, Cal thought. *He saw as well as I. He knows he's hung to a record.*

The rod was a glass half-circle.

"Not much line left."

"We'll run up on him again. Take in steadily, keep the pressure on him."

They'd worked back to the channel edge, and Cal noticed with apprehension that the mahogany speed cruiser which had passed them outbound was headed in again at high speed, bearing directly across their course. He sounded a sharp warning on his horn and saw the bow wave diminish sharply. They hadn't seen him before. He gave his attention to the fish.

With the help of the boat, Bobby had the fish within a hundred feet again, and surfacing. Cal kicked into neutral.

"You **tired** him some; don't let him rest now." He went below **for the** big gaff. When he came topside with it, he saw with consternation that *Tiderunner* was laying to, not a hundred feet beyond the surfaced, thrashing bass. He cupped his hands and shouted, "Ahoy, *Tiderunner!* Move off, please! This fish will run again!"

The man and the girl had taken seats on the cabin to watch the fight. The man gave no sign he heard; Cal saw the girl turn to speak to her companion, probably repeating the message. The man pointed at the fish and said something. Cal shouted a warning again but it was ignored.

"He's going to move again, Cal, I can tell. He's getting ready! There he goes!"

78

The surface leaped and boiled. The bass took line once more and the tip of Bobby's rod was pointed directly at the other boat.

"I can't turn him, Cal," he called.

"He'll pass under that lardhead. I'll swing in an arc around him. Don't pressure him enough to keep him up."

He gunned both motors. He saw the man on *Tiderunner* leap for the wheel and shouted, "Don't start up! Lay where you are!"

The girl waved, but *Tiderunner*'s motors came alive with a roar and the mahogany leaped, crossing *Carey's Chicken*'s bow.

"He's going right over my line!" Bobby shouted.

Cal kicked into neutral, slammed into reverse. *Tiderunner* jumped clear, the man at her wheel shaking a fist.

"He cut me off!" Bobby's cry was anguish. Life had gone from the rod, line drooped from its tip. The mahogany cruiser, her damage done, lay to, motors idling again, and the boy called to her skipper in Cal's own phrase, "You big lardhead!"

Cal said, "Easy. I can do better than that. Reel in your line." He ran over alongside *Tiderunner*, and the man emerged from her wheelhouse. He was younger than Cal had thought, and the girl was better looking. But even so. . . .

He said, deliberately, easily, "You're a no-good son of a bitch. At first I wasn't going to say it in the presence of the lady, but then I figured anyone who'd be palling around with you wouldn't mind an understatement like that. . . . You don't, do you?" he asked, his eyes on the girl.

Her companion had a bull of a voice. "You wouldn't say that ashore, you clam mucker! You haven't got the guts!"

79

"I'd say it ashore, afloat or flying. And with ditto marks. I base on the river at Farrell's Wharf and I'll be there in less than an hour. I'll be glad to say it then and there or any time later, anywhere."

He moved out and headed upchannel. *Tiderunner* passed him, heading in.

"Maybe he'll be waiting, Cal," Bobby said.

"Good. I need it."

"Looks pretty big. In good shape."

"I need a licking. Do me good. Shouldn't have said it—not in front of her."

"She didn't look the kind would be with him."

"Doesn't make any difference. Shouldn't have said it. Don't you ever."

"I won't. . . . Cal?"

"Yuh?"

"How big was that bass?"

"Really want to know? Make you feel bad."

"I want to know."

"Not less than one hundred pounds. Not less than five-and-a-half feet long. Now you can cry in your pillow tonight."

"Maybe I'll get a bigger one."

Cal grinned. "I got me a good mate," he said. He put an arm around the boy's shoulder. "Listen, kid. No sense to tell a man not to feel bad when he loses a record fish. But if you'd caught it you wouldn't have had any fun bass fishing the rest of your life. Imagine that!"

They both laughed. . . .

Tiderunner wasn't in sight when they tied up at Farrell's Wharf.

"Wash down and make up the bunks," Cal said. "I'm going up to see Tom Salter and tell him about that fish, and I'm going to call New Haven and tell Dan Merriman, who's doing striped-bass research at Yale. No sense telling anyone else; they'll just figure we're dreaming. If I'm not back in fifteen minutes get some chow cooking; anything suits me."

"Okay, skipper." Bobby grinned.

Cal found Tom Salter at his boat station and told him of the fish. Tom told of the fish he and Father O'Meara had seen.

"Could be the same," Tom said. "Fish we saw wouldn't stay in the river long."

"How is the Father?"

"No younger. But well enough. And asking for you recently."

"I'll drop by the rectory and say hello. Someone I want him to keep an eye on."

"You won't find him this afternoon. Manuel Riba is giving him some worry and he went up to Manuel's place. That damn-fool chief down at the Coast Guard Station, Maddox—you know him—he's got Father in a frame of mind to believe that all his works are in vain if he can't save Manuel from the devil."

"By the way, you know a sport cruiser, *Tiderunner?*"

"I've seen it lately. Seems to belong up the river. Saw it moored off a new house up there where some professor and his daughter come to live. Why?"

"Quite a craft."

The soft, warm light was going. Cal paid his respects to Mrs. Salter and decided to go back to the boat without telephoning Merriman. He saw the riding and cabin lights were already turned on; Bobby would have something cooking. Maybe later they'd go uptown to the movies. Right now he was hungry.

81

He called when he walked out on the apron of the wharf but Bobby didn't answer. The new tide hadn't raised *Carey's Chicken* much. He swung down four rungs of the ladder and jumped aboard. Bobby lay sprawled on the deck between the engine housings, his head on his hands, sobbing. Cal knelt swiftly.

"Hey, kid, what gives?"

The boy half-turned his head. It was a bloody mess, mouth and cheeks cut, both eyes swollen, nose torn at one nostril.

"What happened?"

"That guy came looking for you. Said you'd run out on him. Called you a yellow bastard. I told him everything you'd said went for me, too. That's all. Except he's awful fast and awful good."

Cal got him sitting up and washed out the cuts. The nose wasn't broken. Nor the spirit.

"I wasn't crying because I took a licking."

"I know."

"It was because I'd lost the fish. Cal, you'd have had him if you'd been handling him. Would have meant a lot for the reputation of the boat."

So that was it.

"Listen, Bobby. I couldn't have done any better than you. Nobody could. You made no mistakes. That rod was too light to kill that fish in anything under an hour. Hadn't have been for that son of a bitch you'd have had him."

"Maybe."

"Come on, let's chow. You want to go to the movies later?"

"Sure, anything you say."

"I say the movies for you. I got an errand to do."

82

Roccus sank to the bouldered deeps off Mashnee. The hooks of the plug were merely an annoyance, the weight of it a nuisance which did not greatly alarm her. She had rid herself of similar lures before. Behind her, as she swam, trailed one hundred and twenty feet of forty-five-pound-test nylon line and three feet of nylon leader. Before dusk all except a foot of the line had been cut off by the sharp edges of barnacles, mussels and rocks. She expelled with an exertion that tired her and somehow caused her to be tense. Awkwardly, she fed through squid though she was not hungry. She sought the reassurance of normality.

In their new house on the river, Stormy Force poured a second cup of tea for her father.

"What happened to Pickman, rushing off so?" he asked.

"Someone snatched his pride in my presence. He's gone back to Bournham to find it." She told him all that had happened. "He heard both requests that we move *Tide-runner*. He felt they were too much like orders, and Pickman won't take orders. We were too close and I told him so, but you know how stubborn he is. Then, when we cut off the fish, he seemed actually elated. . . . Dad?"

"Yes, Stormy?"

"Do you think he was actually glad? Is that the kind of man I'm going to have for a husband?"

"I don't know, dear. But I don't blame him for resenting

being called what he was called, especially with you there. No gentleman, whether he's in the right or wrong, can be expected to take that."

"I suppose so."

She had the dishes done when Pickman returned, jubilant.

"Guess what, Brat? One of them ran out and I wiped up the deck with the other. Taught him a lesson."

"Which one, Pickman?"

"Younger fellow. The one who called me a lardhead."

"Pickman, you didn't! He's only a boy! You didn't hurt him?"

"I hurt him, Brat. Not too much. Just enough to teach him to mind his language. I probably wouldn't have touched him except he got fresh and said he stood by what the other fellow'd said. You save me anything to eat? I'm hungry after that workout."

His callousness was a knife inside her. Workout! The boy couldn't be more than eighteen, and he was at least sixty pounds lighter than Pickman. She wouldn't have minded if it had been the other; what the man had said had been a deliberate affront to her as well as to Pickman, and he was old enough and big enough to take what Pickman might hand out. But the boy!

She said, "I think it was a despicable thing to do."

He reached for her, grinning, but she eluded him. "That means you despise me, Brat?"

"It means I despise what you did."

"Well, you'll get over it."

Will I? she thought. *Will I come to accept his bullying and his arrogance and his childish petulance, and his capacity for hurting others, as undisturbing occurrences in the natural order of life shared with him?*

84

A small doubt that had lived long with her became a formidable, frightening question mark. They had a compatibility of interests, but their approach to them was along separate roads that never seemed to meet. Even her physical desire for him, which she had reluctantly acknowledged to herself, had lessened as she came to recognize his weaknesses. She was aware it could be wholly obliterated.

It came to her suddenly, and with the overwhelming force of delayed realization, that she had no respect for the man she had promised to marry.

He said, "What's bothering you, Brat? Whatever it is, forget it. Give me a kiss."

"No," she said.

Then Professor Force called from the doorway, "There's someone here to see you, Stormy."

She welcomed the interruption and the chance to get away from Pickman, but when she walked into the study he was close behind her. Cal Knight stood there, gray-flanneled back to them, reading book titles. He turned, smiling casually, and Pickman said, "I was looking for you. And you ran out."

Ignoring him, Cal addressed the girl. "Miss Force? My name is Knight. I came to make an apology. I said something this afternoon which I should not have said in your presence. I'm sorry for it."

Pickman said, "If you think a pretty-please will get you out of what you've got coming, you've got another think."

"Be quiet, Pickman."

"My apology was to Miss Force," Cal said. "And it was for having said it in her presence, not for having said it."

"You're a dirty, low-down clam mucker!" said Pickman, wetting his lips.

"In season," Cal said. "At least, I used to be. So was the seventeen-year-old you beat up this evening." He grinned. "That's my favorite second cousin. Going to be a good man when he grows up. Point is, he hasn't grown up yet. Shall we dance?"

"Right now!" said Pickman. "I could beat you to a pulp the best day you ever saw!"

"Say—you might do that." Cal's glance took in the heavy shoulders, the flat belly, the long arms.

"Hold on, gentlemen!" said Professor Force. He was finally getting around to a realization that something of a menacing situation had developed in the quiet of his study. But nobody even heard him. Cal opened the door and stepped into the night and Pickman followed, calling back, "You want to come along and watch the fun, Brat?"

"No," she said, abruptly and fearsomely aware of elation in the thought that if, by any long chance, Pickman should take a licking, she might enjoy it.

Cal said, "There's a street light up by the road a distance and I'd rather see what's going on. You impress me as the kind of skunk who'd use his knee and his thumb."

It was meant to goad. When Pickman rushed him from behind he was ready, side-stepping quickly.

"That you, Bobby?"

"Yuh," said the boy, stepping on deck from the wharf.

"How was the show?"

"So-so. Not too good." He entered the cabin and switched on the light. Cal was in the port bunk, face to the bulkhead.

"What was the picture?"

"Why—guess I didn't notice the title, Cal."

"Guess you didn't," Cal said. He turned over, grinning.

86

He had a purple mouse over his left eye and his left cheek was deeply cut. He said, "You think I didn't know you followed me?"

"Knew where you were going," the boy said. "Say, you messed him up pretty. Thought for a while you weren't going to be able to do it."

"Yuh. He's strong and he knows how to box. And he has more guts than I figured."

"He hit you when you were down on one knee."

"Sure. Expected it."

"How come you helped him up at the end?"

"Just wanted to make sure he wasn't permanently damaged."

"He was damaged good, though. You want something for that eye?"

"No, it's okay. Snap out that light and get your sleep."

The tide was a cat's tongue at the bow.

"Cal, you sure that bass was a hundred pounds?"

"Positive. Forget about that bass."

"Aren't you thinking about him?"

"Nope."

"What you thinking about, Cal?"

"I was thinking how come a swell girl got mixed up with a punk like that."

"You go for her?"

"Might."

"I'm going to think about the bass."

STORMY WAS sure she would never forget her first meeting with Whitcomb Sears. It stayed in the forefront of her memory and she viewed it always with curiosity, sometimes with foreboding.

It had happened on a day near mid-June. Pickman had returned to Boston and with his departure her spirits had lifted. She was glad to have him gone. She felt release from captivity. She was not certain she would welcome his return. His pride but not his arrogance had been injured by the licking he'd taken at the hands of Cal Knight.

She had seen the boatman but once since the evening he'd appeared with his apology—a meeting in the Bournham chain store where he was buying supplies. She'd nodded and he'd smiled pleasantly enough and she felt he would have approached her if she hadn't moved away. Later he had been much more in her thoughts than she had liked.

This had been one of those approaching-summer days, sparkling in forenoon and early afternoon but turning damp in late afternoon as a steady southwest wind piled a high fog of increasing density overhead. Despite a threat of shower she had gone exploring and had come upon the house standing near the narrow waist of the river, well hidden behind a group of pines on a knoll.

The house, a structure of two-and-a-half stories, was bleached and beaten by sun and storm of two centuries, bleak and gnarled and twisted. The pines about it whimpered in the breeze like hounds before a blaze. It might be the home of the Mr. Sears her father had mentioned,

88

she thought, but it was curiosity as much as neighborliness that turned her steps toward it from the road.

No one lived there, it appeared. The house seemed as forsaken as a soul condemned. Uncurtained windows stared like sightless eyes. Nobody had stuffed the broken panes of glass. Its top jagged with displaced bricks, a single chimney poked a forlorn finger skyward, yet made no beckoning to swift or swallow. Wind ruffled the curling shingles of the roof with a ceaseless sound of fluttering as it ruffled the river at the foot of a steep descent behind the house. There a pile of shells, oyster and scallop, clam and quahog, an accumulation of years, gleamed white as weathered bone.

Lilacs, the flowers rusted past bloom, leaned against the rear of the house. Or did the house lean against the lilacs? She could not be certain. Here and there day lilies waved spent blossoms. Golden coreopsis swayed and nodded. Like lanky blondes in a fashion show, she thought. And everywhere, crowding the long and unkempt grass, crowding the lilies and the coreopsis, blowing white and magenta, old-fashioned pinks blossomed in profusion, filling the air with a heavy, aromatic fragrance, a spicy scent which hovered over all. She knelt to gather a few in a small bouquet that would please her father, but had plucked no more than a dozen blossoms when she felt the gaze of someone unseen—knew that sense of being covertly observed which a woman eventually comes to know so well. She rose abruptly. Perhaps there was someone in the house after all.

But there was no one in the house. The man came from an edge of scrub oak beyond the path.

"Careful not to pull the roots, girl," he said. "My wife planted those."

"I'm sorry," she said. "I thought nobody lived here. I'll go right away."

There was something about him which caused her to offer the few blossoms she had picked. He ignored them.

"No need to go," he said. "I'm Whitcomb Sears and this is my home. I'll help you pick a pretty bouquet."

He was a gaunt man, slightly bent, with white hair. Heavy brows arched his deep-set eyes and met above a thin nose. His skin was the color of damp sand and wrinkled by sun and years, and it showed those spots of darker brown, like huge freckles, which sometimes appear on the aged. He wore a light wool shirt, dark coat and work pants, and scuffed black boots which could never have been polished. As he knelt, gathering the long-stemmed pinks, he hummed tunelessly.

"Pretty, ain't they? Smell good, too."

"Just a few, please. Your wife won't mind?"

"It don't make no difference what she'd mind, girl. She's dead." It was casually stated but with the finality of death itself.

"I'm sorry," she said. But he was humming again.

His presence imposed upon her a vague, static unease which increased when, after placing a bouquet in her arms, he said, "You look something like my little girl that went away." His gaze added to her discomfort. "Quite like my little girl," he said.

"Do you live alone?" she asked. He seemed too old to be living alone.

"Oh, yes. All alone. My wife died and my little girl went away. This has been my home all my life. Pretty, ain't it? Best place on the river. Prettiest place, my wife always said." He added irrelevantly, "I been to the pictures. Just got back."

90

"Oh." Then she understood. "In town, you mean. To the movies? Was it a good picture?"

"Dandy picture. I go 'most every day. Work on my cranberry bog in the morning—got a big bog down back—and go to the pictures afternoons. Mostly I go at night, too."

There was only one movie house in Bournham and the pictures changed twice a week. Stormy asked, "To the same theater? Every day?"

"Oh, yes. They have fine pictures there. I walk down and back mostly. Years past I used go in my boat."

She wanted to leave. Unease wrapped her like the fog.

"Look here, have you seen the view?" He walked toward the lip of the decline where his path pitched to the shore. She followed against her wish. An opening in the pines framed a vista of the river, white-capped. All the shore had a wild, a primitive appearance: scrub oak and tangled dwarf pine, razor grass and dunes and long reaches of glistening marsh. Here and there, in the green matting of hog cranberry, there were faint splashes of faded blue which were the last of the wild lupine. A few chimney pots gave evidence of habitation; otherwise this might still be the land of the Nauset-Wampanoags.

Mr. Sears shielded his eyes with his hand and gazed down the river. "A pretty sight. My wife loved it. She used come here time on end just to enjoy the view."

As he spoke, the first drops of rain began to fall.

" 'Most time for Willie-the-Whip," he said.

She had no question; more than ever she wanted to leave.

" 'Most time," he cautioned. "You listen."

Stormy listened, not knowing for what.

"He's late tonight," said Mr. Sears. "We'll hear him soon."

91

He pointed a crooked finger across-river. "You see that hill, girl? That's Burnt Indian Hill, highest point around. When the fog is on it like that, you can know for certain the weather will be fine."

The rising wind made an eerie soughing in the pines and the rain came in a sharp gust, bouncing on the water, noisy in the foliage. Stormy glanced at him quickly to learn if he teased her. His face gave no hint.

"No, girl," he said. "It never rains when Burnt Indian shows like that."

Then she knew he was living in the past. She smothered an impulse to tell him rain was streaming down his face.

"I must go now," she said.

"Do. Do, girl."

"I'll come again some day."

"You come any time, girl. If I'm not here just make yourself to home. Like as not, I'll be working at my bog in the morning and I'll be at the pictures in the afternoon. But you come any time and pick the pinks. Just be careful not to pull the roots, because my wife planted them and they come up every year."

From down the shore, strong on the wind, keen on the wind, came a song of loneliness, the voice of a whippoorwill calling the dusk.

"Hark," warned Mr. Sears. "There's Willie-the-Whip." He drew a thick gold watch from his trouser pocket. "Willie's late tonight. 'Most time I started for the evening picture. My wife loved listen to Willie-the-Whip."

She left him listening to Willie and gazing on the view whose haziness proved it would not rain—and the rain dropped a silver veil between them. She felt like running.

When she reached home her father was in conference with a heavy-set man she had not met.

"This is Mr. Salter, Stormy. My daughter. He has an excellent boat for sale and I think we'll buy it."

She mentioned her visit to Mr. Sears.

"I never heard tell Mr. Sears didn't know enough to get out of the rain," Salter said.

"He spoke of a daughter who went away."

Salter said nothing and she recognized a subject he wished to avoid.

"Anyway, the pinks are beautiful. His wife planted them."

"Lucy Sears planted them!" Salter snorted. "Mr. Sears said that? Lucy Sears never planted anything but an evil thought in a man's mind. The price of the boat is one hundred and ten dollars, Professor, and it's worth more."

On this night of June, in a steady drizzle, Cal Knight and Bobby Meade caught twenty-seven bass to a top of twenty-one pounds, live-lining sea worms in the rip off the Mashnee rocks near a submerged rock where Roccus, circling close to bottom, rubbing, wore thin the cartilage of her jaw where the hooks secured the plug. The presence of the plug was beginning to be a constant worry. She swam awkwardly, fed meagerly, lost weight. The trailing free hooks of the plug caught in sea beard and bladder weed, impeding her. The sudden resultant jerking of her head alarmed her. Occasionally she swam aimlessly at top speed as if in flight from the enemy that clung.

Webb Everly pulled the door to behind him, and Clifton Hartwell, seated by the fireplace, did not rise to greet him.

"I brought yours," Everly said as if in reassurance. "But I brought something else—a little news. That boy that's flying for me thinks he's entitled to a bigger cut."

"What do you think?" the banker asked.

"I think so, too."

"Then why don't you arrange for him to get a larger share?"

"You're willing, then?"

"So long as it doesn't reduce my own."

"Christ! That's what I figured. That kid is taking a double risk, spotting the schools and getting aboard in time for the seining. You're getting the hog's share and you can afford to contribute some."

"I'm not so sure."

"Not so sure of what?"

"That I'm getting all I'm entitled to get. You didn't produce any bills of sale last week. I'm taking your word for the size of the catch and the price you sell at."

"Why in hell don't you come along with us then if you're so goddam suspicious? Bills of sale, bah! I can fake any amount of bills of sale."

"I know it." The banker gave him a smile meant to be soothing. "Don't get your back up. What does my share figure this week?"

"A third with expenses out—*your* share of expenses—gives you seven hundred and twelve dollars. It ain't hay."

"No. That leaves fourteen hundred for you to divide. Neither is that, as you express it, hay."

"I've no kick coming; everything's working out as I saw. There's a lot of bass and plenty big ones just beginning to show. Price will go down some. Some of the sport boats are taking big rod and reel catches and marketing. Few of them are fishing nights."

94

"I was going to mention that. Has anyone been close to you when you've set?"

"Hell, no! If there's boats where the schools are we don't work the area. But mostly there aren't. We work between midnight and daybreak. Before sunup we're on our way to a market where there's no questions asked and the price is only a few cents off the New York Fulton Market quotation. But they're not giving any bills of sale and you can't blame 'em."

"There was something I wanted to mention, and don't take offense, Everly. I think you come here too early. I don't want people to see you coming to my house. It might arouse suspicion."

"Especially if I'm caught," Everly said bitterly.

"Especially if you're caught," the banker agreed.

The seiner counted out and handed Hartwell his share.

"I ain't getting caught. You going to reconsider about kicking in for that fly-boy's ante?"

"No. Nothing to reconsider. We made a bargain."

"You want him to quit and maybe spill his guts?"

Hartwell's voice had an edge. "Have you mentioned my name?"

"Naturally not. You think I'm crazy?"

"Then the concern as to whether he spills his guts is yours, not mine—yours and the others. *You* sweeten his ante."

Everly tried a switch. "You going to buy a drink?"

"Certainly. What would you like?"

"I'll take the brandy. The warmth lasts longer, and after midnight it's still wet and cold. Though you wouldn't know."

The banker poured.

"Here's to crime!" Everly said, gulping.

Long after he had gone Hartwell turned the phrase over in his mind. He'd participated in many a shady deal in his career but in none where the letter of the law hadn't given him protection. Perhaps in the deal with Everly, though it was a highly profitable one, he had gone a little too far. He had no great trust in the seiner. Everly wasn't the type of man—Hartwell thought with an irony he did not recognize—you could trust very far.

Across Roccus' range of vision, quartering like a hunting dog, a torpedo shape streamed bubbles that rose to the first light of the first sun of summer. An eleven-foot length of black and white glided effortlessly, dark snout questing. Behind it, cartwheeling from the surface, came another, tail flukes bent on the plane, dropping like a roller-coaster car. Then over an expanse of more than an acre of water, a dozen such shapes appeared. Roccus took alarm.

These were bottle-nosed dolphins, commonly miscalled porpoises, which on the flood tides had moved into the bay to feed on the alewives and now were returning in the way they had come, to pass through Quicks Hole and journey to the back side of Cape Cod. They were not hungry but were hunting merely for sport, surfacing to breathe and blow, diving to the bottom with thrusts of flippers and flukes. They were barrel-round and hog-fat, and the largest was twice the length of Roccus. This was the leader, Truncatus, who was twelve feet from the tip of his five-inch snout to the flange of his concave, pigmented flukes.

Truncatus was an old dog dolphin who, the year before,

had dropped his twenty-two pairs of teeth from diseased gums. Prey which required much chewing he since had carefully avoided as an aged man shapes his diet to his powers of mastication. He gummed soft food like an old human and like a human, he felt rheumatic twinges along his backbone.

Roccus took alarm at his approach. She feared no single dolphin but, wearied and worried by the plug, she feared the school. As Truncatus dived on her, she drove forward and upward to pass over his head and came head-on with a young female dolphin who habitually followed the leader to take the foods he avoided. Roccus thrust and sinuated, passing above her, surfaced and dived. The commotion attracted another of the dolphins and another, and soon all the school joined in the chase, converging on the bass. Roccus' speed was greater, but the dolphins came from several directions and in her weakened condition panic seized her. One of the smaller and swifter of the enemy gained to within chopping distance and sank his teeth, three-eighths of an inch long, into the wrist of Roccus' tail, receiving a caudal blow which momentarily stunned him.

The dolphins sported, enjoying Roccus' discomfort. They had the nature of otters. In this fashion of play they often attacked sharks, butting and chopping at them until they were lifeless. They tried to butt Roccus but she was too swift. They closed about her, chopping. In a fury of motion she somersaulted and seized a snout in her jaws. Her teeth, in parallel patches along the base of her tongue, tore flesh from Truncatus' snout. She dived under the shaken dolphin and escaped westward, feeling a balance she had missed, a plague gone from her.

The dolphins continued sporting, butting one another

in play—all except Truncatus, who carried, deeply embedded in his snout, the weight and the tail gang hooks of an oversized teakwood plug.

CLYSTIE HARROW, greeting Maddox at the door, said, "I thought Father O'Meara was coming with us."

"He was," Jeff Maddox said. "A problem arose. Father O'Meara always has a problem."

"I doubt that you asked him. It was a pretext to get me to consent to go."

"You have a level head on you and I like the way you use it. I confess, then. I didn't invite Father. He can come another time. Besides, a priest has no business with romance except to make it legal."

"What romance is this?" she asked.

"Ours," said Maddox blandly. "Yours and mine. Did you not admit the other day that you have no husband lurking in the background?"

"I have no husband past or present and I certainly have no romance, nor any wish for one. I *do* have a son."

"Where is he?" asked Maddox. "Is he ready to learn how to catch a fish?"

"Down there on the beach. I wonder you failed to see him."

He'd seen him, all right, but he'd wanted a few minutes alone with her and now he said, "I'll come in while you get squared away."

She smiled. "I'm squared away. Let's go." She tucked a bathing suit under her arm and pulled the front door shut.

"Is it possible you don't trust me in the house? Or trust yourself in the house with me?"

"I have no doubt of myself and I trust you in the house as much as I trust you anywhere, Maddox."

"Not exactly an expression of tender regard. Yet you're a discerning woman."

"No more so than most, surely. You're as obvious as daylight."

"And always a grievous fault. I've never made any progress with ladies because of it. They always expect me to howl."

"And you wouldn't disappoint them for worlds."

"Still, it's not always like a wolf. Take note." He cupped his hands and called, "Ow-wee! Don-nee!"

The small figure at the rim of the dropped tide turned an inquisitive head. Maddox shouted, "Come on, boy, we're going fishing."

The boy came running. Clystie Harrow's son was blond and slim, stretching out. He had a snub nose but otherwise the regular, fine features of his mother, and her long legs. He said, "Hello, Mother. Hello, Chief Maddox."

"I'll feel less like an Indian if you call me Jeff. You want to catch a fish?"

"You bet!"

"And that's an idiom you didn't pick up in France or Ireland." He put a hand on Donald's shoulder. "Look here. . . . Two fishing rods and a box of bait, squid and worms. Maybe we'll catch a striped bass. Can't ever tell."

"I can tell; I'm going to catch one."

They walked toward Rocky Point on the hard sand the tide had surrendered to the warmth of the late June sun. Donald waded in the lisp of water, exploring with a stick for sand dollars and hidden crabs.

99

"You have a nice profile," Maddox told the boy's mother. "I like the strength of it. The upper lip is a little short, but the chin and neck lines are the best. And lurking in the background of my mind there is a sense of having known you before, at least of having seen you under different circumstances."

"Anywhere you might have seen me would have been under different circumstances."

"Yes, I wouldn't have forgotten if I'd walked the beach with you before."

She possessed, he thought, about all the physical qualities he had ever sought in a woman, and he had been, in this respect at least, a demanding man. She had beauty and a bold figure which had made no sacrifice to maturity or motherhood; she was lithe and vividly alive; she had poise and a fine sense of humor as it was displayed in their conversational sparring. But there was about her something else which caused her to be, in Maddox's opinion, a more attractive woman than he had ever sought, and this was a quality which, because it was as much a part of his own make-up as his big hands were part of his body, he had no difficulty in naming. It was the quality of hardness, hers the feminine counterpart of his own; not a cynicism of exhausted emotion but a shell of protection for emotion that has been tortured and shall not be exposed to suffering again, he thought.

As steel may lie under a thin veneer of rubber this hardness of hers lay close to a deceptively yielding surface, but the hidden armor was one that would not easily dent, and had, he thought, repelled the points of many spears. She was not adroit in its concealment and he thought she did not try to be. Her simple statement that

100

she had never had a husband was an example of this hardness, which lacked either defiance or apology. Maddox would have been disappointed had he detected either.

She wore, for their outing, a red-flecked, dark-green skirt of Irish looming and an oversize, yellow cardigan showing wear at the buttonholes. Her legs and feet, well tanned, were bare; she had feet that complemented her long, tapering hands—narrow feet, high-arched, broad at the toes with the toes long and well shaped. He turned to look back at the tracks they had made.

"What is it, Maddox?" she asked.

"I looked to see if the dobbies were following. Do you know about the dobbies?"

"My father told me about them when I was a girl. They live in the dunes. They're like the little people of Ireland. I knew them well before I met the leprechauns. I told you this was my home."

"But little more," he said.

"Because there is only a little more and what there is doesn't matter now. This land was my home when I was a girl. I left it as a girl and now I've come back to it and probably to stay."

"A good place to bring up a boy."

"You've said that before and I think I agreed it is a better place than most, Maddox."

"Has no one ever told you it's unseemly to address a man by his surname?"

"But I prefer it to your given name. Tell me, Maddox, how long have you been on this station?"

"Since after the first war."

"I remember there was a war," she said. "And after?"

"Here until another war."

"A war and another war. And another war to come." A shadow fell across her face. "I wish to Christ, Maddox, I'd never borne a child for war!"

It was a small, intense explosion. He had no sooner felt the shock of it than her demeanor changed. She said banteringly, "Why, Maddox! Two wars for you? You're an old, old man!"

"One adjective will suffice," he said, "and I'll permit you to use it only in comparison with yourself. But yet I'm not so old."

"Can you still run?"

"When the need requires."

"Then I'll race you to the point."

She was running as she said it and it took twenty strides to overtake her, and then, because the rods made running awkward and Donald had joined the race—and because he wanted to watch them—he stopped abruptly. She ran with long-legged, easy grace, head back, hair flying, and though he had stopped running, something within him kept up with her, some tenderness, atypical of him, that she had aroused. It was a new, a strange feeling, and one, for the time being, he would not too closely inspect or try to analyze.

Clystie allowed her son to pass her, then waited, laughing, for Maddox. "I'm getting old, too," she confessed.

"Never say it and no one will ever know."

At the point, in the wind-scooped hollow at the base of a dune where thatch grass grew, Maddox rigged the rods for fishing while she went behind the dune to change into her bathing suit. Donald was an attentive pupil, and when they were ready they walked to the surf and Maddox cast the baits far out to fish the bottom, thrusting the rod butts deep into the sand.

"We set the lines fairly tight," he explained. "The drag is off but the click is on and if a bass takes hold we'll hear the reel clicking."

"I shall catch a striped bass, Jeff," the boy said. "I guess I'll become the best fisherman in all the world."

"You might," said Maddox, "but if I were you I would be content with less. I'd try hard to become a happy fisherman."

"I will be a happy fisherman," Donald said.

"Some of the best fishing days can be those when you catch no fish at all. You'll learn about them. It depends on who you're fishing with."

"But first I want to learn to catch a bass. Then I can learn how to be happy not catching a bass," Donald protested.

Clystie came from behind the dune and Maddox saw her and said to the boy, "Stay here and mind the rods," and went to meet her. The bathing suit was yellow nylon. The skirt of it and the cardigan with which she had cloaked her shoulders were less concealing than she thought.

Maddox said, "I will look once and then I will not look again."

"I will take it as a compliment though it is open to another interpretation. But have you never before seen a woman in a bathing suit?"

"My share. Perhaps never one so lovely."

"A line that no more becomes you than sheep's clothing. Are you going to spoil the picnic, Maddox?"

"I will not," he promised. "I'll say no more."

"Then go to Donald. He has a fish on."

He had. Maddox ran to the boy, who reeled at something heavy. The action of the rod tip told it was no bass.

103

"Keep him coming," Maddox coached. "Keep your rod tip high. I bet you've got a skate."

"What's a skate, Jeff?"

"You'll see. Takes a good man to catch one."

It was a skate, reluctantly dragged into the brown shallows, body cupped, tail thrashing. Maddox turned it over with his foot and extricated the hook.

"That's no good, Jeff."

"Well, it's a fish."

"It doesn't take a good man to catch one."

"Well, sometimes the big ones come hard."

"Jeff?"

"Yuh, Don?"

"I guess I boasted and that's the punishment."

"Why, I don't think anything of the kind. A skate is a miserable kind of critter but I don't guess God put 'em in the ocean to punish anybody. If He did there's an awful lot of punishment waiting for fishermen."

"Who's God, Jeff?"

"Fellow put the fish in the ocean—animals on the land —birds in the air." He was getting into quicksand as quickly as that. "Know what I think? When the tide gets half up you'll catch your bass. Look, now, how these worms are hooked on one hook and the head of the squid on the other with the point up between the eyes. And watch my cast. Like this. . . . Easy . . . does . . . it. You want to try?"

"Next time I will."

The midday sun was hot. When the tide was half in, Clystie swam; and later while she was changing Donald caught his bass, a small one of five or six pounds, handling it well under Maddox's coaching, hauling it finally exhausted and gasping to the edge of the surf.

They gathered their gear and started home, led by a triumphant, sunburned small boy dragging his first bass.

"God's a good guy," Donald said. "He let me catch a bass, Jeff. Next time I will learn how to be a happy fisherman not catching a bass."

Maddox said to her, "A successful day from one standpoint, anyway."

"A pleasant day," Clystie said. "I enjoyed it as much as Donald. In a way you surprised me."

"Perhaps I surprised myself."

"I mean you take things as they are, Maddox, which I like. You are inquisitive but not overbearingly so. You hide your curiosity rather well."

"But deliberately. Someday I will press you for answers to questions—about that elusive memory I have of you, about the boy, about your real name, which, I know, you do not use, and about your home somewhere in this area."

"And I'll give you no answers. You don't need them, Maddox. For what you have in mind for me, you don't need to know."

"What have I in mind for you?"

"Don't you want to name it?"

"I will name what you think I have in mind. It revolves around the theory that an unmarried mother is fair game for any man's hunting."

"I hadn't thought of it so brutally, but that will cover it."

They stopped walking. Donald forged ahead.

"As a matter of fact, I'm confused, Clystie. I hadn't thought about it in exactly that way."

She said quietly, "There could be no other way, Maddox."

"We'll leave it there, then, sleeping. I shall try to

105

awaken it later, perhaps. The boy and I will go again and if you like, whenever you like, we'll let you tag along. And we will take Father O'Meara. Now, here's your house. If your old hag is within, I'll invite myself for coffee."

Roccus' jaw healed swiftly, causing her no pain. As June waned she joined first one and then another of the many schools of striped bass which remained in the area of Cape Cod Canal. Some of these fish were from the Chesapeake region and more were native to the Hudson and its tributaries. There were few from the Roanoke; most of the migrating Roanoke fish had come no farther north than the Jersey coast.

All these fish in the canal area moved back and forth with the tides through the big ditch, driving whiting from the bottom to the surface, where, in the rips, they skitted furiously, heads out of water, terrorized. The bass rose beneath them in pursuit, tail-smashing to stun them.

Day and night the anglers lined the canal riprap to cast for the bass, using eelskins on weighted rigs during the darkness and plugs in daylight hours. Favorite spots were crowded. These were adjacent to the swiftest rips and had been given names common among the angling fraternity. Some of the names were Halfway Gate, Split Rock, The Mussel Bed, The Cradle, Lobster Pound, Lumber Yard, Paddy's Rock, The Beacon, The Herring Run, The High Tension, Portugee Hole and The Basin. There were a score more. Some men fished all night and slept in the daytime in cars parked in a wooded section under the

Bourne highway bridge. Some fished for market, some only for sport; others fished for sport, yet marketed their catch so they could meet expenses and continue to fish for fun. When the bass were choosy, or chasing whiting far out in the middle of the canal, hard to reach, many of the fishermen lived for days on little more substantial than coffee and doughnuts. Restaurants stayed open all night to cater to them, and these, on the slack tides, were crowded with anglers who were waiting for the rips to make up. They had only one subject of conversation—striped bass. There was none but dreamed of catching a record fish. None really expected to. They were a red-eyed, bewhiskered, somewhat odoriferous congregation of zealots.

JUDGE LEANDER WICKETT reached home at five o'clock, having remained after court for fifteen minutes to confer with the chief justice and the district attorney on several matters involved in the administration of justice to a quartet of armed robbers who had spent the loot of a bank robbery to engage certain counsel adept in the defense of felons. Counsel had yanked a few political strings and had manufactured substantial alibis. That afternoon, having watched developments over a period of ten days of trial, Judge Wickett, with a few brief observations, had slashed through a maze of red tape, red herrings and contradictory testimony to expose a plot, nailing one attorney for contempt and eventual disbarment, and two witnesses for perjury. The jury had required only an hour of deliberation to reach a verdict of guilty on all counts in the case of all defendants. He had congratulated the jury; the chief justice had congratulated him.

At home he was greeted by his grandson, Andrew, an eight-year-old who attended private day school. His daughter met him with a smile, a kiss and a glass of orange juice slightly iced. She had been a comfort and joy to him since the death of his wife ten years before and doubly so since her husband, a commander in the Naval Reserve, had lost his life in Okinawa action. She was an attractive woman and, he thought, it might be best if she fell in love again. Now she listened to the short résumé of the day's court proceedings he was accustomed to give each evening. He made no mention of his part in the final determination of the case, but she could sense his elation.

"Do you realize you'll be twenty-five years on the Superior Court bench day after tomorrow?" she asked.

A man of less integrity would have pretended this had escaped his attention. Judge Wickett said, "Yes. I'd thought of it."

"I've something to tell you which I feel you'll think I should have mentioned before. I know you're going to disapprove. You're to be the guest of honor at a small testimonial dinner at the Harvard Club on your anniversary."

"No!" he exclaimed, honestly dismayed.

"Two members of the Supreme Court and the executive committee of the Bar Association planned it. Daley Merrill phoned to make sure you had no other plans and pledged me to secrecy until today."

"Making a show! It's in rotten taste, Sue. We must stop it."

"You can't stop it now, darling, and I don't think it's

108

in bad taste at all. There's nothing irregular provided irregular persons aren't allowed to attend."

"No," he said. "There are too many people who want too many things. I'll phone Merrill after dinner."

They had a quiet dinner prepared and served by Roma, a colored girl who doubled as maid and cook. Andrew was, as usual, encouraged to monopolize the conversation and dwelt upon the day's highlights at school. There had been fun in mathematics class when the teacher was guilty of an error in multiplication while working a problem on the blackboard. There had been fun in the gym, where Andrew had chinned himself a thousand times.

"How many, Andrew?" his mother asked.

"About a thousand. Johnny Wright could do it only half as much."

"Not a thousand," Sue protested.

"About," he persisted. "I didn't count."

"Nobody can chin himself a thousand times."

"I can," he countered, slightly sullen.

She glanced appealingly at her father. "Well, now," said Judge Wickett, "I think the best way for Andrew to prove how many times he can chin himself is actually to count the number of times. He can do it again tomorrow and report to us."

Andrew brightened. "That's a cinch," he said.

"We'll be going to Bournham the end of this week. Are you looking forward to it?"

"Yes, sir."

When he had gone to bed his mother asked, "How many times do you think he can chin himself?"

"Oh, maybe a dozen or fifteen. I haven't any idea."

Something else bothered her. She asked, "Do you think he'll give us an honest count?"

"Of course," said Judge Wickett. "It's natural for children to exaggerate their accomplishments. Put them on their honor and you'll get an honest reaction. Now I must phone Daley Merrill."

He presented his demurrer to Supreme Court Justice Merrill. Judge Merrill thought he was being overcautious, leaning too far backward. The dinner would be very small with no political figures except the Governor in attendance. There would be no publicity. It was too late to cancel the plan. Judge Wickett, unconvinced, acquiesced with all the graciousness he could muster.

Next evening Andrew reported he had chinned himself nineteen times, almost twenty.

"Maybe someday I can do it a thousand," he said.

And on the following night, Judge Wickett was privately feted. The Governor and the Chief Justice paid him high tribute. He was honestly embarrassed, and he knew, following the presentation of a solid-silver coffee service and a set of golf clubs, that he spoke inadequately in response.

No member of the press attended because the event was a well-kept secret. Yet three days later the political column of a Boston morning newspaper reported:

> The heavyweights of the bench and bar dined Judge Leander Wickett in secret at the Harvard Club on the 25th anniversary of his appointment to the bench. The Governor attended and the event has especial significance in the fact that there will be a vacancy in the Supreme Court, through retirement, perhaps before the fall term.

Judge Wickett had the note called to his attention by his clerk. He read it with repugnance. Yet, during a morning devoted to cleaning up small affairs in anticipation of

110

summer recess, he caught himself speculating as to which justice might retire. Daley Merrill likely. Merrill was in ill health; he was fond of him and he carried weight at the State House. And Merrill had instigated the dinner. . . . With the stern discipline of the years, Judge Wickett arrested this mental wandering.

FATHER O'MEARA closed his breviary and removed his specs.

"It seems to me, Maddox, you are trying to tell me something you haven't yet put into words. That is unlike you."

"Yet it could be." Maddox was no longer sure of himself. He walked to the rectory window and stood there, back to the priest, and spoke as if addressing someone outside. "What I said of the boy is the truth of what I feel about him. Don't you like that expression, 'God's a good guy!' Father?"

"I love it," said the priest. "God *is* a good guy."

"This boy is old enough for spiritual guidance of some sort, your own or another's. I choose you because you are less faker than most. At least you believe you teach the truth. You have something to offer him which in my youth was never offered me. Anyway, I never came in contact with it."

"It's never too late, Maddox. Is that what you call trite?"

"For myself I'm not seeking it now. And if I've ever felt the need of a faith I couldn't muster, you wouldn't expect me to confess it now, would you? And as a friend you wouldn't pursue that line of inquiry any deeper. You're

111

free to draw any conclusions you may from my request so long as you accede to it."

"But I had no least intention of doing otherwise, provided his mother has no objection. The instruction of a boy is not only a pleasure but a duty. There was something entirely different troubling me."

"I might guess it." Maddox turned to face him.

"You need not. I'll state it. What is the relationship between this boy's mother and yourself?"

Maddox grinned. "I did guess it! I'll be completely honest with you if I say that's a question also troubling me. I don't know the answer, Father. This is a woman who attracts me as no other has ever done. Yet her own estimate of our relationship is that any unmarried mother is fair hunting for any man. She said so."

"She said that?"

"She expressed it as a thought that must be paramount in my own mind."

"And is it?"

"I can't say yes and I can't say no. I don't believe it is. It's there; it exists. But I'm fairly sure it doesn't dominate."

"You mean, Maddox, that it has occurred to you that you might marry this woman?"

"Now that you've said it, yes. But it has also occurred to me—and in a way it has been made evident to me, at least hinted—that she wouldn't marry. Me or anyone else. You must meet and talk with this woman to understand her, Father. She's tougher-fibered than I am. She's been through more suffering and my guess is that it doesn't only concern the boy. There's a hard shell there and I haven't much idea of what may lie beneath it. Either she's lost all capacity for normal emotional outlets—or else she's drained of emotion itself and there's only emptiness left."

112

"What is her attitude toward the boy, Maddox?"

"So far as I can observe it's the normal attitude of a mother toward a son."

"Then how can you ever speak of emptiness? All you have pictured to me is a woman who has lived in fear and sorrow, without God, for a long time. I have known many such. I suspect, Maddox, you have too. Perhaps I can help her as well as the boy."

"Perhaps you can. She asks nothing from anyone."

"What are you going to do about her?"

"How do you mean?"

"What are you going to do about her?"

"All right, then. I'm going to make love to her. If she wants to be married I'll marry her but I'll make love to her anyway."

"Why couldn't you leave her alone, Maddox?"

"Why should I leave her alone if I love her—if I have what you'd call an honorable intention?"

"I doubt that you have any such thing. Subconsciously you anticipate a rejection of your honorable intention and the acceptance, in substitution for it, of a dishonorable act. You mean to sleep with this woman by one means or another."

"I hope to."

"And this about the boy. . . . How much subterfuge is there in your professed interest in his welfare?"

"None whatever, Father, regardless of what you think. I'm fond of him. I never had a kid of my own—that I know of."

"You are a hard man to talk to, Maddox, because you always try to bring the plane of the discussion down to your own amoral level, deliberately to place me at a disadvantage. I don't complain of it; I merely mention it to

113

let you know I'm aware of it. What respect I held for you was based on your interest in the welfare of your fellowmen, certainly not on any interest you had in your own future in this life or the hereafter. This respect is under severe strain. I ask you to leave that woman alone."

"I won't promise you that." Maddox raised his voice for the first time.

"Will you leave her alone until I've visited her?"

Maddox considered. "If you don't take all summer getting around to it," he said.

Rosie appeared in the doorway and frowned at Maddox. Maddox made a face at her.

"Tom Salter telephoned," she told Father O'Meara. "He says Manuel Riba would be in need of a visit from you."

"Thank you, Rosie." The priest sighed and got to his feet with some painful effort. "I don't make much progress there, Maddox. Perhaps I won't make any more with the mother of this boy."

"I'll drive you out to Riba's."

"I'll go alone if you don't mind."

"I might be of help. I'm not due back on station until three o'clock. Have I offended you, Father?"

"There's no offense to me," said the priest. "Only to God. No, Maddox, it's just that you're the last man in the world I want as witness to my failures."

WHEN THE phone rang, Professor Force answered. "For you, Stormy," he called.

"This is Stormy Force."

"Miss Force? This is Cal Knight."

114

"Oh?"

"Do you remember me?"

"We cut off your big fish."

He laughed. "That wasn't exactly what I referred to. I thought you might like to go out in the boat someday. We've been having good fishing and you might enjoy it."

"I haven't fished much, but I suppose I could learn. My father might enjoy it."

"I'm sure he would. Bobby and I have a free day next week—let's see, that's the last day of June. We'd like you along if you can make it."

"I'll talk to Dad and let you know. Can I phone you?"

"No, but you're downtown fairly often. You could leave word with Tom Salter if our boat isn't at the wharf."

"I will," she said. "And thank you."

She said to her father, "We're going fishing, Dad."

"Are we? With whom?"

"That man who had the fight with Pickman—Cal Knight."

The professor had been on the verge of saying he'd prefer not to go, but the name, and something in the tone of Stormy's voice, caused him to change his mind. "That's excellent," he said.

"Dad?"

"Yes, dear?"

"How would he know I'm downtown often?"

"Why, I don't know. I suppose anyone of normal intelligence would know you must go in to shop."

"Dad?"

"Yes?"

"What would you think if—if Pickman and I decided to break up—if I decided to break up with Pickman—if we didn't get married?"

115

"Do you want a perfectly honest answer?"

"Of course, Dad."

"It would be the very nicest thing that ever happened to you—or to me."

After he said it he completed the best essay he'd ever written.

THE BLUE-SILVER butterfish were in the surf. The bass schools were herding them. Three fifty-pound fish—females, mistakenly called bulls—worked with Roccus. The sun in Cancer wheeled for deep summer with the end of June.

July

MANUEL RIBA awoke in the night, nauseated. He had been in a stupor for more than two weeks since the back-lash of his carefully designed plot to silence the mockery of Nick the Greek. During part of this period he had sweated and groaned through nightmares of delirium during which big lobsters chased him down streets lined with crowds seeking to impede his progress, tripping him, laughing at his terror. There were children as well as men and women in the throng. All the lobsters bore tags announcing their individual weights as eleven-and-three-quarters pounds, and they all wore the leer of Nick Constantos.

Sometimes he had seen the face of Father O'Meara and realized that the presence of the priest was not a part of his dreams. Once, he knew, the priest prayed over him. He was also aware that at least once a doctor had attended him, sticking his arm with a needle, and now, his fever subsiding, the alcohol gone from his brain, he remembered occasionally having seen the hard, uncompromising features of Maddox.

117

Manuel's shack was a frame, tar-papered structure, flat-roofed, supported on cedar posts sunk into the mud of the marsh. A flimsy wall that did not quite meet the unfinished ceiling partitioned it into kitchen and bedroom. The kitchen held a table and two chairs and a range that burned wood or coal. In the bedroom were an old pine chest and a full double bed with tarnished brass ends. In this bed his parents had slept while he occupied a nest of blankets on the floor. Following his father's departure, Manuel had shared it to the extent of a third with his mother. Since her death he had shared it more generously with many a girl. Though not yet with Maggie Blynn.

He swung his feet to the floor with an effort that started his head pounding and was sick out the door opening on the marsh. Like a pointer on running pheasant he quartered the kitchen, seeking whisky. There was none. The shelf over the table held an assortment of canned goods, mostly soup, and there was a loaf of reasonably fresh bread. His stomach felt as if a bilge pump sucked it; he knew some hot soup would help. Reaching for a can, he saw the slip of paper protruding from between two cans, and in the light of the kerosene lamp he spelled out the contents of a note:

> There's one drink left in the bottle under your bed. Call Father O'Meara. You are a no good bastard if you worry him again.
>
> Maddox

He found the bottle and drained it and felt his blood come alive. Then he opened a can of tomato soup and, unable to manage the kindling of a fire, spooned it cold from the can. He pulled on slacks and a light cotton shirt and sneakers. Summer had come without his noticing.

His battered clock, which someone had kept wound, said it was two-thirty in the morning. Of what day he couldn't guess except it was a day for black coffee, hot black coffee. He was leaving when the thought of fishing occurred to him, and he turned back for his flat wooden reel, on which was wound a length of tarred cod line with a six-ounce lead and a 7/0 hook. With the long-bladed sheath knife on his belt he cut the hook from the leader and re-tied it with shaking hands.

From his shack he had a quarter-mile hike to the tarred road and an equal distance to The Trickle, an all-night lunchcart in Bournham. He negotiated the half-mile with only one stop to relieve his abused stomach. Except for the counterman who had the midnight to eight duty, The Trickle was empty, so Manuel knew the canal rips had made up for the best fishing.

It had not occurred to him up to the time he ordered black coffee that he might not have any money. He had a vague recollection of having sold his big outboard for whisky, but he also hazily recalled having spent this money, a sum unknown to him. He fished his left trouser pocket and found it empty; and in quick alarm, because he knew his credit with the counterman was nonexistent, he explored the right. What he felt was reassuring. There were a five-dollar bill and another note. The note said:

Talk with me about how you spend this money. I bought your motor back from the man who cheated you and you can pay me later. Yours in Christ,

Father

The priest's kindness warmed him more than the coffee and by virtue of it he had a second cup. Then he ordered a hamburg. Father O'Meara hadn't told him not

119

to spend it, only to talk with him about how he spent it. Father would certainly want him nourished. He thrust aside a small yearning for a drink of whisky and had a third cup of coffee.

From the restaurant he walked a short distance to one of several bait shacks near the canal and roused the owner, who, having dealt with him before and having only just dozed off after the departure of a better customer, resented Manuel's knocking.

"Got squid?" asked Manuel.

"Frozen," said the bait man, yawning.

"I buy three squid."

"Sell 'em by the carton. Half a buck. Depends on the size of the squid how many's in 'em. You know that."

"All I want three squid," Manuel persisted.

"Take the old ones?"

"Oh, sure."

From a soupy carton outside the shack the baitman dumped three squid, slimy, onto a brown paper. The unmistakable fragrance of ripe squid rode the night air.

"Take 'em as is for a dime. Don't ever get me up again." Resentment prodded his memory and he grinned. "Say! You bought any more big lobsters lately?"

Manuel said nothing. He wanted to wash the other's face in the squid, but that would mean a further expenditure for more bait at another shack. And he didn't feel up to it physically. He left with the squid dripping a trail behind him and he saw again the crowds trying to throw him in front of pursuing lobsters. Everyone from Bournham to Provincetown would have heard the story of the lobster and how Nick Constantos had shown him to be a liar and a fool.

Walking to the canal bank he put this idea from his mind by a series of thought manipulations climaxed by the conclusion that he had served Father O'Meara well in not having wasted the squid by using them as a washcloth. He had thus conserved a portion of the priest's investment in him. Yet Maddox, he thought, would have cheered the waste of the squid in such good cause. He had told neither the priest nor Maddox about the episode of the lobster—he hoped, though he could not be sure.

When he reached the canal he turned left along the engineers' road, a hard-surfaced single-lane road close to the banks above the plunging riprap. All cars except those used by the guards on radio patrol were forbidden use of this road. Many anglers wished they might use it and resented the restriction, but Manuel, having no car and no expectation of one, was not one of these.

From the elevation of the road above the uneven granite blocks Manuel observed through the glow of the canal lights that many were fishing. East and west of the oil dock that hid his lobster pot he heard reels singing and, far out in the oily whirlpools, the unmistakable splash of eelskins tied on heavy rigs. Once he heard a fish struggling on the surface, twice he heard the thump of clubs on fish. Anglers were silhouetted by the lights against the moondrift on the gurgling rips, and to two he called, "You catch luck?"

Nobody admitted anything but bad luck, yet he knew there were fish hidden in riprap or grass, or staked out in the water. He knew the fishermen lied; and though they would have lied to anyone, it was in his mind that they withheld the truth only from him, from Manuel Riba. From Double-It-Up.

121

For a short distance beyond the east dolphin serving the oil dock there were fishermen. One hundred yards east of the dolphin there was nobody. There, about one hundred feet offshore, was a reef of mud and boulder, several hundred feet in length, that was the curse of the night eelskin fishermen. Thousands of deep-running rigs lay embedded in it. Between reef and shore there was a varying depth, no greater than twenty feet, which the night anglers had learned in recent years to avoid. Yet in years gone it had been a productive water on an east tide to the daring man who would creep up a plank ladder to the dolphin top and live-line a worm bait toward a backwater eddy inside the reef.

The plank ladder was long since gone with a storm tide and had not been replaced. It was no longer fashionable to fish with live bait. The bass, unaware of changing fashion, except in the variety of lures presented to them, most of which they avoided, still used the backwater inside the reef.

Manuel knew this. He knew that on an east tide as now prevailed bass would turn in from the outside rip over the reef to the shoal where bait worked continually. It was a favorite spot of his and there were seldom others to challenge him for elbowroom. Halfway between the east mud bank that turned the tide to backwater and the dolphin, which marked its start at a setback of riprap, he climbed down the irregular stone facing with the aid of his hands, being none too secure on his feet, and located a flat rock near the tide's edge. Here he unlaced his tarred line, baited his single hook with the head of a squid and hurled it out after winding up for centrifugal force with three overhand, clockwise circles of the heavy sinker.

Thereafter he reclined uncomfortably in the riprap be-

122

hind him and tried to doze off. He had a turn of line around one finger. His head was beginning to ache again.

When the bass mouthed the bait he was wide-awake, clearing the turn of line. He waited on a slow, mental count of ten, and jerked the running line. Life struggled at the end of it. He felt a small bass. He hauled the fish in, hand over hand, and at the edge of the water beat its head on a rock. Then he hid it in the riprap.

From the engineers' road someone called down, "Anything doing?"

He looked up and saw two men with rods. "Not yet," he called.

This was the essence of the answer he had always received to similar questions. He thought: *To hell with them!*

When the pair had passed along he rebaited and cast out again. He dozed for close on an hour, awaking as day came, framed in the arc of Bourne highway bridge—a watercolor. Suddenly it was light enough to see scores of casters up and down the canal on both banks. None was close to him. Terns came from the west, querulous, diving on small bait. Big gulls swooped over the whiting driven to surface in the canal center. He had another strike. A bass picked up the squid bait and moved offshore twenty feet. The fish felt the hook and dropped it before Manuel could set up. He rebaited with his last squid head; he had no faith in the squid bodies unless the bass were thick and famished. He felt a little better. He sat tense, determined not to miss another chance.

It was light enough now and the stirring of the back-water was sufficiently lessened by tide pressure so that from his perch on the canal bank he could see down into twelve or more feet of water off the riprap—see to the bottom. There were innumerable cunners drifting. He saw four or five red crabs, one having trouble with a starfish. He saw a small lobster move forward, pull back, disappear in a drift of weed.

Then he saw a school of spent herring. They had climbed the fish ladder at the herring run, spawned in Herring Pond and had dropped back into the canal again, thin and scarred, to work their way seaward. They were weakened and had turned into the backwater for rest. Behind them swam a great bass.

At the first sight of Roccus, Manuel trembled with quick fear that the alcoholic distortions had returned to his brain. Then, realizing the bass was a product of true vision, he trembled with excitement. Except for the tremor he did not move. The huge fish passed directly below him not three feet under the surface, her lateral stripes sharply delineated. Her tail seemed hardly to move. One big round eye seemed to stare at Manuel. For the better part of a minute she remained in sight. Then the pod of herring darted away from the riprap and the giant followed, unhurried, and was lost to view.

The trembling of Manuel's hand agitated the line. He tried to stop it and could not until he grasped right wrist in left hand, elbow on left knee. What if the fish should seize his bait? Big bass liked squid. He shook from head to foot.

Five minutes passed and nothing happened except in his thoughts. He knew that water and conditions of light often magnified objects beneath the surface, but he had watched bass swimming many times and he knew he had seen a fish the like of which few anglers ever had reported. At first he told himself that the bass was at least ten feet long and two hundred pounds in weight.

124

Thinking of Father O'Meara, and of Maddox, and of their advice, he lessened this estimate but he could not reduce the size to less than six feet and one hundred pounds. He knew this to be the truth before God and he could not contain himself any longer. He snagged an end of the wooden winder in a cleft of rock and ran down the engineers' road to the mud bank where two casters were at work with plugs. A bass of about thirty pounds lay on the bank, and both fishermen were concentrated on the capture of another.

"Big fish!" Manuel cried. "Coming this way!"

One caster turned. "Yuh?" he said.

"Big, big fish!" said Manuel.

"How big?"

Starting to say how big he abruptly realized he couldn't answer. St. Peter might have answered truthfully without fear of disdain, disbelief, scorn or ridicule. Manuel Riba could not; not Double-It-Up Riba whom none believed.

He felt nausea again, knew he would be sick. He said, apologetically, "Big." He turned back toward his handline, puked in the grass, went waveringly along the road, his little strength suddenly drained. Opposite the small white grass stake where he had fished he went down the riprap backwards, lowering himself with the support of shaking hands.

He found the rock where he had stood to cast—or thought he did—found the cleft where he had wedged his wooden reel. The reel wasn't there. He could, he knew, be mistaken in location. He climbed the riprap to the road and walked along it, east and west, seeking his line, which, now in the full daylight, would show against the water. It was not to be seen.

125

Then, belatedly, he remembered the bass he had caught and stashed between rocks. He returned to the point of his original inspection and found the fish where he had hidden it. The same cleft he had previously inspected was, he knew, the one he had sought; it was vacant of his reel and line. A fish had taken his last squid and his gear had gone with it. It could have been the great fish, Manuel thought. Then he knew it could have been any one of lesser fish.

ROCCUS WENT east with Manuel's gear trailing and rid herself of it quickly. She had taken the ripe squid head on the bottom because its richness had pervaded the waters and drawn her to it. She had been hooked only lightly when the hook came taut against the snub of line. She had lost the wooden reel at the edge of the reef, and later she had circled a boulder west of the herring run, snubbed the trailing cod line, and jerked the hook free without seriously tearing her jaw. Then, as the sun rose, she sank to the bottom with the schools of smaller bass.

MANUEL WALKED into Bournham with his bass. When a fish market opened he sold it for two dollars, at the rate of twenty-five cents a pound. The story of the big bass rose in his throat but would not come out. Then he felt the proprietor was cheating him; the price should be twenty-eight cents a pound. This thought was in his mind when he left. Actually, he had received three cents more per pound than the buyer paid for other fish later the same day.

Outside The Trickle he had a need for more coffee, but the place was crowded with anglers who had deserted the rips after the morning show of fish. He thought if he entered he would blurt out that which was demanding release at whatever cost. He knew the reception the story would receive. Too many knew Double-It-Up. Too many knew the story of the lobster. He moved along for St. Peter's.

Father O'Meara had begun the mass; the church was comfortably filled. Manuel found a place well in the rear on the aisle so that he could quickly escape if his stomach misbehaved.

"Munda cor meum ac labia mea, omnipotens Deus, qui labia. . . ." Father's rich voice filled the edifice. He was no mumbler.

"Cleanse my heart and my lips, O almighty God, Who didst cleanse with a burning coal the lips of the prophet Isaias. . . ."

Manuel's mind wandered. He had only a vague understanding of the ritual of the mass, though Father O'Meara once had explained it in detail. It was not the type of information his mind catalogued. He thought of the great bass. He might get to tell Father about it. In an incongruous switch of thinking it came to him that he might tell Maggie Blynn. He thought of Maggie Blynn and with an effort put her out of mind, and at the act of consecration returned his attention to the priest.

"Hic est enim calix sanguinis mei. . . .

"For this is the chalice of my blood, of the new and everlasting testament: the mystery of faith: which for you

127

and for many shall be shed unto the remission of sins. As often as ye shall do these things ye shall do them in memory of me."

Manuel was one of the first to leave, going directly to the rear door of the rectory, which Rosie Carmody opened to him, then barred with her thin body.

"Why do you come here, dirty and smelling like a fish market?" she demanded. "You have the whole river at your front door and with no charge for the water. Is it soap you wish to borrow?"

Shame seared him. Despite his weaknesses he was by nature a man of cleanliness and neatness; he realized he must be foul. He sorrowfully touched a finger to his forehead and started away.

Shame also touched her. "Wait!" she commanded. "Come in as you are. If I sent you away I should never hear the end of it from Father."

At her direction he washed his face and hands at the sink and took a chair near the electric range. Coffee was perking and water boiling for eggs.

"Is it coffee you're after?" Rosie asked.

"To talk with Father O'Meara."

"Nevertheless I'll give you coffee and perhaps you could talk better for it."

She poured and he sipped gratefully. Father appeared for a moment, still wearing his alb, greeted Manuel and disappeared to remove the vestment. He was hungry and cheerful when he reappeared.

"Put in the eggs, Rosie—two for both of us—and time them three minutes and a half. Like rubber they were yesterday."

"Yesterday you were fooling around with a fishpole and wouldn't come to breakfast," she said without rancor.

128

"And the toast—have it well browned. How is it with you, my son?"

Manuel managed a smile. "Better than it was, Father."

"Still, it will be better yet. Drink your coffee."

"I brought the five dollars, Father. I bought some breakfast and some bait but I caught a fish and sold it."

"For the money there will be time enough later. Tell me about your fish."

The priest's tone expressed genuine interest.

Manuel condensed it. "Eight pounds on a squid head in that backwater inside the reef where not many fish."

The priest nodded. "A good place."

"Had another strike but didn't set quick."

Father O'Meara clucked his tongue. Delay in setting a baited hook was one of his own weaknesses.

Now I will tell him about the great bass, Manuel thought. The story drove past the constriction in his throat and was on the tip of his tongue. Yet it would not pass through his lips. The mental block became the physical barrier; his lips were a tight line, whitening. There was greater fear here than he had known outside the crowded restaurant. Father might pretend that he believed, but how could he? Manuel could not face the possibility of disbelief. If the priest doubted, who would ever believe? He ate his eggs, which pushed the story back into his throat.

"Your outboard is in the shed," the priest told him. "Maddox said he'd drive it down to your place when you're ready. I'll phone him and he may get it down this afternoon."

The sale of it was a dim detail his subconscious mind wished to avoid, yet he said, "Bad if I go back on bargain."

"There is no question of a bargain," said Father O'Meara. "It was recovery of stolen property. You sold it in a bad moment for twenty dollars." He thought of a way Manuel might be spurred. "That will be twenty-five you owe me, so you better start quahogging. Will you have more coffee, more toast?"

"No, thanks, Father. When you telephone Maddox thank him for coming with you to see me."

"Maddox was not with me when I visited you," the priest said.

Manuel thought of the note and the heel of jug under his bed.

Back at his shack, he bathed in the river, then shaved. He swept and did a washing, including blankets: these wouldn't dry before night but the night promised heat. Shaving, bathing, cleaning, he thought of the great bass he had seen; he thought of his vanished throw line. The great bass might have taken it.

In the afternoon Maddox brought his motor. He thought he might tell Maddox of the great bass, but he could not. Maddox did the talking.

"I've decided you're none of my goddamned business hereafter. I hope Father O'Meara comes around to the same conclusion. If you had any strength left after your bat I'd hammer hell out of you."

He propped the motor against the shack and turned to his car.

"You need anything?"

"No, thank you, Jeff. Who paid for the doctor?"

"What doctor? You better get to work."

Though it was late on the tide he ran his sled to the bay. He didn't have enough strength to use a bull rake; he had barely enough to tong. He boated a bushel of quahogs before the water got too deep. All the while he worked, the great bass swam through his mind—the great sight he couldn't share. If he couldn't tell Father O'Meara and Maddox, his only friends, who could he ever tell? The thought came to him again that he might, if conditions were right, tell Maggie Blynn. Then he knew he would not tell her. He would never tell anyone of the few for whom he had affection because their disbelief would hurt him too cruelly to bear. He would not mind so much the disbelief of those who had belittled him for years. These were many and eventually, he knew, he would tell one. It might be wise to select the lowest in this order. Nick the Greek! He might tell Nick because Nick's reaction, in view of what had gone before, would hurt him least.

DURING THE first week in July, Donnie Harrow caught his first bass on a plug, an eleven-pounder that golluped a bucktailed red popper over the Rocky Point hole at high water. Maddox aided only in the manipulation of the star drag.

"Now you're a man," he praised, "and we'll shake on it."

They shook hands. The boy was trembling all over.

"Cold in this heat?"

"No, sir. Just silly nervous, Jeff."

"Think nothing of it—happens to men of all ages. Let's take your fish up to your mother."

But Clystie Harrow was moving down to them.

"Mother—look!"

"Wonderful," she said. "I watched you catch it."

"God's still a good guy."

131

"I remember when you said that before."

"Jeff is a good guy, too."

"In our different ways we are okay," Maddox said. "Father O'Meara will explain the difference to you."

"Perhaps you'd better rest now," Clystie said.

"I want to catch another, Mother. All by myself. May I?"

"I guess you may try."

They watched him for a while, and Maddox suddenly became aware that she was crying, silently.

"What will he be like when he grows up, Maddox?"

"Stop blubbering and I'll tell you. Tall, inclined to be fair, with some of your good looks but not as handsome as I am. Yet he'll be wise with the lessons I will teach him."

That did not stop her quiet weeping.

"Once before, I thought you were going to cry when you spoke of the boy and the war. Why don't you get it off your chest? You had a bad experience. I had some, too. Let me tell you about a dame I met when we were in Liverpool getting set for D-day."

She said in quick anger at herself, "I don't want to hear. I'm a fool for crying. I haven't cried for a long, long time and I shall never cry again."

"Yes, you will cry again," he said.

"If I ever do, Maddox, I'll tell you why."

"Then you'll not need to cry any more. Let's fetch Donnie."

STORMY SAID, "Pickman, I've said I was terribly sorry that it turned out this way. I can't say any more."

There were anger and hurt pride in him, and a sense of frustration he had never known, and he said, "Yes, you can. You can be honest about it."

They were in the cabin of *Tiderunner* at the Force landing on the river. Brown had insisted, over Stormy's protests, on coming down. She had written breaking their engagement, had sent his ring, and had confirmed her decision by telephone in response to several pleadings which, giving further evidence as to a mental attitude resembling the pouting of a punished juvenile, convinced her she had made a belatedly astute move. She had argued that a quick, clean break was best, and that a further meeting was not only futile but from several standpoints unwise. Nevertheless he had arrived aboard the cruiser, and a few hours later—with Professor Force absenting himself at the movies in what he believed to be a good cause—they were having it out.

"I have been honest about it," Stormy protested. "I've said I don't love you and it won't work. Let's leave it there, Pickman."

"If you were honest you'd tell about Knight," Brown said.

"There's nothing about Knight to tell you. I've been fishing with him and I like him and that's all. That has no bearing on you and me."

She sat on the starboard bunk and he moved restlessly back and forth across the deck. He said, "Brat, I believe it does have a bearing. I think this person has gained some kind of hypnotic influence over you. You've become infatuated with him and you'd live to regret it—if I let you."

The phrase aroused her curiosity without alarming her. "What do you mean, 'if I let you'?"

"Merely that I won't let you. Precisely that I won't."

"I abhor precise people. And you have nothing to say about it."

He took a bottle of brandy from the port locker, cut the seal and poured a drink. Stormy declined and he drank it in a gulp and poured another.

"I mean this," he said. "I fell in love with you a long time ago. You fell in love with me. We became engaged and I took myself out of circulation. So, I thought, did you. I've been devoted to you. Reasonably enough, I think, I looked forward to our wedding."

"I did, too, Pickman. Up to a certain point. You must understand that. But it changed; my own feeling toward you changed, or I was better able to estimate its worth. Whatever it is—and I'm not good at explaining it or you wouldn't be here—what we planned just can't be. It's ended."

"Is it?" He poured another brandy. "I don't think so. Not just because this dreamboy father of yours moved you down into a God-forsaken country and you fell in love with a clam mucker."

"That isn't true!" She was on her feet. "It's over because I don't love you, Pickman."

"But I love you, and that's enough."

"No, you don't. I know it now. It's yourself you love and all you've ever felt toward me is the reflection of your own self-esteem."

134

She was being unkind to him, and not entirely truthful, and she realized it but thought it the better way. There was a tension building up but she ignored it.

"Knight's in love with you," he said.

"If he is I don't know it." She was angered.

"And you've some crazy idea you're in love with him. Brat, let me tell you something. I've loved you more than that son of a bitch ever could."

He put his big hands on her shoulders. His hands were warm and wet. "At ease, Brat," he said.

She was not at ease.

"I can give you everything. I want to give you everything, Stormy."

He stooped to kiss her and she evaded him. He laughed and let her sit again on the edge of the bunk and poured himself a drink. He put the glass behind him, and his hands on her shoulders again could not be avoided. His fingers hurt. "Everything you want, Brat," he repeated. "Kiss me."

He leaned and fumbled. She was too quick. She was up to one side, moving away.

"I'm getting off, Pickman. It's all over. It will make everything easier if you sleep aboard tonight and leave in the morning. Good night and good luck."

His right arm held her, not close. He said, "No. It's not over between us; it's just beginning."

"Nothing's beginning. Everything's ended."

"This is beginning." One grip on her wrist, another in her hair, forced her to him, hurt her. His big mouth was hot on hers. She struggled, gasping, fought free of his lips but not his hold. His mouth was a slit, white-rimmed, and his eyes were hard.

"Let me go. Are you drunk?"

135

His hand in her hair twisted her head again. "Drunk? On a couple of drinks? I've never been drunk on a dozen. You little fool, what did you think? That I'd let you play around with a clam mucker? Stand by and see him take what I've always wanted? You've gone to bed with him, Brat, haven't you?"

"Your mind is foul and I think you're insane! You're hurting my arm. Pickman!"

"I mean to!" His mouth was close again, his other hand forcing, and she knew him suddenly for all that he was and panic seized her and the frenzy gave her strength. She fought to her feet and he yanked her down and when she tried to scream his hand smothered the sound. She bit his fingers and he swore and cuffed her hard, backhanded, across the face, leaving a smear of his blood on her cheek and nose.

"Please!" she whispered.

His hand at her throat tightened. No sound came from her. She thought, *Dear Jesus, dear Jesus.* Her arm, freed from his grasp, would not respond to the will to move it. She became suddenly conscious of small things—the cruiser lifting gently with the tide, an oppressive heat in the cabin, the tick of a clock. She heard his voice and it seemed far away: "Brat, I can't lose you. . . . Stormy, please!"

Then there was a better voice and it seemed closer though it was distant.

"Anyone aboard *Tiderunner?*"

She felt the deck thumped by a leap from the landing. "Anyone aboard? Went to the house . . ."

Brown said, "Get . . . off . . . fast!"

Cal Knight stood balanced on the deck, regretting he was aboard.

"Cal!" she said. The way she said it was enough.

Knight said, "There's blood on your face, Stormy."

"From his hand. Where I bit him."

"Get off, Knight!" Brown shouted.

Cal asked, "Can you walk, Stormy?"

"Yes. I think so."

"Then get off and start walking for home."

She moved slowly from the cabin, her hands pressing her cheeks.

"Get off." It was Cal's, yet a stranger's voice. He helped her to the float. She felt his hand pat her shoulder. He might have been patting a dog. She started along the float toward shore and heard him say to Brown, "She's gone. I'm staying on. I'm taking this hunk of mahogany down the bay."

She didn't hear Pickman Brown's answer, but Brown said, "Over my dead body!"

"You may be right. Because I think it's a good time to kill you."

Cal was moving. Brown started from the cabin to meet him, the bottle of brandy cocked in his right hand.

"That's good," Cal invited. "I was going to warn you— anything goes. My knee in your balls and my thumbs in your eyes. Swing that bottle, you bastard!"

The shouted admonition made Brown swing too soon, as Cal had hoped. He caught the weight of the bottle on his left shoulder, heeled Brown's forward instep hard, sank his left fist into Brown's stomach and snatched the bottle with his right hand. As Brown bent with the force of foot injury and belly punch, Cal hit him on the back of the head with the bottle. Brown merely continued to fall forward on his face. Cal's glance was on him only a moment. He pressed the starter for the engines, held them

137

in neutral while he cleared the lines. He jumped aboard again and headed *Tiderunner* down-bay.

Brown might be dead, he knew. It seemed to make no difference to him. Knowing what the cruiser could do, he did not open up the engines. Even with the trip half behind him, his emotions cooling out, he did not speed up. Brown didn't move a little finger.

Off the wharf Cal nosed uptide outside *Carey's Chicken* and Bobby secured his lines.

"Got a patient here," Cal shouted. "Got himself hurt in a winch. Want you to run to a phone and call a doctor. Go to Father O'Meara's or Tom Salter's, doesn't matter."

Bobby was off like a deer without having spoken.

Cal went to the galley and put water on for coffee. He didn't go near the figure on deck and he was startled when he heard Father O'Meara calling from the wharf. Going topside he beckoned the priest to cross over *Carey's Chicken*.

"Bobby came to phone the doctor and I thought I might be needed," the priest said. He saw the sprawled figure. He bent over it and made the sign of the cross and began the prayer of the last rites.

Cal brewed coffee. When the priest had finished Cal said, "Don't move him unless he's dead. Doctor'll be right along; I think that's his car now. Bobby must have waited by the road to direct him."

The doctor made only a brief examination, exploring pulse and wound. To himself Cal would not admit that the diagnosis was important.

"Possible fracture," said the doctor. "Bad concussion anyway. Some time in a hospital. Town has an ambulance."

"I'll phone from the rectory," Bobby said.

138

Father O'Meara stayed on after Brown had been re-moved. In the summer dusk he ate coffee and browned hash, a worry on him.

"Make the lines, Bobby. Tide's falling."

The boy moved from his empty plate, knowing that the talk to follow was not for his ears.

"A bad wound," the priest invited.

"From a bottle of brandy."

"A waste of good spirits."

"It did not break. If it had it would've served in good cause. . . . Father?"

"Speak up, lad."

"What should a man do when someone rapes or nearly rapes a girl he loves?"

"Seek the counsel of God."

"That I will have from you. What I mean, if you were not a priest—if you were in love—can you guess what you might have done in my place?"

"Hit him a trifle more gently!" said Father O'Meara. "But I am not pleased with you."

"Why, Father?"

"Your concern is for someone all the nurses in a hospital are attending. Your great consideration should be for someone else."

Cal returned to normal thinking. "You're right. Thank you, Father."

When he phoned her home, Professor Force said, "I'm sorry, Knight. She's indisposed and she's been in bed for more than an hour."

"It's awful important I talk with her," he said.

There was an indecisive silence. Stormy's indisposition had puzzled the professor; she was rarely ill.

"I think it will do her good, sir," Cal pressed.

139

"Hold on, Knight. I'll see if she feels like talking."

When he returned he said, "I'm sorry. She can't come to the phone."

He wouldn't take it. "Listen, Professor, it's important I talk to her. Will you tell her that?"

"I will." The professor, too, felt it was important, even urgent, without in the least knowing why it should be.

"Hold on again," he said.

Stormy's voice, frightened, came through. "Hello."

"Hello, lovely," he said. He heard a small sob. "I've wanted to call you that since the first day I saw you."

"Cal . . . I'm not lovely now . . ."

"That's just it," he said. "Today never happened. Today's out of the calendar. I want you to know that. For both of us. Stormy . . . Well, it will keep, I guess."

After a little she said, "It *was* important. You'll never know how important it was, Cal. Do you know it?"

"I said it."

"I guess you do know then."

"I guess. See you tomorrow. Got a charter. Be through early."

"Cal?"

"Yuh, lovely?"

"Thank you. Thank you, darling."

ROCCUS SCATTERED the stars and seized a compressed slab of moonlight, swallowing it.

The July moon beamed on waters slapped by the tails of late-arriving menhaden moving inshore along both sides of the Cape. There were many thousands in each school

140

and there were countless thousands of schools. Into one dimpling over three fathoms Roccus drove again.

Other fish were feeding on the pogy—many other bass, squeteague, late pollock, the first of the bluefish, blue and hammerhead sharks, bonito, dolphin and, in deeper waters, broadbill swordfish and whales. Nearly all life of the ocean fed on the menhaden. Lobstermen seined them for bait. Fleets of white vessels seined them by the millions for oil and fertilizer. They swam fin to fin, tiers deep, the most abundant species in the Atlantic fishery. They were late arriving because the sea on the shoals had been late to warm. Now they would summer in the bays and harbors, the inlets and surf, waxing fatter and oilier on algae, sediment of organic decay and minute crustacean life, and their enemies from the land and of the sea would deplete their numbers by millions, yet fail appreciably to deplete their population. For each mature menhaden moving inshore had spawned more than one hundred thousand eggs. They were a countless streaming under the stars of the tide, showering as Roccus drove again.

"THERE IS a little trick to this, Father. Do you know it?" Cal Knight asked. "Do you, Stormy—Professor?"

"I never live-lined a pogy," said Father O'Meara.

"Nor I," said Stormy Force.

The professor had never live-lined anything but an essay.

"Bobby'll show you. The rods are rigged with ounce-and-a-half sinkers and treble hooks. The idea is to cast into the pogy, jerk until you foul-hook one and then let

141

him swim with the school on the lightest possible drag. The bass lie beneath the pogy, and the weight sinks the hooked fish down nearer them. Bobby, make a cast and show them."

Carey's Chicken drifted with the light tide in the fulling moon. The cedars along the shore were silhouetted against the sky. Cal had wanted the priest and Stormy together.

Bobby cast easily, not far, and began his retrieve, jerking the rod tip. He felt life and handed the rod to Stormy.

"Pogy's on. Let him go. If he starts going awful fast, put your thumb on the spool and set up." He cast for the professor. The priest made his own cast.

Cal said, "Pogy working back around us after being frightened."

They all had swimming pogy on.

"How well do you know Mr. Sears?" Father O'Meara asked the girl.

"Not well, but I'm crazy about him," she said.

"I may want you to help me with him."

"If I can I will be happy to help."

"Do you know Clystie Harrow who lives in the dunes?"

"No, Father."

"I will want you to know her. Time enough."

Was there? he wondered. Was there ever time enough?

Stormy felt the line running swiftly under her thumb and set back hard on a heavy fish. The priest, watching her as she played it, felt she would do.

"About twenty-four," Cal said, gaffing. "Nice fishing, Stormy."

"I would like to meet this Clystie," Stormy said. "Harrow, you said?"

"I'll take you," said Father O'Meara. He set a fish and passed his rod to the professor. "Try that," he said. The

142

professor tried it and mastered his bass despite contradictory coaching.

"About twenty," said Bobby.

Cal said, "Steady all!"

About sixty feet off the port beam the sea bulged in the moonpath and erupted silver. A great head, mouth agape, thrust through the fountain of slabs and stars twenty feet above the surface.

"God protect us," prayed the priest.

"Finback whale standing on his tail," said Cal. "Hold on."

The head of the monster fell forward, the closing jaws spewing light. Cal kicked the idling motor into gear and turned the bow to ride the wave.

"A great sight!" Professor Force exclaimed.

"It cost you your fishing," said Cal. "Scared everything off. Sometimes they come on the shoals with the first of the pogy."

"I'll take you to meet Miss Harrow," said the priest to Stormy, "though first I mean to meet her myself."

Father O'Meara didn't look like a priest on a mission of duty. There was no way to fasten a Roman collar to a sweat shirt. He wore old sneakers and salt-whitened khaki pants and carried a surf rod over his shoulder. He was hatless and the dome of his head was a mass of freckles fringed by unruly tufts.

Between the Coast Guard Station, where he made sure of Maddox's absence, and the house in the dunes he made only one cast and this merely to keep his hand in. There was a woman stringing a wash behind the house but a glance told him that, unless a great change had come over Maddox, this would not be Clystie Harrow. He walked up from the hard sand and she came out front to meet him; she had an ominous eye.

"Good day. I'm looking for Miss Harrow."

"Are you now? And who might you be?"

"O'Meara is my name and unless my ears deceive me you will recognize it."

"There was an O'Neill had devil's ears, too," she said. "My home was in the north."

"Still you would know of Rory O'More."

"There was a plot to seize Dublin castle," said the woman.

"It failed," said the priest. "Where is your mistress?"

"Resting and not wanting to meet fishermen."

"I'm Father O'Meara."

"A priest? Is that so? I wouldn't have guessed in the disguise. But now that you've told me she's *still* resting. Go away and leave the girl be."

Father O'Meara had had enough. "I'm sent for, woman. Kindly tell Miss Harrow."

"I'll tell her," she granted without grace. "I'll also tell her what I think of priests who go running around without their collars." She went in, slamming the door, while the priest thought that though Miss Harrow hadn't really sent for him, Maddox had sent him.

The door reopened soon enough and the Father knew Maddox's eyesight remained good.

"Good afternoon, Father O'Meara. Won't you come in?"

"I thought you might care to walk the beach," he said. He liked the voice of her. "The day is gentle. There might be a fish. And we could talk."

144

"Of course. I wish Donald were here."

"Where is the boy?"

"Maddox drove him in the jeep to visit aboard a fishing boat, the *Carey's Chicken*. Do you know it?"

"Well, and the skipper, Knight, and the young mate Bobby, who will be good for your son. You will come with me and meet them, too, sometime."

The priest was tired and his knee bothered him. He would have liked a chair in the house and a cup of tea, but any discussion in the presence of the crone would have been impossible. Maybe they could sit in the sand up the beach a ways. They started out.

"Maddox takes an interest in the lad," he said.

"I appreciate it. And also, to an extent, his interest in me."

The priest smiled. "I see I will have no trouble here. There will be no need to go around the forest to get home."

"None at all. I will be perfectly frank with you in the things that must concern you. I was christened and confirmed in the Catholic Church and left it at the age of sixteen. Now I have a son approaching the age where religious instruction is indicated, and I would like to have him return to that which I left."

"Alone?"

"Alone."

"I'll make one cast and we'll sit down."

"And catch a renegade?" She laughed and settled on the sand, and Father O'Meara made one long cast, retrieved his plug and joined her.

"You would not come back with him?"

"No. Not unless I should have unexpected reason to change a mind that has been made up on the subject of the Church for years. But does that matter so far as Donald is concerned?"

"Not so far as it concerns the boy and the Church. Only the boy and the mother."

"Do you want to know if his father was a Catholic?"

"Only if you want to tell me."

"He was not."

"It makes no difference. What I have in mind is that a boy brought up in the joy of God can never understand a parent who will not share Him. I have a duty to urge you."

"I understand. I cannot return."

"But you will nevertheless see that he applies himself diligently to his study of God and conforms to the precepts of the Church?"

"I will do that. It need not be mentioned again."

"It will be my great pleasure to superintend his instruction. Does he fish? I could help there, too."

"Maddox is teaching him and Donald is fascinated."

"Shall we discuss Maddox then?"

"Of course. I expected to."

But he remained silent, and after a while she said, "Do you find it difficult to begin?"

"A little. With a woman. But I hesitate also because I suddenly realize I have never thoroughly analyzed Maddox. We have been friends since he came on this station a number of years ago. He has no religion. His concept of right and wrong differs in many respects from my own. I was going to say, nevertheless, that Maddox is a man of high moral integrity who possesses few morals, but that is a paradox impossible of existence. He's a pagan and much of a man. I respect him if for no other reason than that he is concerned with the welfare of his fellows. His

146

belief in what is good or bad for them differs sometimes from my own but does not lessen my respect. I have never challenged his sincerity. But yes, once I did. And I was wrong. That was where your boy is concerned."

She started to interrupt, decided not to.

"Maddox is a being of toughness, born in adversity as he has told me, raised in poverty, thrown early upon his own resources, hardened in action in two wars. Yet he does not abuse his personal dignity. He has self-respect by virtue of the fact that he does nothing he himself recognizes as sin. Yet there is sin in the Maddox code. Being weak is a sin, being a coward an unforgivable sin, being a celibate a sin of omission."

He paused, and Clystie Harrow said, "Most of the things you tell me of Maddox I recognized in him at our first meeting."

He said, after deliberation, "So you might have done."

"I will help you, Father. Isn't it about Maddox as Maddox concerns me that you wish to get into? You said there would be no need to go around the forest."

He matched her smile. "So I did. Yet found it the easiest way. Will you speak for me?"

"I will. You are tormented by the thought that having taken Donald under your instruction his mother will become Maddox's mistress."

"I would have tried to put it more delicately and would not have said it so clearly."

Her steady gaze met his. "It could happen."

Sorrowed, he said nothing; waited.

"It could. But I don't think it will. I have a regard for Maddox not born of my appreciation for his interest in Donald. Maddox has some feeling for me. He likes my body, which he has not touched. He likes my mind, which

147

he has touched lightly. He likes what he calls my toughness. His regard is probably as close to love as Maddox may approach. If he should sufficiently arouse within me any emotion approaching his own, and if I feel the relationship would not harm him, I might very well become his mistress."

Father O'Meara thought of saying something about harming the boy but he said nothing.

"Maddox hasn't awakened me, Father, in that sense. I could not come any closer than Maddox to love as you envision it."

He had some hope. "If Maddox should ask you to marry him . . ."

"He won't. If by any chance he should, I would not marry him. If he should mention it to you—" she was reading his mind—"and I know he confides in you, please tell him this: that that which he seeks in me others have known for stronger reasons than I could muster in his case. Will you tell him?"

"I will not."

"*I* will, if the need arises."

"I doubt it would make much difference to Maddox."

"Perhaps not. I hinted it to him once. I will be more explicit if I must."

"Maddox described you as a tough-fibered woman."

"He is observing."

"And guessed that under your armor there might be emptiness."

"There may be."

"No. Your toughness is not to protect you from outside attack but to protect others if you explode within. There is something in you that must someday burst the shell."

148

"Perhaps you are more discerning than Maddox, Father."

He gave her his hand and helped her to her feet. It did not surprise him that her cheeks were wet.

They started back and she said, "I told you one lie."

"I do not mind."

"It was about my feeling for Maddox. I think I'm in love with him. I'm not sure, perhaps, because I never loved anyone before."

He was eagerly hopeful. "Then you would marry him?"

"I couldn't."

"You might if you exploded."

"I couldn't, ever. Will you watch out for my son?"

"With God's help."

"With God's help," she repeated.

"There is one question," he said. "Where were you confirmed, child?"

"In your church, Father—St. Peter's. By you."

"I suspected as much. I am trying to remember."

"I hope you will not remember. . . . Father?"

"Yes, Miss Harrow."

She couldn't say it. She ran for the house.

He went on, his own emotions agitated. He did not remember, surely, but Tom Salter might. Of one thing he was certain: Clystie Harrow, or whatever her name might be, was a woman of even greater worth than Maddox might suspect—Maddox, who sought from her what she said she had given to others for better cause.

149

"Somebody's seining bass," Tom Salter said.

"You have the evidence, Thomas?" asked Father O'Meara.

"Enough to convince myself, and I could make a pretty close guess who's doing it."

"You and I might guess the same but the evidence is all circumstantial," Cal Knight said.

They sat on a wharf stringer, legs dangling close to the rail of *Carey's Chicken,* which was lifting with the evening tide.

"I've heard seining discussed every year," said the priest, "but no one ever came up with the evidence around here. What's your evidence?"

Salter gave it. "Big schools in an area one day, gone the next. My fishermen all report it. There's plenty bait to hold the schools."

"I agree," Cal said. "Bobby and I have marked down schools many an evening and been unable to locate them next daybreak. Furthermore the fish aren't moving into the canal on the east tides as they should be. I'd like to have somebody down from the Marine Fisheries Division."

"A wild goose chase unless you have a substantial lead," said the priest.

"Webb Everly is a substantial lead," said Salter.

Cal said, "I'll go along with that."

"Everly's a seiner and a law-breaker from 'way back," Salter continued. "He brought his vessel up from Cape May early this year before the mackerel moved north and while prices were still high. He fired all but four or five

150

of his crew. One of those he kept on flies a plane out of Wareham. Everly comes in once or twice a week and anchors off Higgins Neck, never ties up at the pier. He and his crew go ashore in a dory and always leave a watch aboard. He always gets out during darkness. He never comes in through the canal, though all the big mackerel schools are north of the Cape now. He ain't seining mackerel but he's seining something, and I suspect he's selling down New Bedford way or likely in Rhode Island."

"If that's all, the verdict is not guilty," said Father O'Meara.

"It's not all," Cal said. "Twice lately Bobby and I've seen Everly acting suspiciously. One morning just before first light over by Bird Island he had a seine boat out and I'll swear it was starting to circle bass. He spotted us and called his boat back. About a week or ten days ago we saw him in close to the beach at Butlers Point about the same hour. No boat out, but he wouldn't be there for anything except bass."

"It's still no good," the priest said. "Maybe he's seining pogies."

Salter snorted. "The damn pogy fleet is cleaning them up and they're mostly in Cape Cod Bay."

"There would be evidence on his vessel—the seine and bass scales. You can't rid a boat altogether of scales and you can't mistake them. If you could find them you might have a case to interest the marine wardens."

"And who's to find them?"

"Why, myself," said Father O'Meara. "Because if he is breaking the law and taking the bread and butter out of the mouths of my people there is good reason for me to be concerned. Next time his vessel's in I can get aboard when there's only the watch."

The subject was closed so far as the priest was con-

151

cerned. He turned to Cal. "How's Stormy coming with her fishing?"

Cal laughed. "She has been teaching me. Tom sold them one of his skiffs and we've been live-lining the narrows upriver. More good fish up there than I thought."

"There's a lady I want her to meet. Name of Harrow. Lives near the Coast Guard Station with her son. Perhaps you would take them fishing one day when you're not engaged."

"I'll be glad to," Cal said.

"I might go myself if you asked me."

"Then I might ask you."

"And Maddox—do you know Maddox at the Coast Guard Station?"

"Yes, but I've never had him out. He never indicated he'd care to go."

"Merely say to him that Miss Harrow is going and he'll care to go."

"I will then."

"And forget to say I'm going too."

"Sounds like a plot, Father."

"Merely a fishing expedition. Come on, Thomas, it's time I ate whatever Rosie has mishandled tonight."

The priest and Salter set off toward the church.

"How are you making out with Riba, Father?"

"Manuel has a new plague on his mind and I can't get through to it, though I've tried. I think he wants to tell something and is afraid to."

"Still on the bottle?"

"Yes. Tell me, Thomas, do you think I would be wise to find a parish elsewhere?"

"I wouldn't like it. Many others would miss you. What are you thinking about?"

"An offer of a permanent pastorate in Worcester."

152

"You'd miss the bass fishing."

"I would miss my friends. Yet I have a feeling that most of my best work here is done. Another might accomplish for Riba, and all those others for whom he somehow stands as a symbol in my thoughts, more than I have been able to accomplish over the years. And by the same token I might prove more effective in a new field among people not so aware of my weaknesses."

"I would be sorry to see you go."

"I know, my friend, and I am grateful. Tell me, Thomas, is the name Harrow familiar to you?"

"It is not. I thought of it when you mentioned it to Knight but I know of no Harrows hereabouts."

"Here we are. Will you come in and sample Rosie's wares?"

"I'd better not. I've still got a couple boats out and May will be wondering where I am."

"Good night, wise man," the priest said.

He went in but he did not eat for an hour, during which his supper sogged on the range. In his study he pored over the record book back down the years until he found what he sought—a name, a date. They made a little click in his mind.

THOUGH SHE had told Father O'Meara she was entranced with the eccentricities of Mr. Sears, Stormy Force was never wholly at ease in his presence. That which had first drawn her to him was undoubtedly a natural curiosity provoked by his deep preoccupation, his unawareness of current events, his disinterest in happenings and people. She came eventually to recognize that though he

153

moved in the present he lived only in a past which was crammed with memories of a beautiful woman who was dead and a little girl who had somehow, somewhere, forsaken him.

During their acquaintance he never gave indication that he knew her as Stormy Force or that she lived on land adjoining his. She was "girl" to him and when she took friends to visit him, to show him off as a special character, he always ignored introductions and addressed them as "girl" or "mister." Nor did she ever hear him addressed as Whitcomb, or Whit, or identified in the third person other than as Mr. Sears or "that queer old man who lives up the river." With few exceptions he had outlived his generation. He had erected about his life a bull-brier barrier of remoteness that few tried more than once to penetrate. With his cranberry bog and with the movies at Bournham his attention seemed entirely absorbed, with these and the memories he kept alive and bright with the burnishing of his imagination.

He told her many times she resembled his little girl who had gone away, told her of the fine picture showing at the movies, told her of his cranberry bog deep in the woods below the river road. Only once did she ever venture into the woods to locate his bog, a day of deep July when, not having found him at the house, she crossed the road and started down a narrow, vaguely defined path which led through scrub oak and brittle pine and salted cedar toward a lowland swamp. Wild sweet peas were in late blossom, the Scotch broom faded. A short distance in from the road a vast stillness seemed to smother the way. The breeze seemed not to penetrate. The scrub pressed closer. There was no bird song, no hum of insect life. She had ventured a far way and was thinking of turning back when she saw Mr. Sears approaching up the path. He stopped in his tracks.

"What do you want here, girl?" he demanded.

"I was just coming to visit you at the bog," said Stormy. "I didn't find you at home."

Anger left his face. "You're the one looks like my little girl. You mustn't come in here. It's a dangerous place. There's big moccasin snakes and poisonous spiders. It's a bad place for a little girl."

Stormy realized that this was so. She walked ahead of him to the road, wishing she had not come. But he seemed to have forgotten her intrusion when he reached his yard and insisted on showing her, with pride, his vegetable garden. It was a small plot on the south slope of the knoll beyond his woodshed and though she had noticed it before she had not recognized it as a garden. It had been partially turned over, perhaps with a clam rake. Witchgrass and purslane made a rank growth about a few undernourished spears of corn. There were some bean leaves already yellowed and perforated by beetles. There was nothing else but dreams.

"Grows good, don't it?" he said. "Didn't get to plant much this year. Ain't no use to plant when you have to give most of it away. My wife used have the best garden on the Cape. I never see such a woman for a garden. All this slope was corn and potatoes and strawberries and cucumbers and melons. Best berries you ever tasted—a Marshall my wife crossed herself. My, oh, my, the jam she made! I still got a few jars left. Maybe you'd like one."

"Oh, no, thank you," Stormy said.

"I'll fetch you one and, by gorry, you'll taste the best jam ever made."

He led the way to his back door and bid her wait there

155

and was gone a long time. When he reappeared he held a small jar gray with dust and green with mold.

"There, you take that home. I bet you never tasted a berry jam like my wife made."

She could visualize her father's dismay but was gracious.

"Well," said Mr. Sears, "you best go now, girl. I'm going to the village to the pictures. Fine picture there this week."

"Don't you have any lunch?" she asked.

"Sometimes I do, sometimes I don't. When my wife was alive she always had a hot dinner for me when I come home from the bog. My, the good things my wife could cook—clam chowder and quahog cakes and sea clam pie! And how she could make a lemon pie! Best cook on the Cape my wife was. She could broil a bass that would melt in your mouth. Cooked it with the scales on to keep in the juices."

His gaze went down the bay and his thoughts down the years.

"When I think of those things it don't seem much sense I should try to make a dinner for myself. Well, you go, girl. Come again any time and make yourself to home if I'm not here. But keep away from the bog."

Invariably when Stormy went to the movies she would see Mr. Sears. When the summer folks and natives lined up in front of the box office Mr. Sears would be among the first, standing aloof between raucous, horseplaying youngsters, showing no impatience but with a certain eagerness on his face. Once inside, he moved swiftly to a seat in a front row. If children occupied these seats before him he was obviously annoyed, casting angry glances about him until the lights dimmed. Stormy was near-sighted and often sat close to him and observed his attitude during

156

a picture. He sat forward, tense and rapt, and no action on the screen appeared to escape him though he might have attended several showings of the same picture. Sometimes Stormy sought to draw him into a discussion of the feature, but he never seemed to recognize the title or the name of a star or the sequence of a plot. He was always evasive. Eventually she concluded that he was never aware of what happened on the screen.

Soon after noon and in the late afternoons he would pass her house, walking the brushed-out edge of the road, looking neither to right nor left nor heeding any car unless it stopped beside him. He had a quick step, far livelier than his years warranted, but he always moved faster going to town than returning home.

"There goes your friend, Mr. Sears, to the movies again," the professor would say. Or, "Here comes Mr. Sears back from the movies."

The interval between afternoon and evening shows gave him little more than time for the round trip unless he caught a lift. When a motorist offered him a ride he never refused. The professor and Stormy picked him up many times and the routine of his behavior never varied. He would shield his eyes with his hand in what appeared to be an effort at recognition—as if he might refuse—and he would say, "Well, now, don't mind if I do. Don't want to crowd you, though." He would be climbing in as he said it. Then he would remark on the weather: "Fine sweet day, ain't it?" or, "Mean day, threatening. Don't know as ever I remember such a summer for mean weather. Bog set a lot of blossoms, though, and I'll have a big crop of cranberries if the worms don't get 'em." Then he would hum a little and, in the manner of a boy

157

imparting a secret, say, "I'm going to the pictures," or, "Been to the pictures. Fine picture this week." Then he would hum again. Near the home of George Blenn, who displayed a sign advertising eggs and fowl, Mr. Sears always chanted, "Georgie Blenn's a big fat hen." And at a fork of the road beyond Blenn's place where there was a tall and twisted apple tree, unpruned for a decade, Mr. Sears would caution, "Slow down, now. You see that tree? Prettiest tree on the Cape when it's in blossom. My wife used walk 'way down here just to see that tree."

Stormy found it useless on these occasions to try to carry on any conversation with him. He listened only to his own voice and the urgings from his past.

He didn't drink or smoke. Of fishermen who came to use his leaky skiff he always inquired whether they had alcoholic drink. None ever admitted he did, either knowing Mr. Sears' antipathy or fearing, if he were a newcomer, that he might be asked to share his bottle. But it was the rare fisherman who used the skiff and did not pay his dollar for it, though he found it necessary to shove the money into Mr. Sears' pocket. Stormy came to know that the stranger who accepted formal refusal of the money as final never got to use the boat again.

If Mr. Sears were home when a successful angler came ashore he usually managed to wangle a bass from him.

"Well, now, aren't those pretty fish. Best eating fish there is to my taste. Been a long time since I et one."

"Have one of these, Mr. Sears."

"Well, now, I don't want to rob you. Leave me the smallest one. It's not like when my family was here."

One day in his woodshed Stormy found three bass spoiling from the flies. "Don't care much for fish any more," Mr. Sears explained. "Can't cook 'em like my wife did."

158

That was the hot Sunday afternoon he invited her in for tea. "I always make tea of a Sunday afternoon when there's no picture," he explained. So, for the first time, she entered Mr. Sears' home.

In his kitchen a battered kettle of water steamed on an old-fashioned warped and rusted wood stove which glowed red despite the day's heat. Against the inside wall stood an old pine table, on it an ironstone sugar bowl and an oversize shaker of salt. Above the table hung a lumber-company calendar depicting an unfortunate angler emptying half a trout stream from a rubber boot. The month on fly-specked display was August; the year was 1930. On a mantel above table and calendar was an old chime clock whose hands had stopped exactly at the hour of eleven of what bygone day or night there was no guessing, unless it was a time in August of 1930. There were two ladder-back pine chairs at the table. There was a gallon water jug that Mr. Sears filled daily from a roadside spring. There were a few iron cooking utensils, pitted and rusty, hanging by the stove. There was nothing else.

"Sit and wait," said Mr. Sears. He vanished into an adjoining room and reappeared with two cups of pale blue, delicately laced with white. The professor collected pottery and Stormy had a smattering of knowledge about it. She felt there was no mistake: these were Wedgwood jasperware, unglazed, decorated with Flaxman's reliefs.

Mr. Sears fetched a canister of tea from a tiny closet and into each cup dropped a thumb-and-two-finger pinch of leaves. Over these, while Stormy held her breath, he poured boiling water. The cups made no protest.

"There, girl, when that settles it'll be ready to drink."

"The cups are beautiful," Stormy said.

He looked pleased. "Pretty, ain't they? My wife liked

159

them. My wife was a great hand for pretties. You drink that up and I'll show you."

The tea was bitter strong. Stormy strained vagrant leaves with her teeth. Mr. Sears blew in his cup and drank noisily and arose.

"You come with me," he said.

In the sitting room were a horsehair sofa, a Boston rocker and a large cabinet of five shelves which held, behind glass doors, a collection of great value—more Sandwich and milk glass of intricate design than Stormy had imagined existed, more Wedgwood. And ancient pieces which had been shaped on the potter's wheel in the far places of the earth in centuries past. There were a faïence vase in rich blue and cream, an Italian majolica saucer presenting the profile of a crowned lady, a pot of Böttger porcelain, a glazed earthenware with what seemed to be Italian relief, and what Stormy wildly guessed might be a Spanish-Moorish majolica jug. There was a pitcher with tree and cupid and butterfly relief, fashioned with infinite grace from upward sweep of handle to downward curve of lip. There were several score pieces of varying degrees of beauty and value, all collectors' items.

"Pretty, ain't they?" asked Mr. Sears.

When her eyes could leave those pieces, Stormy saw adjacent objects in an incongruous setting—a brass plate, souvenir of a world's fair; two or three cheap, torn fans; a set of china dogs from the five-and-ten; a pair of plaster book ends, broken; cheap, silver-plated salts and peppers.

"Pretty?" Mr. Sears pressed.

"Some of them are absolutely beautiful," Stormy said. "They would bring a fortune."

"Not to me, girl. Money couldn't buy them. They were my wife's things. You follow me upstairs."

160

She had no choice, though she was ill at ease. Behind him she climbed the narrow stairs which at the top opened into opposing rooms. Mr. Sears turned left into a square room over which hung a platinum haze alive with millions of particles in the slant of sun through broken windows—the undisturbed dust of years. From the braided rug on the spattered, wide-board floor it rose like a fountain beneath their feet to settle over a pine ball-poster double bed which had been overlaid with a coverlet of a color that could not now be guessed. A woman's slippers, scuffed and heel-worn, were near the foot of the bed, one on its side, the other upright. As if kicked off in a hurry. A discarded robe lay in a heap near them. On a night table beside a pillow stood a candlestick and a yellow vase holding black stems, headless, brittle as frozen glass; long ago they had been old-fashioned pinks in blossom. A sconce of tarnished brass on the wall beside the bed held a half-burned candle. In and about the room and over all its contents the dust of the years rose and settled and rose again, dry, pungent in the nostrils. Stormy put a finger against her nose to stifle a sneeze.

"Pretty, ain't it?" Mr. Sears asked. "Just like it was when my wife died. You come with me and I'll show you my little girl's room. There ain't anyone been there since she went away."

In the opposite room were a matching single ball-poster, a huge old ironstone pitcher and basin on a pine commode, two small braided rugs. There were several framed, unglassed, dirt-smudged pictures—a setter scratching behind an ear, a long slant of meadow with doe and fawn near a stream, an etching of a small girl swinging on a gate beside a stand of hollyhocks.

"Pretty, ain't it?"

161

Stormy had a practical curiosity. "But where do you sleep, Mr. Sears?"

"Oh, where do I sleep? Well, girl, when you get old you don't need much sleep. Sometimes I nap on the sofa downstairs but mostly I just doze a little in a chair. Time I get back from the pictures it's 'most midnight and I'm around before daybreak. There's chores to tend, fetching wood and water, before I go to the bog. Bog keeps me mighty busy these days and I had to sand a lot this year. Worms is pestful, too. Most like I'll get a small crop this year."

He seemed eager, now that he had shown Stormy his house, to get her out of it. She could tell he was anxious for her to leave. He consulted his watch. He glanced from a window toward the lowering sun. He opened the back door and listened for Willie-the-Whip. It was, she realized, getting on toward the hour when he would be starting for Bournham and the Sunday-evening movie.

Yet she was reluctant to leave.

"Don't you ever see your daughter—the little girl who went away?"

"I used see her once in a while," he said. "Not recent. I may see her soon. You best go now, girl."

Next day she called on Georgie Blenn, the big fat hen so obliquely disparaged by Mr. Sears. She went on the pretext of buying eggs. She found him an aging, thin man with tired eyes set at angles under a tight brow. When he fetched the eggs she told him Mr. Sears had suggested that he sold excellent eggs.

"Whitcomb Sears said that?" he demanded incredulously.

"Why, yes," she fibbed.

"That cantankerous old cuss must be getting softer in his years."

"He told me you were his age," she prodded.

"To hell you say, miss!" He peered closer at her. "I got a short leg to pull. Whitcomb Sears is ten years older'n me and he never said a good word for me or my hens or anyone else."

"He says a good word for his wife. He's a lonely old man with his wife dead all these years and his daughter gone."

He regarded her quizzically. "You know any nursery rhymes?"

"All of them," she said, and did.

"You'll remember Peter then."

"The pumpkin eater? He had a wife and couldn't keep her."

"That's it." He moved as if to close the door.

"Wait," she said. "What do you mean?"

His grin showed stubs of teeth. "Whitcomb Sears was like Peter. Married a young girl when he was getting along. Town girl—a Frenchie, she was—and pretty. Too pretty. He couldn't keep her."

"But she died," Stormy said.

He grinned again. "She didn't die no more than you nor me. You ain't dead. I ain't dead. She ain't dead. Leastwise she wa'n't when she quit him. That was a story he made up because she left him. Everyone knew she was going to leave the old fool. It was just a question who she'd leave with. Made up the story of her death to save his pride, though likely he believes it now himself. I dunno."

So, Stormy thought, here was an understanding of him. "Didn't he have a pumpkin shell?"

"Don't know as Mr. Sears ever went in much for pumpkins. Don't know if it would have done him much good

163

if he had. She had a will and a way and she was a young
one set on her way and he was too old for her. It was best
for him, miss, when she cleared out with the youngster."

"But she must have loved him," Stormy said.

"Go on from there," said Georgie Blenn.

"He told me about her."

"She loved herself. I guess he gave you a wrong impression of Lucy Sears. She wa'n't nothing but a small-town
tart always on the lookout for something better'n she had."

"She had a good man in Mr. Sears."

"Pretty, most of that type," said Blenn. "At least one
like her in every town. Never marry except some old fool
like Whitcomb Sears takes a fancy to them, and then for
no good reason. Lucy thought he had a fortune and he
had a collection of old china." He laughed unpleasantly.

"But the things she did he tells about," Stormy protested. "She gardened and preserved. He's always telling
what a cook she was."

"All that's just part of Whitcomb Sears' pride. They
did have a garden once but she never planted it nor
tended it. He done it. He always had. If they had pre-
serves he put 'em up. And he got most of the meals himself. She had other things on her mind, Lucy did."

"She did collect fine old china. I've seen it."

"I tried to tell you that old stuff he has was in the Sears
family for generations. Sears clippers brought it home
mostly. If you see any junk around the house, that's hers."

Stormy thought of those things so blatantly out of place
with Wedgwood pitcher and faïence vase.

"Anyway," she said, "he loved her."

"I ain't saying he didn't. But I ain't saying I blame her
for running away from the old cuss either."

"What was the little girl like?"

164

"Nice enough youngster, I guess. Not much like Lucy then. Maybe later she was."

She thought of many things to ask, phrased no questions. "Thank you for the eggs," she said.

"Don't take offense, miss. You asked about Lucy Sears. Maybe I shouldn't have told you."

On the way home she kept hearing Mr. Sears' voice: *"My wife planted those. . . . I never see such a woman for a garden. . . . Best cook on the Cape my wife was. . . ."*

Was it pride alone from which such dreams were fashioned?

WHEN THE July moon filled, Roccus returned to the lie by the Bird Island boulder, gorged with pogy, and at two o'clock of a morning, when the light on the water was one-six-hundred-thousandth of the brilliance of the midday sun she moved into the circle of a seine. She felt it against her tail before she saw it; she felt it against her side. Lesser bass, also trapped, began in excitement to mill about her. She surfaced and found no escape; she sounded and encountered wide-mesh twine. She swam the closing circle of the seine, brushing against it. Some of the smaller bass were gilled, thrashing, floundering. But she was not greatly alarmed. In the Roanoke, in an arm of the Chesapeake, once in the Hudson, she had been in nets before. From traps, like most bass, she always found her way; these were the offshore weirs with openings never closed except on low water. This trap was different; its opening already had closed, its diameter was closing.

165

Bait fish, mostly sperling and small herring, escaped through the wide meshes. Whiting also pushed through. A few pollock, a few cod were caught. The remaining fish, in scores, were striped bass.

Roccus swam to the center of the closing circle and, accelerating, drove her head against the net, bulging it. A male bass of six pounds, gilled and doomed, slapped her with his frenzied tail. She swirled and drove the diameter of the circle at full speed, rising, and leaped the rim of the net into free water. She did not hear Webb Everly's voice saying, "That sounded like a truck falling off a bridge. Free fish, boys. Hurry the seine boat; man the skiff!"

CLOSE ON to midnight Webb Everly arrived, and Clifton Hartwell, having dismissed his housekeeper, admitted the seiner and led him to his study without a word of greeting. There was a showdown due and he wanted Everly to speak first. When the door had been closed, the thin-mouthed skipper did. "A fine July night. Fine night for seining."

"And there's talk about it," said the banker.

"How do you mean?"

"There's talk among the sportsmen that there's seining going on—that seining is making the bass scarce."

"You ever known a season when there wasn't such talk? That's common gossip about the pogy fleet."

"This talk is different," Hartwell said. "It's being said by substantial men. I hear it in the bank. Are you acquainted with Tom Salter?"

166

"Old fellow runs the boat place? Sure, I know him."

"And the priest is another—some Irish name, O'Hare or O'Meara."

"It's O'Meara."

"They carry weight in the community."

"Hell!" Everly said. "Salter's seeking an excuse for the customers who don't catch fish and that priest is a bug on fishing. The priest is a bug, period."

"Nevertheless they are respected and I don't like the talk. I'm wondering if your crew—anyone in your crew—is getting loose-lipped. Do they drink?"

"Drink? You ever know a crew that didn't drink?"

"How much are they roaming the towns and shooting off their mouths?"

"They ain't. None of them. They're all too smart."

Hartwell wiped his chin. "Do you realize what it would mean to me if it ever got talked about I had any hand in bass seining?"

"Mean the same thing to me if we got caught. Boat confiscated, heavy fine, maybe jail."

The banker shuddered. He went to a locker and produced a bottle and glasses.

"I'd have to leave town if it became suspected I was in it."

"There's other towns."

Hartwell burned. "That's a careless observation. I was born in this town and all my forebears going back to the seventeenth century were born here, too."

Everly grinned. "Some were slavers and some were opium runners, and that's worse than seining fish."

Hartwell poured with a hand shaken by anger. "Everly, I don't like the talk and I don't like the seining. You're not giving me a square shake."

167

"That's a goddamned lie!" The skipper put his glass down. "I'll make you eat it."

"No, you won't. And keep your voice down. You're seining and selling more fish than you're reporting to me and you *have* been for several weeks."

"Why, you fool, I told you the schools had dropped off and you know the New York market has been flooded with shipments. The price is off some, varying daily."

Hartwell paced the floor. "*I* know you're holding out. The talk of seining is a result of poor fishing and the poor fishing is a result of your seining heavy catches."

The skipper gulped his drink. "If you're scared and suspicious, why in hell don't you pull out? You've about got your investment back."

"I haven't any of my investment back."

"Your take is almost six thousand dollars so far."

"That's not paid on my investment. Don't you remember the agreement? I hold your note for a loan of seven thousand. That comes due on demand when the bass-fishing season is over."

Everly knew this to be so but chose, as a man selects a red herring from a stick, to pretend otherwise. He dropped his thin jaw. "You mean to say the dough you been getting hasn't been paying off on the note?"

"Naturally I mean to say just that." Hartwell felt elated. "I made a loan to establish this business and entered into an agreement, based on my ability to finance it, to accept one-third of the profits. But not to be applied as payments on the note."

"By the Christ! Do you think I'd have agreed to a third share for you if it wasn't to be applied on the note?"

"I know what you did. You gave me a demand note and you've been paying me my share of profit—or some of my

168

share—in cash for which you hold no receipts. No matter what I've been paid or will be paid as a third share, you'll still owe me seven thousand dollars."

Everly yanked the visor of his cap. "You intend to milk the profits all summer and stick me up for seven grand when the fishing's over?"

"Stick you up? That's a bad phrase. This is a perfectly legal agreement between gentlemen."

"Gentlemen, crap! I'm no gentleman, Hartwell. If you look at it through the small end of the glass, we're both crooks and you're the smarter one."

The term aroused fear in the banker. "I'm not smart if I let you trim me on my share of the profits."

"If that's your story you can choke on it. Anyway, to hell with this. I'm going fishing."

"Didn't you bring any money?"

Everly counted out two hundred and sixty dollars. "That's your share for the week."

"All of it?"

"All of it."

"What was yours?"

The question caught the skipper unawares. "None of your goddamned business," he said.

He slammed Hartwell's back door. It was true enough that he had been holding out on the banker. But not so much as he now would. And he had no intention of paying off on the note even if he had to threaten to incriminate himself by revealing an illegal agreement. He knew Hartwell well enough to know he would not stand up against that threat.

The banker, sipping another drink, knew this as a thought in Everly's mind. He knew he stood to be bilked more in the future. He hadn't been smart to show anger.

169

It might be smarter, he thought, warmed by whisky, to trail Everly some night and confront him with proof of his deceit. He turned this over in his mind. There might be a safe way to do it.

Judge Wickett's summer began auspiciously with beautiful weather. There was early July heat but his estate was situated to take advantage of the prevailing southwest breeze. To the somewhat restricted summer colony of which he was the recognized leader the persons he best liked and admired had returned. Here, as in all the circles of his professional and social life, he was respected, looked up to for guidance, held up as the shining example of integrity, a man who practiced privately the stern code of morals he publicly enunciated from the bench—the very soul of honor.

He quickly relaxed from the strain of adjudicating issues involving man's freedom or imprisonment, his life or death. He played golf regularly at Dunetrap, where he was chairman of membership, and made two early trips to Oyster Harbors and Eastward Ho. He sailed in the yacht club's week-end races, paid a friendly call on Father O'Meara, walked the dunes a good deal with his daughter and grandson, joined the colony picnics, swam regularly.

A New York contractor, a Boston insurance broker and a marine artist were his regular golf companions. They were a high-handicap quartet which never fired the course. Originally they had played dime Nassau and engaged in other small wagers, but this practice had been discontinued the previous summer at the Judge's request because he had presided over a trial at which the moral code of the public with relation to anti-gambling statutes had been raised in issue by counsel for a notorious bookmaker, who had contributed heavily to the campaign funds of at least two elected state officers. Defense counsel had suggested naïvely in final argument to the jury that perhaps even His Honor had, at one time or another during his exemplary life, been a party to a transgression of the hypocritical law that permitted wagering at race tracks and forbade it elsewhere.

On the fairway, although his drives often strayed, the Judge pursued an objective course within the boundaries of the rules, calling penalty strokes on himself sometimes to the annoyance of his partner, the broker, who was given to taking his score a little more seriously. During the first game of the summer the Judge played and won two holes before discovering that he was playing a lost ball, and these holes he insisted upon forfeiting though none but himself could have been aware of the mistake.

He was a fair sailor though not a dusty one, given to taking few chances. The *Sailfish* was too wet for him but he managed one or another of the smaller one-man or two-man crew classes. In the windward position he never gave way in a luffing match, but on the other hand he never tried to jockey out of position a boat which had the right of way. He did little maneuvering while awaiting the starting gun, being content to cross the line with the trailers, who used no stop watches. Sailing alone in the second meet of the summer, he scored a rare victory due to an unexpected offshore slant of wind, but he reported disqualification, having fouled the turning buoy.

"Tried to jibe, should have known better," he called over to the judge's boat at the finish.

171

There had been no official boat at the rounding mark and no competition nearby. The yachting reporter for one of the Boston papers dwelt on the incident, and the same paper subsequently carried a brief, trite editorial evaluating sportsmanship and honesty.

Judge Wickett wasn't an angler and didn't expect to be one. Certain of the yacht club crowd had tried on occasion to convert him. These were, in his subconscious estimate, the slightly less desirable members of the colony who drank a little too much on regatta days and fished all night after the sailing. In response to their importunities he said he was getting along in years—though he was in fact younger than many of them—and fishing was too much like work. Moreover, he couldn't seem to get excited about any of its prospects.

Striped-bass fishermen, the Judge had observed, lived more on hope than realization. They lost sleep and were likely to be boors. They exaggerated, both about the size and number of fish caught and those they just missed catching. They were, of course, fine sportsmen and completely trustworthy about everything except fishing. They were far from trustworthy as regards the location of fish taken and lures used to take them, and some were not above changing lures to misguide late arrivals.

"Anyone who fishes places his reputation on the block," he observed to an angling golfer—and that was still his opinion this daybreak of waning July when he looked down from the master bedroom of his fieldstone house to the long reach of shore and dunes emerging from half-light into what promised to be a beautiful day. Terns were working, their discordant cries alive with hunger. The tide was close to flood. It was an hour when, with none on the beach, he enjoyed a dip. He would, as was his custom,

172

swim approximately fifty yards parallel with the beach and not over his depth. He'd float on his back, kicking his feet for a minute or so, duck again and run up to the house, where, after a warm-to-cold shower and a once-over shave, he would breakfast on orange juice, black coffee, one slice of dry toast and a three-minute egg.

He felt vibrant. He pulled on the khaki shorts he used for swimming and thrust his feet into old sneakers from which the laces had been removed. Quietly, so as not to disturb Sue and Andrew, he went downstairs and, in a little dogtrot because he felt so good, to the sand.

Approaching the near jetty he observed without annoyance that his favorite swimming spot was in use by a fisherman whose presence he had not observed from his window. He decided to swim a few hundred feet beyond the angler, where a sandy point thrust from a headland into the bay. His course took him through thatch grass behind the fisherman where, he noted, a sedan with a New York license plate had been parked at the foot of a wooded road. This was his own property but he did not post it, and anyone of good behavior was welcome to use it.

The angler was a heavy, tanned man about the Judge's age. He had a full head of iron-gray hair and an energetic thrust of belly above a pair of blue shorts, his only attire. He was bottom-fishing with bait, using two rods, one of which he set in a sand spike after making a long cast. As the Judge watched, he baited a second hook with sea worms and walked down the beach about fifty feet to make a second cast beyond the lazy lift of rollers. Then he walked up to his knees into the curl of surf and stood waiting with the rod butt between his legs.

The Judge called, "Good morning! Any luck?" This was

173

a question which, without having any interest in the answer, he invariably asked all fishermen.

The angler half-turned his head to show an unshaved jut of chin and said, "How in hell could I have any luck when I just started?" The unexpected answer brought a smile to Judge Wickett—a reasonable enough reply based on logic, he thought.

"Any bass around this dump?"

"Why, I've seen bass caught in that very spot," said the Judge. "I'm not a fisherman myself."

"You're not, huh?" All the disdain of the zealot for the unbeliever was in the three words.

The angler lifted his rod tip and retrieved a few feet of line. The Judge was about to pass along when the other grunted like a rhinoceros, set back on the rod and shouted, "By the Jesus, they're here!"

Then he began a variety of contortions which entranced Judge Wickett. He backed up onto the beach, reeling like mad. He raced down into the water up to his hips. He backed up again and ran along the beach. His rod, tip high, arced toward the surface and his line made a sizzling sound cutting the water. "Big son of a bitch!" he shouted.

"Well, good luck to you," the Judge called. Though his curiosity was aroused, chiefly by the other's antics, he was still not sufficiently interested to remain and watch the outcome. He had started to pass along when he became aware of a steadily burring click below him and, glancing down, he saw the second rod jerking violently in the sand spike, line whipping off the reel.

"See here!" he called. "You have a fish on your other rod."

The angler half-turned to shout over his shoulder, "Well, grab it and sink the hook in the bastard!"

The Judge involuntarily started down the beach, then stopped.

"I can't do that. I never handled a rod, never caught a fish."

"You grab that goddamn rod and fast, or by the Jesus, when I beach this fish I'll chew your ass out!"

This was one of the few times the Judge had been profanely addressed and certainly the first time in his life anyone had ever threatened to chew his ass out. He was more than mildly startled. Then, not under duress, wishing merely to be helpful, he hurried to the free rod, lifted it from the holder and felt life pulling distantly and viciously at the line.

"Set the son of a bitch! Jerk back on him!"

The Judge jerked back, felt the heavy tug, felt a line burn across two fingers of his left hand.

"Hook the bastard? Good. Snap off the click and tighten up the drag."

Judge Wickett had not the slightest idea how to snap off the click and tighten the drag, but after experimenting with the handle and the axle nut he finally threw out the click and the screaming ceased.

"The drag, goddamn it—the drag! Turn down on that little star thing on the right side under the handle. Turn it away from you."

The Judge, working under these instructions, suddenly felt the rod take terrific strain, nearly tear from his grasp.

"Loosen up on the drag, goddamn it. Not so tight. You'll pop that line."

The Judge loosened up. The distant fish ran parallel with the outside rollers. The Judge moved into the water, following. In a few minutes he was up to his waist and the fish was close to the end of the jetty.

175

The angler called, pumping his own fish, "Don't let the son of a bitch get around those rocks; he'll cut the line. Tighten up and turn him!"

The Judge tightened up, felt the tail rap on the line. Within him an excitement awoke. His arms ached. The bass stopped a few feet from the jetty and turned back. The Judge felt an exultation. "Turned him!" he yelled.

"Well, keep the son of a bitch clear of my line."

The battle lasted about fifteen minutes. The Judge, mortally engaged, was aware when the other backed up on the beach lifting his silver trophy on a wave crest, beaching him. He was aware a short time later that the other stood behind him.

"Here—take over," he gasped.

The other backed away. "Not on your obscene life! Go to work on him. Tighten up a little more, he's tiring."

The Judge went to work on him. He discovered that by properly adjusting the drag, lifting the rod tip and dropping it fast while reeling, he could pump the fish closer as it tired. He saw the bass roll green inside the rollers. He reeled like mad.

"Now back up on the beach! Take the bastard easy. Not too fast! Not too fast! Lift him in the wave and I'll grab the leader. That's it! That's it! Goddamn!"

The fish was dragged to the dry sand, its life all but ebbed. The Judge, perspiring, his hands trembling, his blood pumping faster than it had in many a day, walked over to inspect the prize. The angler dispatched it with one rap of a loaded club. It lay gleaming silver-green, a beautiful fish, with bluish-brown stripes darkening.

"Nice goin', kid," said the angler. "Nice fish you got there. Bigger'n mine. Weigh more than twenty pounds."

"Is that all!" the Judge exclaimed. "I thought he must

weigh forty at least. He looks more than you estimate."

"They're deceiving. But he fought like a son of a bitch, didn't he?"

"Like a son of a bitch!" said Judge Leander Wickett. It was a phrase he hadn't used since his college years.

"Well, we'll bait up and cast out again. May be a big pod of fish in this hole."

The angler baited both rods, cast one. The weighted rig described a parabolic arc and splashed distantly. "Go ahead, cast out."

"I might break something, you know. I'd prefer you to."

"Christ's little kittens! Here, let me show you. Right thumb here. Be sure the reel is on free spool. Take it back easy like this. . . . Now forward quickly with just a little snap of your right wrist. Don't move your left arm. . . . No, not that way. Jesus and all hands around!"

The Judge had moved adequately, but had not kept sufficient thumb pressure on the unspooling line, and the result was a grandfather of backlashes and a ten-foot cast. The angler unraveled the bird's nest to an accompaniment of words not often heard in a courtroom. He again demonstrated form and the Judge responded.

"Now you're cooking. Haul in and try it again."

The Judge, cooking, showed definite improvement.

"Okay, let it lay out there. Hit hard if a fish picks it up."

The new excitement did not diminish. The Judge fished for an hour longer, twice changing bait. He was taut with the expectation of a strike and tense with the memory of his battle with his first striper. It was the angler who finally suggested that, tide having turned, it was probably useless to fish longer in daylight. The Judge helped his companion carry the rods and fish to the car.

"Hey, that's your fish, kid."

"Oh, no," said the Judge. "It was your equipment. It's your fish." He wanted to say that he didn't want the bass, but that would be a misrepresentation—he wanted it like he wanted his right arm.

"Hell, you caught it. I never took another man's fish yet."

So Judge Wickett let himself be argued into it. He introduced himself by name only. The other responded: "My name's Popowski. Got a junk yard in Brooklyn."

They arranged to meet and fish the following morning, and the Judge started home with his fish. He was vaguely disappointed that he met no one on the beach, but the colored maid, rolling her eyes, greeted him with enthusiasm.

"What do you think of that? Caught him myself."

He went to the foot of the stairs.

"Oh, Sue—Andrew! Come down and I'll show you really something."

His daughter came down in her robe, his grandson in his pajama bottom. The Judge held his prize aloft, his fingers, cut, in its gills. The fish dripped blood on the rug.

"Oh, boy!" said Andrew.

"Well, Dad! Who caught that?"

"I caught it," said the Judge. "Caught it myself. Man, regular fellow, Pop-something—runs a junk yard—let me use his rod."

"What's he weigh, Gramp? Fifty pounds maybe, huh?"

The Judge was tempted to let the estimate go uncorrected—merely state that he didn't know—but that ingrained sense of integrity brushed temptation aside; there must be integrity in angling as in all else.

"Oh, no, Andrew. Perhaps twenty pounds, twenty-one. Not more. But he fought like a son of a bitch."

"Dad!"

"Sorry." He was genuinely grieved and amazed at himself. "I'm awfully sorry. But he did fight like the very devil. Vicious fish—courageous." There was a new gleam in his eye.

In such fashion Judge Leander Wickett of the Massachusetts Superior Court became a convert to the art of the angler. By evening the entire summer colony was aware he had caught a twenty-pound striper and planned to fish next day with a companion who, through some transition not of the Judge's making, had assumed the social and financial stature of a steel tycoon from New York.

The Judge moved that day into the circle of the veteran bass addicts whose company he had rather studiously avoided in years past. He listened to their fishing stories, told his own. Joe Hartley, a night caster, invited him along some evening and he accepted gratefully, though he knew Joe always had a bottle in his plug bag. His day was full of discussion of rods, glass blanks, reels, the merits of a wide spool, nylon and linen lines, popping plugs, underwater plugs, wagtails, block tin, barracudas, butt harnesses, gaffs, sand spikes. The zealots welcomed him with open arms and hymns. Merely because he felt exalted, uplifted, he sipped two Manhattans instead of his usual one before lunch. He went to the golf club but excused himself from his foursome on the ground that his arms ached and he must save his strength for possible battle the next morning.

Before night he had put through a phone call to a New York sporting goods house, ordering an expensive assortment of tackle to be shipped air express to Hyannis, where he would pick it up. In the evening, seated on his veranda and reliving in memory the dramatic fight of the

179

morning, he received a visit from Clem Hartley, Joe's brother. Clem was generally recognized as a hot bass fisherman. His wife was known as the Striped-Bass Widow, which is worse than being a golf widow because golfers sleep at night, as a rule. Clem had heard he had caught a bass and was calling to congratulate him. The Judge recounted the circumstances for at least the tenth time.

"Good fish, they tell me," Hartley said.

"Twenty pounds or so," said the Judge.

"Weigh him?"

"No. The man whose rod I used estimated the weight."

"They're hard to guess. Fool you, unless you've been at it a long time. Look heavier than they are, most of them. Care to show me?"

The Judge led him to the kitchen. He felt a misgiving lest, in Hartley's opinion, the fish would weigh less than twenty pounds and he would be placed in the position of having misjudged or exaggerated. The maid had cleaned and gilled it for baking and, in the freezer, the Judge thought his fish appeared smaller. But Hartley said, "Better than twenty when he was caught. Closer to twenty-two."

Judge Wickett felt better, but when Clem had gone he realized he had talked too much about the fish all during the day, probably boring a lot of polite people who hadn't the slightest interest. He determined to watch out in the future—let his fish speak for themselves.

Next day he caught no fish. The tycoon of rusted steel departed Brooklyn-ward, his vacation ended. The day following, in the same hole, fishing alone, the Judge hooked a big fish and lost it. He made no mention of this to anyone. His tackle arrived and he spent hours testing it out, casting various lures from the beach, learning to give

180

action to them. He caught a small bass on a plug, took another night-fishing with Jeff Hartley. He played only one round of golf during the last week of July. He didn't sail in the week-end racing, but joined the anglers in the rocking-chair fleet as they talked their preparations for night excursions. He ordered a fourteen-foot lapstreak skiff and a five-horsepower outboard motor. He put his golf clubs away in a closet. He was a goner.

IN THE moon's last quarter Roccus re-entered the canal, following schools of spike and tinker mackerel, feeding only at night, lying on the bottom with lesser fish during the hours of sun. Her appetite diminished and she was easily satisfied. She no longer pursued the darting whiting to the surface to whack them and gorge them. She moved lazily after eels, not eager for their taste. As the water warmed her stripes darkened from brown to deep blue, and a reddish hue appeared on the edge of her gill covers. Sea lice left her for fish traveling to the surf. A benign lassitude of old age crept upon her.

EVERLY AND three of his crew went ashore about noon, leaving one man aboard the seiner riding anchor off Higgins Point, the black seine boat swinging at her stern— the only black seine boat to be observed in all the bay. The man left on watch had an early lunch on a half-pint he had cached against such a situation, and now he dozed

181

on a hatch cover unaware of the approaching skiff until the boat bumped the seiner's hull and a voice roused him. Then he was on his feet, alarmed and ugly.

"Good day, friend," called the man in the skiff, shipping his oars.

"Keep off, you," warned the watch. "Stand clear. Nobody comes aboard."

The man in the skiff stood and grasped the seiner's rail, and the watch saw in surprise that his caller was an elderly priest, at least a man in priestly garb, black-clothed, wearing the Roman collar under his round, tanned face.

"Can't come aboard. Sorry, mister," said the watch less severely.

The priest, smiling, seemed not to hear. He tied up and climbed stiffly on deck, rubbing a knee.

"Good day," he greeted. "Just getting my exercise and thought I'd pay my respects."

"Skipper says nobody's to come aboard. You'll have to go."

"I don't always hear well," said the priest. "Are you a Catholic, my son?"

"I ain't anything. You'll have to get off."

The other, smiling, said, "Good," and nodded, obviously mistaking the order.

The watch barred his way and lifted his voice. "You'll have to get off!"

"Well, that's all right then. I just need a little rest. This a lumber boat?" He walked to the hatch cover and sat on it, rubbing his knee.

"Fish!" shouted the watch. "Skipper finds you aboard, I'll catch hell."

"There is a hell, friend." The priest smiled. "Do you have sails?"

182

"Engines. Look, mister, you'll have to go."

"When I was a boy I sailed a boat on a lake. Now everyone is in a hurry."

The watch glanced shoreward apprehensively. Apparently he could rid the vessel of the old fool only by force and he knew better than to use that.

The priest's glance went to the masthead barrel, his finger questioning.

"Lookout," said the watch. "Man watches for fish."

"Fish? Now I understand. It was in the back of my mind this was a lumber schooner. What fish is that, cod?"

"Mackerel, mackerel!"

"I like a cod, boiled, with an egg sauce." He stood. "I grow more stupid in my old age. This indelicate perfume should have told me this is a fishing vessel." He lifted the hatch cover with a quick movement of his foot and thrust it aside. The high sun shone on a section of wide-mesh seine silvered with big scales. The priest pointed another innocent question.

"Net—catch mackerel," shouted the watch, hastily replacing the cover. He sat on it and the priest rubbed his knee again.

"You'll have to go."

"Go?"

"Get off."

"I must leave?"

"The captain don't like strangers aboard."

"Oh. You should have told me, friend. I would not want you undeservedly punished on my account. I'll leave."

He moved to the rail and climbed gingerly into his skiff. He smiled and waved a hand and rowed away awkwardly.

183

MADDOX SAID, "That was a good trip yesterday even if we didn't catch fish. I was surprised to find you aboard."

"Were you?" asked Father O'Meara. "I merely wanted to observe you and Miss Harrow together, and I wanted Stormy especially to meet Miss Harrow. I think they might be good for each other."

"You are conniving to what end I can't make out. It was obvious yesterday you're up to something. How's Donald making out?"

"Well. As all children do. They have minds open for the reception of truth. I shall not burden him with complexities for yet a while, as much as I would like to speed the process. I may be leaving you soon."

"Tom Salter mentioned as much to me. Don't go, Father."

"Do you need me, Maddox?" The priest smiled.

"No man is sufficient unto himself. All men need friends. But I could make out without you. It's Clystie I'm thinking of."

"She will make out, Maddox. She may need you more than what I can provide. I'm very sure of her."

"If you are, you must know what's inside that shell."

"Something of it I have figured out—part of it. There is something else perhaps only you can get at. All in due time. Are you kind to her?"

"She doesn't want kindness."

"There you are in error. Kindness is her only need."

"Not love then?"

"All love is a generous flood of kindness and under-

184

standing and forgiving. Be kind to her, Maddox; no one else has been."

"She has told you something then."

"Nothing."

"Nor me. I will take her as she is, without explanation."

"No," said the priest, shaking his head. "She might give herself to you but you would not take her."

The Chief paced the floor, agitated, angered.

"I'm sick of riddles, sick to hell of them. Speak out."

"All of it I don't know, none of it I will tell you. One day she will tell you all of it if you will listen with her close enough to your heart."

"Ahhh, hell!"

"And not in bed."

The priest put a hand on Maddox's shoulder.

"In that way I am not so sure of her as I am of you."

"You know I love her."

"I pray each night you do. My bad knee suffers from it. How's Manuel?"

"Not good, not too bad. Why change the subject?"

"Riba is a subject constantly with me, the symbol of all my weaknesses, the gout of all my excesses, the scab of all my wounds. Sometimes, may God forgive me, I fear he could be the dwindling of my faith. Maddox, in what of all earthly pleasures do I indulge myself the most?"

"Why, your fishing, Father, I guess."

"That is so. I merely wanted confirmation of my self-analysis."

"Why do you ask?"

"It is something I have been turning over in my mind. I'm going out to Riba's. Are you coming?"

"No. If I go I'm afraid I'll break his jaw. Go along, Father. I'll be seeing you."

OUTSIDE THE Tavern of the Sun, near closing hour, Manuel Riba stood making up his foggy mind. He wanted a glimpse of Maggie Blynn. He wanted another drink. He wanted to tell of the great bass which was stuck in his parched throat. The fear of ridicule stayed his hand on the door and he turned away toward the package shop.

In his austere room, beneath the crucifix, Father O'Meara knelt in prayer for the mending of Riba's ways, for the soul of a small boy, for the peace of the woman who had borne the lad out of what sorrow he could only guess. He kissed the cross on his beads.

Whitcomb Sears jogged through the darkness along the river road toward home, another night at the movies behind him. But he turned away from his house down the pitch of lane toward the bog.

Clystie Harrow dreamed again of the shots and awoke, sitting upright. There had been the sharp raps of the Luger, a single blast of shotgun fire. She rose without a light and moved softly to Donald's bedside and knelt there, an arm across his sheet, her head upon it.

Judge Wickett slept fitfully and dreamed a dream of a school of wooden plugs swimming in the surf of a lonely beach. He roused once and snapped on his light to check his alarm clock, which was set for three o'clock fishing.

Maddox, in his shorts, climbed the tower stair to check the lookout's vigilance, stood for a minute gazing on the moonlit roof of the house in the dunes. Then he went for a swim and the warm water was ice to the pulse of fire within him.

Banker Hartwell, from his captain's walk, trained a night glass on Webb Everly's seiner still riding off Higgins Point. Even as he watched he heard the snort of her Diesel coming alive, the sound of anchor chain hauled inboard.

Cal Knight rose once out of habit to check his mooring lines and adjust a bumper. He stood at the stern gazing up the thin moonpath toward the narrows until he heard Bobby stirring in his bunk.

In the canal the east tide met the west flow and the rips dissembled and the water was quiet, and in a crevasse of a submerged ledge near the Bourne highway bridge Roccus shifted position, nipped a questing crab, relaxed. Westward the tide began to run, the rips making up in the swirling current of the change.

187

August

THE GREAT fish devoured Manuel Riba. The secret of
Roccus which he could not share burned like a fever by
day and night in both his sober and his drunken moments.
His appetite for food vanished. His wiry strength, which
had withstood the abuse to which he had subjected his
body for so long, would not withstand the onslaught of the
fire in his mind. He lost weight. He aged swiftly. He could
not drive from his brain the image of the bass, or the
compelling urge to shout of her existence or the conflicting knowledge that the telling of this truth would subject
him to more scorn and ridicule than ever had been heaped
upon him as the result of his exaggerations.

Tell he must, eventually, or there could be no escape
from torment. This he realized subconsciously. Over and
over he weighed again the idea of telling Father O'Meara
or Maddox, or both. He could not risk the disaster of the
disbelief of those who, alone in the community, had any
faith in him or any kindness for him. It even occurred to
him that he might tell the priest in the confessional; the
priest would know he would not desecrate the confessional with a lie. This course he could not follow. He had

too much to confess and he had forgotten the act of contrition. Yet he might still tell the priest.

In the end he returned to his original idea of telling his most unbelievable truth to Nick Constantos, his cruelest detractor and belittler. This became a final decision when, in an unsober moment, the thought occurred to him that the feverish secret might be passed along to infect the hated Greek. Later, when he was sober, the idea persisted.

Twice during the shimmering heat of the first week in August Manuel went to the Tavern of the Sun with his mind made up to spit the story of the great bass into the teeth of the man he could depend upon to react most violently to it. Twice he lost the nerve to do it as Nick baited him for previous tall tales. Twice he got drunk instead.

On Tuesday of the second week in August he prepared for the third attempt. He had quahogged for five hours through a small tide, his physical exertions a mechanical habit which left his mind free to torture him. He knew he could go on no longer without release.

In the evening he sacked his quahogs in the creek, bathed and shaved and dressed in his best slacks, his loafers, a fresh shirt of green rayon. The sheathknife which he always wore on his belt he removed from the belt and shoved inside his shirt under the waistband of his slacks. He did this automatically without inspecting the reason why he did it. If someone watching him do it had inquired the reason, he could not have supplied an answer. It was not an act of conscious thought. But he did it. And when he had done it he strolled slowly into Bournham through the first dusk.

He turned toward the Tavern of the Sun, yet turned away from its door and went on to the rectory and, conscious of his immaculate self, approached the front door.

189

When Rosie Carmody appeared he said, "Will Father O'Meara talk with me?"

"He's gone," said the housekeeper. "He's not home."

"Soon maybe?"' asked Manuel.

"I don't know," she said. "I'll tell him you called. Can anyone else help?"

"Thank you," said Manuel. "Nobody else. Maybe I come back, maybe not."

He turned away.

In the Tavern of the Sun the early patrons had gathered, most of them sipping cool beers that made them hotter. Manuel saw Nick behind the bar and knew that this was a night for telling. For the Greek was in a surly mood and wore a dour frown, the consequence of a quarrel that afternoon with Maggie Blynn. Maggie had threatened to pack and get out but she was still working. Manuel observed that she was more responsive than usual in her repartee and surmised correctly that she was deliberately prodding Nick's jealousy. She greeted Manuel with unexpected warmth and a demand to know why he hadn't asked her out recently.

"Don't give up on me, Manuel." She patted his shoulder.

She awakened no response in Manuel. He glanced neither at her face, nor her breasts, nor her legs. He kept his gaze on Nick and walked directly to the section of the bar opposite him.

"A beer in the bottle," Manuel ordered.

Nick served him without a word and Manuel poured a third of it but did not taste it.

He said, "I got something to tell you, Nick."

Nick sloshed his counter cloth and said nothing.

"I got something to tell you, Nick," Manuel repeated.

"Go ahead, by God, and tell it," Nick responded.

Manuel's hand trembled around the glass. He licked dried lips. He opened his mouth but no words came out.

Nick grinned, having his first fun. "I believe it, by God!" he said.

Manuel ground his teeth, parted them, breathed noisily and blurted, "I see a striped bass weigh a hundred pounds!"

The words were as loud in his ears as an explosion. Actually he had managed only a whisper, running the words together. Nick said nothing and he thought Nick hadn't understood. He ground his teeth again and wrenched his body like a woman in labor, and said clearly, though with a tremor in his voice, "I see a striped bass weigh a hundred pounds."

Nick gave him a glance of black anger but he said nothing.

Manuel waited, trembling. He managed a sip of the beer. He was prepared for anything except Nick's continued silence. Nick ignored him and moved down the bar, sloshing his rag. Manuel, as if drawn by a magnet, followed opposite.

"You say something," Manuel gritted.

Nick's heavy-lidded eyes searched his face.

"Sure. What you want me say?"

"I said I see a hundred-pound striper."

"By God, I hear you say that twice before."

"Now you say something—your turn to say something."

"Hokay. I say something. Anything you like. What you like I should say?"

Manuel coaxed, "You say I'm goddam liar."

Nick blotted the bar thoughtfully. "No," he decided, shaking his head and thrusting it forward. "Why I say that? I think you see that hundred-pound striper!"

He grinned.

Six inches below the grin Manuel stuck his knife to the hilt. He turned, running.

LOVELY AND peaceful beat the sea of summer, cruel with death. Schools of small tuna were annihilating squid. Giant bluefins were decimating the mackerel shoals. Stalking the big tuna came the killers.

Through the canal with the tide east-flowing Roccus moved under Sagamore Highway Bridge, past Paddys Reef, past the dolphins in the mooring basin across from The Blinker, past breakwater and sandcatcher and into the surge of Cape Cod Bay, where the half-flood kicked a chop of seventy-one-degree surface water against the current disgorging between the riprap. A light easterly behind the fetch of sea added to surface commotion at the canal's east entrance. Roccus felt an uneasiness. She moved across the Sagamore bar where sand eels and sperling silvered the surf.

The school tuna harassing the summer squid were between twenty and forty pounds in weight, fish which in the larval stage three and four years before had measured only a quarter-inch in length. Several hundred of these in two or three distinct schools had moved higher along the bay arm from the Barnstable traps where they had gorged on herring. Now they moved through and under acres of the small red squid, gorging again.

It was not coincidence that the adult members of their family were in the same area. Departing from the fathom curve of their migration highway between the tip of Cape

192

Cod and Nova Scotia, they had moved in from Wood End to intercept the mackerel which swam with the east wind. They raced at great speed effortlessly. Between their bullet-shaped heads and their tails of tremendous power there was no line of water-resistance; their giant fins fitted into grooves in their bodies. Sun rainbowed the spray above them when they surfaced, sporting; they made a slick caused by the slimy substance adhering to their tiny scales. The slick made a pattern of betrayal on the water.

Orcinus, the killer whale, was leader of a pack which had sped south with the Labrador Current, then followed a bent course inside the Gulf Stream to a point three miles off The Race. There they had been sighted, an even dozen of them, and reported by two draggers inbound from the Georges Bank. They had been seen in combat with a finback whale of sixty feet which they had mortally wounded but upon which they had not fed. They had come south to feed on the tuna.

Orcinus was twenty-nine feet long with huge rounded flippers, great tail flukes and a dorsal fin, curved with age, more than five feet in length. About three-quarters of his scaleless skin was black, but his chin and belly were white and there were white oval patches above each eye. In his pack were six males only slightly smaller. The five females were less than half as large, and their flippers, flukes and fins were disproportionately smaller, perhaps a quarter of the size of the males'. These were the gangsters of the Atlantic and their molls, unmatched in ruthlessness, working with a mob instinct that struck terror to the hearts of the largest whales and sharks.

Off Barnstable the killers had intercepted the trail of the tuna and soon began to take toll of them in all sizes.

193

A forty-pound schoolfish was a half-bite appetizer for Orcinus, a five-hundred-pound bluefin a two-bite hors d'oeuvre. Despite the speed of the tuna the killers overtook them at will. Yet they did not harry them ceaselessly. They withdrew as their appetites were satisfied, so that the bluefins were not completely stampeded.

Now, having swum outside the tuna for several miles during half a day while the bluefins, their alarm diminishing, resumed feeding, the killers drove toward the land again and the giant tuna fled before them among the schoolfish. The schoolfish turned over the shoals in terror.

Inside Roccus there was no hunger except a yearning which had no significance for her senses. She moved leisurely across the Sagamore bar and onto the shoals off Scorton Harbor Creek in Sandwich. There, encountering extreme shoaling, she finned farther off the land. And farther off the land, where the water deepened to eight fathoms, Orcinus hit her.

The bass had brief warning. A tuna of about twenty pounds arced into her vision, leaped and twisted and turned offshore again. Roccus followed from curiosity and met, nearly head-on, a giant tuna in a glide of frenzy, in flight before the closely following killer.

Orcinus saw Roccus only as a blurred shadow suspended where no shadow should be. He chopped at her with one side of his jaw in the flash of his passing. His twenty-two conically pointed teeth on that side sliced into the caudal peduncle of the bass—nearly to the backbone—just failing to sever.

Tuna and killer whale vanished as quickly as they had appeared. Roccus, seeking shallower water, swam slowly and with great exertion. Her broad tail, the propeller of her normal action, was fouled and its driving force drastically reduced. She was severely injured.

194

From the surf the red summer squid leaped onto the beach, squirting water and ink, contracting and expanding futilely. A cloud of gulls shrieked above them.

"I CAME as soon as I heard," said Maddox. "Have you seen him?"

"And heard his confession," said the priest. "The confession of his sin that is also a confession of my failure."

They walked the path downhill from the rectory. The river ran red with the last of the sun.

"He could not bring himself last month to come to me with a problem that tortured him. That is my personal failure, not the failure of the Church."

"So you blame yourself because he was jealous of the Greek over a two-buck trollop. That doesn't make sense to me and it shouldn't balance in Jesuit logic."

"I am no Jesuit and this was not the result of jealousy—and who are you to sit in judgment on a woman?"

Maddox had deliberately invited the rebuke in an effort to rouse Father O'Meara from a depression of self-condemnation. He was pleased with the result.

"Where did you see him?"

"In the jail at Barnstable, awaiting quick indictment by the grand jury."

"What will happen to him?"

"He will spend the rest of his life in prison, either a long loneliness behind bars or a short loneliness in waiting for the archaic form of public vengeance we still cling to in this state."

"The loneliness will not be new to him," said Maddox. "He was always a lonely man. I will pay him a visit."

"He would like it. But I doubt they will permit you to see him."

"Tell me when you heard of it."

"In the night, late. I had just returned to the rectory from—from being elsewhere. The police came to tell me. He was still sought. They thought he might come to me. I, too, thought he might come again but he did not, a further manifestation of my failure."

"With all due respect to you, Father, you take it too personally. What do you think you should have done— moved in with him to watch over him day and night? He'd been heading for something like this for a long time."

"That I feared. That is why I must take at least a share of blame for my own nonfeasance."

They stood at the river edge. The sky was an encaustic painting, its colors seemingly fixed by the heat rising in visible waves from the marsh beyond the calm of the estuary.

"You intend to leave us. Your mind is made up."

"Not entirely. If I go it will be with a heavy heart because of Manuel. But there is still a burden of duty for me here. I must be sure I am not running from it."

"Some of it concerns me, no doubt?"

"It does, Maddox, it does."

"And Clystie—and the boy."

"You three are often in my prayers."

"A strange thing," said Maddox. "I said a prayer the other night. I have not prayed since I was a boy."

"And it was for a boy you prayed."

"Right, Father."

"Pray for yourself, Maddox. Denying Him, you have always believed in Him. And pray for her."

"All I know is that for the first time in my life I need

196

a help I cannot summon from myself. Perhaps I pray merely on the chance there is a God."

"Many do, in fear. But not you, Maddox. Do you want to tell me of Miss Harrow?"

"Only that I haven't violated whatever small confidence you had in my feeling toward her."

"That will be in consideration of the boy; but nevertheless it is recognition of right and wrong as God decreed it. I have faith in you, Maddox—not faith without fear, but faith."

"I won't destroy it."

"If you mean that, I will have faith without fear " The priest ran a handkerchief along a wilted collar. "How are the boy and his mother?"

"The boy blooms. I wish to your Christ the blood in him was mine. . . . The mother has a torment she will not share. She reminds me of a swimmer, going under again. You do not go under for long without drowning."

"Someday," said the priest, "she will share the torment, and I think it will be with you. Some of it I already know. Some of it I can guess. She will share it with you because she loves you. Then she may need me Bring her to me."

They took a turn toward Tom Salter's bait shack, the priest's hand on the other's arm.

"When do you go to Barnstable again?"

"In the morning, I hope."

"I could send Manuel a message through you?"

"It depends upon the message."

"You could tell him that Maddox has come to believe in your God. That might help him."

"Do you?"

"I'm hoping I do."

"I will tell him, gladly. He looked up to you and it

197

will help him in his own faith. His own faith in God will
be his only consolation during the remainder of his life."

"Perhaps that's the only reason I said it."

Maddox felt the hand lifted from his arm. "I'm sorry.
It's an old habit and I couldn't help prodding you."

" 'Be sober and watch: because your adversary, the
devil, as a roaring lion goeth about, seeking whom he may
devour.' Who said it, Maddox?"

"I wouldn't know, Father."

"The saint, Peter, called Simon in his fishing days. Not
a very good fisherman until Jesus intervened and made
him a fisher for the souls of men. I don't think you will
be devoured, Maddox."

ON THE second night after being wounded by Orcinus,
Roccus swam awkwardly with the tide in the starry shallows past Sandwich Harbor Creek to the deep of the
canal's east end; and as the west tide began to flow, she
gave her hurt self to the pull of it and, dropping deep,
moved through. The wound on both sides of the wrist of
her tail attracted two lampreys which she brushed off
on a mussel bed, but cunners followed her, as did dog-
fish, drawn by the flow of her life in the tide's life.

Her life was a life of great tides and currents but this
life of the moon's tide was small; the moon was in quarter
stage, and the rips were slow to make. This was a windless
night when the eel-rig bouncers got much distance in
their casts but took few bass. Roccus saw a dozen slow-
moving, blue-backed, white-bellied skins, inflated with
water, move within her striking distance and withdraw

with tantalizing tail action. Hungry, she might have struck. She did not hunger.

Before the new day crept under the span of the railroad bridge she had reversed her journey through the canal and was again in Buzzards Bay.

The wound confused her, rather than pained. The alarm building within her was the result of confusion.

JUDGE WICKETT gassed his outboard and loaded his skiff: wooden bucket of plugs ready at hand, tackle box of weighted lures, bag of swivels, snaps and leaders, wire and heavy nylon; two rods, a light stick of glass with a fast action tip for plugging, a seven-foot split cane for trolling. He double-checked the load, stepped into the stern and shoved off the yacht club float.

"Don't catch 'em all, Judge," Weston Bartlett called from his veranda rocker.

"No danger, Weston. The fish are sulky. There's been a school lying off the west jetty for two days, but they're not eating anything I've offered." He pulled the starter and headed out.

Jeremy Thatcher, the aged caretaker, nudged Bert Rowell, the young assistant steward. "The old fart's bit bad by the fishing bug."

"Does all right, too," said Rowell. "One thing about him, you don't have to listen to a lot of bullshit from him like from most of the fishermen."

The passing days had demonstrated that the Judge had, indeed, been badly bitten. It was also true that, as in most things he tackled, with the exception of golf, he had done all right; he had taken his share of stripers. He fished with an enthusiasm and energy which brought cries of "uncle" from many a younger angler who tried to keep up with him. He had dropped golf altogether, hadn't even been at the club except to preside over one meeting of the membership committee. The sailing of his two small boats had been turned over to his daughter and grandson. As tide and condition served he fished morning, noon and night. He fished daybreak, sunset, dark, eager, untiring. It was as if, having discovered a true love late in life, he was trying to make up for purposeless years. There was no point of satiation. He had long since reached the point of no return. He must go on—fishing, discussing fishing, careful never to exaggerate or to overtax interest, dreaming of big bass.

This evening he planned to fish a rocky ledge where, at daybreak, he'd noticed bass swirling. There had been, he estimated, at least a dozen good fish boiling there, fish that would go better than twenty pounds. He had worked over them without a strike, using plugs, nylon jigs, trolled eelskins. He was returning without having disclosed this secret, the anticipation of battle gleaming in his eye.

It was going on eight o'clock, with about an hour of good light left, when he shut off his motor two hundred feet to windward of the ledge and began a drift, casting into the rocks. The breeze was just right to move the boat along gently. He snapped a plastic swimming plug of amber shade onto the leader of the glass rod, made a tentative short cast upwind to be sure of even spooling. Then he made a long cast toward the rocks. He moved the plug with a slight lift of the rod tip as the lure hit the water. He retrieved slowly with now and then a succession of short jerks. The plug rolled slightly and wigglewobbled its tail. Enticing.

200

As it neared the boat he was reminded of what Clem Hartley had told him about swimming plugs: "Get them with a thick tail for action. They look like the throw of a woman's fanny as she walks when they're working right." So they did, Judge Wickett thought. He cast again.

As the plug started action he thought he detected a small swirl behind it but he felt no strike. He cast a third time. Nothing showed. He switched to a popping plug and had a slow swirl, just a follow.

By then he was close to the ledge. He moved out again, using the oars, to make a second drift. He rigged a wag-tail undersurface runner for only one cast, returning to a swimmer of amber plastic. He bent the plane a little for more roll. On his second cast the water behind it bulged a foot, making a tremendous swirling boil. His heart popped into his sunburned throat. He reeled fast, then slowly. The bass seemed to move slowly.

A V of unbelievable proportions appeared behind the plug. Vanished!

He shook all over like a wet setter. He made another cast, backlashing slightly from buck fever so that the plug lay lifeless on the water while he picked out the snarl. When he started his retrieve the sea boiled again. He reeled steadily, slowly, whispering to himself. The great V-ream appeared again, following.

"Take it, take it, take it!" whispered the Judge.

The plug jerked closer, the wake of the fish behind it. Roccus was fifteen feet from the boat when the Judge saw her clearly. Her spiny dorsal cleaved the surface as she moved lazily behind the plug, curious about its action, having no urge to taste it. The Judge loosed a shout. His knees knocked together. Roccus boiled and vanished, throwing spray.

The Judge sat, not trusting his legs. He bent the plane

201

of the plug with fingers he could barely control. He took a deep breath, stood, cast again, again backlashing. Still, when he began reeling, Roccus followed, fanning leisurely, swimming closer, closer, closer, twenty feet off from the boat, fifteen, ten, nine.

There swam a greater bass than the Judge had ever dreamed existed! He saw her sharply delineated, a memory he would never lose—the great green head, the golden-black eyes as big as aggies, the pink-tinged sheen of gill plates wider than the full expanse of his two hands. The injured tail as broad as a barn door! No! Careful now! How broad was that tail? Fifteen, sixteen inches, probably more. This time Roccus came within six feet of the skiff. This last time she vanished without a swirl; she sank from sight.

Judge Wickett slumped again. He changed plugs, stood uncertainly, made a poor cast, raised nothing. He cast again without luck. He stayed there fishing, casting everything in bucket and kit, and trolling, till long after dark. He did not see Roccus again.

On the run back to the yacht club the Judge turned over carefully in his judicial mind's eye all the evidence of that fish, reviewing it as carefully, as dispassionately, as ever he weighed the evidence in a courtroom at trial of a capital case. He considered the light, magnification of water, proximity, his own unimpaired vision, his own emotional reflexes—everything which might have had bearing on judgment. In the end he settled for six feet of length, at least one hundred pounds of weight. Six feet! One hundred pounds!

On the float Sue waited with Jeremy Thatcher.

"I was getting a little anxious because you said you'd be in quite early."

He tied up, covered his motor after inspecting the stars, lifted his tackle out for Thatcher to give a hand with.

"Sue, I saw a perfectly amazing fish tonight. A fish that would go one hundred pounds! Twice followed my plug close to the boat."

"What kinda fish, Judge?" Jeremy asked.

"Striped bass, Jeremy. A bass that was six feet long. Had two clear views of him."

Thatcher made no reply, went up toward the lockers with the burden of tackle.

The Judge's daughter said, "Too bad you couldn't catch him, Dad. Come along up, now. I let Roma go to the movies and Andrew's alone."

"Sue," he said, "one hundred pounds, not a pound less!"

While eating a sandwich he phoned the Hartley brothers, talked first with Joe, almost calmly recounting his experience.

"Come again on that size, Judge. Guess I didn't understand you."

"Sorry, Joe. Mouthful of bread and tongue. Joe, he'd have gone at least one hundred pounds!"

There was a little silence. "Well, now, that's some fish, Judge. The record is only seventy-three. They've netted some over a hundred but that was years ago and a long way from here. Don't know as you'd ever find a fish like that in these parts."

"Damn it, Joe, I tell you I saw it as clearly as my hand in front of me here."

"Look a lot bigger at dusk. Hard to guess when they're in the water."

"Damn it, Joe, put Clem on here." He heard Joe speaking to Clem, heard Clem say, "Hi, Judge, Joe says you near hung a big one."

"He tell you how big?"

Clem temporized. "How big, Judge?"

"I'll conservatively estimate one hundred pounds."

After a silence: "You had dinner, Judge?"

"What's that got to do with it?"

"Find they put on twenty, thirty pounds every cock-tail."

Judge Wickett shouted, "Damn it all to hell, you listen here!" Clem couldn't listen because the Judge, in a reflex of anger, had involuntarily disconnected.

For the first time a tiny doubt assailed him. Not doubt about what he had seen, but doubt as to the acceptance of his word; it had been almost his lifetime since his honesty or even his judgment had been placed in doubt by anyone.

He slept fitfully. He dreamed once of a striper with the body of a locomotive chasing him down a railroad track with the speed of a streamliner.

He rose two hours before dawn, made coffee, returned to the ledge with first light. He fished five hours without raising any bass.

Upon his return to the club a little group walked down to the float to greet him. The Hartleys weren't among them, nor was Thatcher, but it was obvious from their greeting that they had been.

"You connect with that hundred-pounder, Judge?"

"Didn't see him this morning. Didn't see a fish this morning."

"Tell us about that lunker, Judge."

There was challenge here not to be ignored. Perhaps a more serious challenge than he had ever encountered. His response was as weighed and measured as any instruction ever delivered to a jury which, in his practiced eye, was wavering from the course of justice. He told,

204

without embellishment of superlatives, of the fish he had seen and his failure to hang it and his disappointment in his failure. He recounted Roccus' approaches to the skiff trailing the plug. He told of bulge, boil, V-ream, injured tail. Eagerly he searched their faces as he talked, and they were the faces of many juries he had instructed in the law and in the admissibility and application of evidence.

He noted, as he had noted in juries of many a courtroom, the glances which passed from one man to the next, from the next to another. He guessed the reason for these glances. He must be at his most convincing best without appearing to convince, to sway, to influence in the slightest degree, as he was in his charge to the jury in an important case. Yet, abruptly, he realized he was not only adviser and instructor but defendant as well.

"Gentlemen, I want to give you my word of honor on this. To the best of my judgment—my not infallible judgment—I'm speaking the absolute truth. That bass would weigh more than one hundred pounds!"

He reached for his rods and there was a silence. Someone cleared his throat and spat alongside the float. Someone else said, "All I got to say, Judge, that's either some fish or some story."

He moved through the group trying not to show anger, went quickly home.

"Sue, do you believe I saw a striped bass of one hundred pounds if I say I did?"

"Why, Dad, of course. Why wouldn't I?"

"I don't believe it." This was Andrew calling from the porch. "Tommy Hartley says there ain't no such bass."

"Andrew! Of course, Dad. I was even telling Mr. Beal about it when he was trimming the hedge."

"And what did Beal say?"

205

"He said such fish could exist without anyone knowing."

"What else, Sue?"

"He did say that in bad light you could have been mistaken."

"Goddamn it!"

"Don't say that, Dad. You've been saying it a lot lately. You never used to swear."

"Sorry. There was plenty of light. It was long before dark. What else did your friend Beal say?"

"Dad, he's not my friend. He's the man who takes care of the grounds. Remember? Why, he said it could be a case of mistaken judgment. He said everyone knew you wouldn't exaggerate. Oh, what does it matter? Come on to your breakfast."

That afternoon, sidetracking an urge to fish the ledge again, the Judge drove to the club with deliberate purpose, knowing the story would be ahead of him—the challenge he must go to meet.

"Hi, old hundred-pounder!" It was Quint Warring, the president who had succeeded him. A merciless ribbing began, principally from the robust imbibers who had always resented his temperance and hoped in his story of the bass for evidence of departure from it. The Judge took it all in the best humor he could muster, slightly bewildered. He saw early that it was purposeless to protest; the more he protested, the stronger the doubts expressed. There wasn't any bass of the size he described. There never had been. There never would be. Then Clint Powers came in from the bar.

Clint had had two in excess of his capacity for rum-and-cokes, and he had never liked the Judge anyway though the Judge had never guessed it.

"Why, you old she-goat! Who you trying to kid?"

For the first time in his mature life the Judge felt an impulse to violence. Strike! Strike hard! He fought it down, forcefully displaying the best courtroom smile he could muster. Clint was led away. A small crisis passed. Judge Wickett realized that for once he was disbelieved, refuted, disavowed. His own folks, his intimates, his more-than-casual associates through thirty-odd summers, called him a liar, not with the word but with slow smiles of disbelief, with covert glances, with sly smirks.

It came to him that his feeling could be akin to that of any innocent defendant whose story had been placed under attack in the courtroom.

To Sue, at the end of the next day, he said, "Daughter, there's not a single person in this place who believes my story about the big bass. I'm so damn mad I could murder the whole kit and caboodle of them!"

"Dad! It's not like you, darling."

"You believe it, don't you?"

"Of course, darling."

She said it too quickly.

For a long time he said nothing. He mixed a cocktail, sipped.

"To hell with them," he said. "I'll catch that fish and hang it in the living room!"

Roccus sought the shoals. The wound inflicted by the killer whale was a constant harassment. The flesh in the wound had tightened in texture, making a callous or soft scab outside the backbone, but its apertures were foul

with plankton which caught by accident in the project-
ing tissue, and tiny crustacean life that deliberately
fastened there. The worry was vitiating.

On a night when she sensed an abrupt turn of weather
and a possible buffeting on a lee shore she turned from
the western approach to the canal into the side current
that took her into the river.

STORMY AND CAL, on their way to fish the evening tide in
the narrows, walked the skiff as far as Mr. Sears' cove and
climbed up the hill to the house.

"Who are you, boy?" Mr. Sears demanded from his
doorway.

Then he saw Stormy.

"I'm Cal Knight, Stormy's friend."

"Is that so? Well, you look all right though you never
can tell. You want to come in and sit a minute? I'm going
to the pictures soon so you can't stay long. Been to the
berry bog most of the day. Looks like a good crop but the
price won't be up to last year's."

Cal had observed him often, never met him. They went
into the kitchen and Mr. Sears fetched something in a
paper bag from the next room.

"Here," he said, "your wedding present."

"Oh, we haven't made any plans, Mr. Sears," Stormy
said.

"I guess you made plans but haven't talked 'em over,"
Mr. Sears said.

The Wedgwood cups and saucers were in the bag.

"They're beautiful," Cal said.

208

"My wife liked 'em," said Mr. Sears. "You think you can manage this girl?"

Cal didn't share Stormy's embarrassment.

"Manage her? Guess I can try."

"You want to try awful hard, boy, awful hard. Well, I got to go in to the evening picture. You best get along."

"We're going to fish the narrows," Stormy said. "May we leave the cups here?"

"Oh, sure. But you ain't going to fish long. Storm is coming."

There wasn't any sign of it but when they walked down to the boat, Cal said, "I think the old boy's right at that. Seem to smell a change of weather. Apt to get it on these big tides."

It was still light when they anchored in the narrows in the first of a horsing rip.

They saw Mr. Sears close and secure his back door and start for town.

"There's some brittle, artificial quality about him," Cal said. "I can't put my finger on it."

"It's because he lives on dreams. The woman he loved ran away from him. He's convinced himself she died."

"No, there's something else."

She felt a quick, hard strike on the live-lined sea worms but missed the fish.

"They drop through fast in this current," Cal said. "Must be four knots running here now. Stormy, I think we should go."

"Let's get that fish first."

It had blown southwest all day, but with the new dark, instead of falling off, the wind shifted into the southeast and began to come fresh, pushing the river ahead of it into the funnel of the narrows. The skiff yawed.

209

"All right," she called. It was a reluctant agreement; she wanted to stay; no sense of danger yet intruded. She reeled in swiftly, her rod butt pried at an inboard oar and sudden leverage from hook-fouled seaweed shot the blade outside the gunwales, where a wave struck it broadside. Cal lunged too late. The arcing butt struck his cheekbone and the oar pitched overboard and was gobbled up by the current.

"Are you hurt, Cal?"

"No." He grinned. "But I don't like what we've got."

"We can drift up after it onto the marsh."

"Later. Right now we'd swing broadside and capsize. Got to wait till the wind and tide slack off. We'll ride it out awhile."

He crept forward into the bow to let out more riding line; the bow worked deep against the hissing current. A quick squall gust rocked them. The pressure of the rip was a slavering. They took a wave over the windward side on the swing and then the wind came roaring as the black sky sucked the last of the shadows from the river.

Cal shouted, "Sit in the bottom of the boat, we'll be okay." He was bailing. She was surprised they had taken so much water. The skiff was working like a lassoed colt, wildly weaving, yanking its head.

Cal said, "I could cut but I think we better not. You're not frightened, Stormy?"

"No. But I'm sorry about the oar."

"Forget it. We'll be all right. This won't last."

She felt they would not be all right and the wind was a fearsome tumult.

"The shore's only a hundred feet either way," she shouted. "I'm sure I could swim it, Cal."

"Sit tight, we couldn't make it. Even if the wind keeps

210

up the tide will slack off in an hour or so, enough so we can try the drift."

A wild swing nearly buried the bow and they took a heavy wave inboard. Cal bailed steadily, silently.

In a half-hour she asked, "Hasn't the wind gone down some?"

"A little."

She knew it hadn't; it was stronger, if anything.

"Let me bail awhile. You must be tired."

"Don't move. Don't move, Stormy!"

She didn't, but the skiff climbed a comber, parting it, and the sea rushed on them. She felt Cal's hand in her hair as she went under. She thought, *How warm the water seems*. Then she tasted air. Cal held her by one hand, his other grasping the rocketing submerged gunwale of the overturned boat.

"Work toward the bow with me," he shouted. "Easier hanging at the rope."

She sputtered, trying to be nonchalant, "Careful of my curls."

They inched along to the line secured to the bow eye-bolt. Each put one hand on the rope and the overturned boat rode more comfortably.

Cal shouted, "Wonder if anybody'd hear if I called for help."

He called out three or four times.

"Father'll hear," Stormy said. She knew he wouldn't. He'd be in his study, expecting them to fish late. And he was never weather-conscious.

"Doubt it. No sense yelling. Wastes strength." He had one hand in her hair again and she said, "You're scalping me, darling."

There was a relentless force in the wind and tide, each

striving to outdo the other. There was no diminishing.

"You're getting tired," he said.

"No," she shouted. She had been tiring for what seemed a long time. Her arms, shoulders and stomach were a vast ache from buffeting. She thought: *When the time comes I must let go quickly and he won't know I've gone.* As if he sensed the thought, Cal inched around to her side of the heaving bow and put an arm under hers.

"When Mr. Sears comes back we'll see his light," he shouted. "We'll both call out and he'll hear us."

Though she had lost a sense of time she knew it would be long before the movies were over. It would be much too late. It was almost too late already.

She slapped her hair from her face. "Cal?"

"Yes, lovely."

"It didn't make any difference about Pickman?"

"It didn't. It never will. I told you it never happened."

Her lips sought his. "It's not good-by," she said, "not ever, Cal."

He said, "Hold it!" shouting.

The feeble beam of a flashlight poked out from the north shore of the river and touched them faintly. A voice croaked distantly, "Hold on there. I'm a-comin'."

"It's Mr. Sears! Hi, Mr. Sears!"

Mr. Sears wasn't having any conversation. He thrashed along the edge of the noisy rip hauling his skiff, which must have been full of water. He didn't use his light again until he had emptied the skiff and, far uptide from them, pushed off into the current. Stern-first his skiff sped down on them and the fixed beam of a flashlight showed him rowing wildly.

"He'll never make it," Cal said, "but God bless him for trying."

212

"Grab a-holt of my stern!" cried Mr. Sears.

When, in the last moment, a collision of the boats seemed unavoidable, the old man's strength held his skiff stationary in the rip, kept it clear of the leaping, capsized craft. They transferred handholds. As they clung there, still fearful of the boat behind them, Mr. Sears rowed like the stroke of a college crew and gained the few feet necessary for clearance. Then, easing his exertion, he let the skiff work back with the current, keeping his bow in the gale. Stormy's numbed feet felt sand and seconds later Cal carried her to the bank. Then they waded downshore and Mr. Sears led them to his kitchen. He put a match to the kindling in the range.

"Can't build much fire a night like this," he said. "Stove heats up and the pipe ain't sturdy. Do blow a gale, don't it? My, oh, my!"

In the light of the kerosene lamp, with the water streaming from him, he seemed to be of the gale's own fury.

Cal said, "Thank you for our lives, Mr. Sears."

"Hush, boy. You'd have made out."

"I'd have drowned in another minute," Stormy said.

He gazed at her steadily, a spark leaping in his eyes. "That so? You mean I really saved your life."

She kissed his wet cheek.

"My, oh, my! My little girl used do that afore she went away." His expression changed. "Don't you ever tell nobody about tonight."

"We'll certainly tell everybody," Cal said.

To Mr. Sears' eyes there came a cold, bleak anger.

"Boy," he warned, "don't you ever tell living soul Whitcomb Sears got you ashore. If you do I'll hear of it and, Lord A'mighty, I'll make it hot for you! A man does a bad thing and a man does a good thing and maybe the good

213

offsets the bad. Maybe it does. But he don't go blatting it around, neither the good *nor* the bad."

Cal was too flabbergasted to reply. Stormy asked the time and Mr. Sears produced his big watch. It was only ten thirty-five.

"You didn't go to the movies after all," she said.

"Oh, sure. Fine picture. I was in the picture house when I heard you hollering for help. Left quick and come a-runnin'."

"You mean you weren't home then?"

"Oh, no, I was to the pictures."

"But that's nearly two miles away. You mean you were in the movies and heard shouts for help—heard us so far away?"

"Oh, sure," said Mr. Sears. "Heard you plain as day. Say, boy, guess you'll be able to manage her. Don't forget them cups."

STERNA, the roseate tern, was fishing. From her lookout on the high bank of the point near where Roccus rested the bird watched the schools of bait fish congregating near shore. The sun lay slightly behind her, past its zenith.

When there was a sufficient concentration of the small prey milling about, Sterna performed the Trick of the Menacing Shadow, launching herself and swooping to within a few feet of the water. Her shadow panicked the bait, which showered ahead of it, and the tern of greatest symmetry dipped to scoop baby herring and sand eels, some of which she took from the air.

Lying under four feet of water on the warm silt bottom, Roccus watched this performance for an hour, at the end of which Sterna had had her fill. The bass moved slowly to feed on wounded, fluttering bait.

THE ROCKY POINT dunes snuggled in the blanket of fog which had rolled in high at sunset and settled to the land as the breeze died.

"Now this will make two of us in a fog," said Maddox. "Soon I'll not be able to see your face."

"It doesn't matter," said Clystie Harrow. "Tonight I'll let you touch it."

He said, "I'll check the rod again. Crabs may have eaten the squid." It was as if he had not heard her.

But for the first time in years her mind and her heart were reconciled. She said, "Leave the rod, Maddox." She took his hand and ran his fingers along her cheek. "You have not touched me before."

"No."

"I have wanted you to."

He had no answer.

"Have you not wanted to touch me, Maddox?"

Still he was silent.

"Now you're being stubborn and I'll not let you be." She moved his hand to her sweater and cupped it under her hand. She felt the quick, rough pressure, as quickly ended.

"What is it, Maddox?"

"Just that I love you," he said.

He said it only with his voice and it was a long time before she replied. "Do you, Maddox? Of all who wanted

215

me, none ever loved me. Of those who had me, none ever loved me."

He said, "You are a tough woman, Clystie Harrow, but I'm a tougher man. You will say, if I ask you why you try to hurt me, that it would be better for me to be like the others. So I'll not ask you that. I'll ask you about the men who had you—not because I care but because there is something in you that compels the telling. Who had you, Clystie?"

"Take my hands and pull me up," she said. "Thank you. Put your hands in my hair."

"It's damp with fog," he said.

"Now your hands on my cheeks, Maddox—tight! Kiss me."

Her lips lay gently under his.

"Will you take me first, Maddox?"

"No," he said. "The priest stands between us. Keep away!"

She did not keep away and he struck her lightly across the cheek with his palm and she drew apart from him. She said, "You will not want me when I've told you. But thank you for your love, Maddox."

She sat and he knelt beside her, not touching her.

"Will you hold my hand? Sit there."

He took her long fingers in his big fist. He said, "Who had you, Clystie?"

Her voice was a small voice, distant. "A Nazi General Staff oberleutnant, quartered at St. Sauveur, was the first. There was an urgent need for identification of German Occupation units in Normandy. Some nights he talked. Then there was a U-boat commander on leave at Le Mans. When he returned to service I knew his orders. There was a Luftwaffe ace, a commander of Panzer élite.

216

There was a general in command of forts at Metz. He was Donald's father."

"Who else?"

"There were no others, Maddox. There were too many as it was."

"Father O'Meara guessed it was the war. Perhaps he guessed you were a spy."

"A bad one, a failure."

"So now you have told me and it makes no difference. Let's both forget it."

"Can I forget my son, Maddox? Can you?"

There was something he wanted to say without quite knowing how. Finally he said, "The world is full of wonderful children who were not conceived in love."

"But how many in futility and hatred and deceit?"

Her fingers stirred, quieted.

"Tell it then," he said.

"My home was here as I've told you. It wasn't a good home. I had to run from something. For two years as a kid I'd played summer stock on the Cape. I had a small talent. I went to New York and after a year I had bit parts in two flops. Then to Hollywood for small parts in B pictures. Then I played the part of a French girl in the road company of a Broadway hit, a small part which suited. My mother was French. I was a good French ingénue.

"We played London in 1939, then Paris in the heat. I loved Paris. I had a knowledge of the language from my mother and a facility to absorb it quickly. We disbanded at the end of our run in Paris and though I'd accepted an offer in pictures again I stayed on. I was in Paris when Hitler went into Poland. In Cherbourg I had a ten-day wait for passage home. I wish I had come home, Maddox.

217

But British Intelligence had a need for women agents in France. You've heard the drums and bugles?"

"A long time ago."

"And I was running from something. Before I knew it I was in a London school learning those things we had to know: code, radio transmission, target-area analysis, how to estimate strength by observation of transport, identification of planes and tanks. Hitler was in Norway when the training ended and one night in June of 1940 they dropped three of us in the region of Saint Lô, where the French underground was forming. My contact was an agent outside Carentan at La Haye-du-Puits, an observation post for Cherbourg. Pétain's betrayal was at hand. Belgium and the Netherlands had fallen. The Heinkels were bombing London . . . I am trying to excuse myself, Maddox. Do you understand?"

"It's all right. Get it out if you must."

"For a long time in Normandy it was chiefly observation and report, transmitting from an old farm wagon, getting through once a week without being ranged by the detectors. Then the character of the Occupation changed. The Nazi cruelty began to show. He took the butter to grease his guns. He stole the buckwheat or burned it while the children starved. The Gestapo raided nightly. The black swastikas on the white discs were everywhere. The *miliciens* dealt with the SS Corps and we watched the betrayed marched off to concentration camps or gas chambers. In the beginning the work was chiefly a means of escape but as the cruelty came to the surface it became a kind of personal crusade. There was no means I wouldn't resort to if I could hurt the Nazi. I was a hard woman, Maddox, cold and determined and selectively promiscuous. Sometimes I wished I'd been a wanton. My mother was a wanton. I told myself it was like being wounded in battle, but a wound either heals or kills. There was no healing. I'm trying to tell you, Maddox, that as tough as I was and as determined, I still despised myself. Do you know?"

"I know," he said. "Leave it there."

"I have to tell you of Metz because Donald is Metz. From a month before D-day until December of 1944 my assignment was Metz. I was a wine girl in Metz in May and on D-day I was mistress of the commander of Fort Jeanne d'Arc. My orders were to determine the strength of the fort garrisons and the morale of the personnel but to attempt no radio contact until invasion in the West. Shall I name him, Maddox?"

"No," he said quickly.

"Jeanne d'Arc stands west of the city. Devaux and Drïant to the south were also under his command. First he lodged me in the city but within a month he took me to his quarters in Jeanne d'Arc. When the Third Army broke out of Brittany I had the intelligence needed and sent it—the actual strength of five forts, an accurate estimate of fifteen others. Morale was at high level.

"The Metz transmission principal was a priest from St. Vincent's. The runner was a Metz boy who played the idiot and came to the fort to rummage food from the garbage cans. My messages went out in the garbage. . . . Maddox?"

"It's all right," he said.

"Except once he was no more cruel than the others. He was not much older than you."

He tried to shake her from it. "A fine comparison. I'll bet I'm handsomer."

She would not leave it.

219

"At the end of the third week in August, Patton's Fourth Armored Division was across Loing River, driving for the Metz-Nancy corridor. Reports of swift German retreat streamed into the forts. There was a distinct change in morale. Patton was traveling too fast.

"That was the week I knew there was going to be a baby. There isn't supposed to be any baby in a story like this."

"End it there," he said again.

"Maddox, you have to know all of it. When Patton bypassed Melun and Montereau the Nazi high command decided against the defense of Metz. The personnel of the forts was sent back to the Siegfried Line. This was vital intelligence and I sent it out in duplicate messages which the idiot boy took away. I felt almost elated.

"We remained with a skeleton force at Jeanne d'Arc. A week later a determined Boy Scout troop might have taken twenty forts. But the Third Army didn't appear. I sent another message underlining the urgency of a quick strike. There were reports Patton was stalled for lack of gas and oil. Nothing happened. And at the end of another week the forts were regarrisoned and the Nazi had a new lease on death."

Her hand seemed very small.

"The opportunity for the bloodless capture of Metz had gone. And then he told me, Maddox. Nothing I'd sent had ever been transmitted. He'd known about me all along. The priest had been shot. The idiot boy had always been their agent. He said, 'They wanted to shoot you but I wanted you for my bed.'

"I'd failed, Maddox, and many were going to die because I'd failed. If the messages had gone through, if Patton had come on, there would have been at least some consolation for that growing weight inside me. Instead there was nothing but a sense of complete futility and a black despondency that blanked out everything else."

He felt her fingers groping.

"I didn't want that life born, to be always the symbol of ugliness and failure. I didn't feel I could go on any longer myself. I'd had enough and I made up my mind.

"He carried poison in a paper behind the cover of his wrist watch and he always removed his watch at night. That night when he finally slept I groped to the bureau. His brushes were there, his comb, a bottle of lotion he always smelled of, his Luger pistol. When I touched the watch the bed light snapped on and he sat there blinking, asking what I was up to. There wasn't time for the poison but the pistol was there. I said, 'I'm going to kill myself so I won't have your baby.' He'd started toward me but he stopped. He repeated what I'd said. Then he sat on the bed rocking with laughter over that great double joke he'd played on me. Maddox?"

"Shall I end it for you?"

"My first shot hit him in the stomach. Then I shot him in the head. I blacked out before I could kill myself. Metz didn't fall for two months. Jeanne d'Arc and Drïant and Fort St. Quentin held out until December. They knew the best ways to hurt me. When Jeanne d'Arc was liberated I was five months pregnant. They sent me to Paris and Donald was born there. When he was a month old they sent me to Myra in Ireland."

He took both her hands and pulled her to her feet.

"You see it doesn't make any difference," he said. "You've lived with it inside you so long you've lost your sense of perspective. I'm going to try to make you forget."

"No," she said.

221

Her hands were against his chest, her head against his sleeve. She cried in quick fear, "Maddox! What's that light?"

He turned swiftly, fear in himself. For the fog down the beach, down toward her house in the direction of the Coast Guard Station, was an orange haze. A flame leaped.

She cried, "Donald! Myra! Maddox—my house is afire!"

He was gone from her, running.

SUN BEAT down on the surface of the river. No wind moved that surface, no fish, no bird. The tide had reached the peak of the salt mark on the marsh grass. Bait fish kept to the cooler depths over sand, worrying shell lately turned by the quahoggers. Plankton clouded the iris-blue water. A kingfisher swooped but held its dive over a cloud of minnows too deep to reach and returned with a cry of angry frustration to its lookout at the brittle tip of a dead cedar.

Blue crabs crawled the bottom and in the weed crept up on partially opened seed scallops, and on the bars snuggled with their hinges against small rocks, waiting for clam snouts to show. They could move fast and in any direction. A late-spawning horseshoe crab pushed sand like a bulldozer. Fiddlers, their homes flooded, crept along cautiously, hunting shrimps and sand fleas and the broken clams gulls had dropped for cracking when the tide was down.

In a hole fourteen feet deep, off an old windwheel once used to make electricity for a pump, Roccus rested with her chin in mud, expelling water at an accelerated count,

222

turning on one side, then the other to present the healing wound at the base of her caudal to the black ooze, the warm and salving ooze. So she had rested for days moving into weeks since Orcinus had struck her, feeding lightly and not more than twice a week. She wasted away. She was still a great fish, but her depth and thickness had diminished, the deep bulge of her belly had vanished; she was flabby in her underside, there was an unhealthy sheen on her gill covers and no sea lice sought her as host.

BOATSWAIN'S MATE GATELY speared a pork chop and poured black Joe. Beyond the windows of the Coast Guard messroom the foggy dawn was breaking late.

"Cartwright, get your pencils and let's see if you're a yeoman. I want it all in the record and I want the record straight."

Gately chewed. Cartwright pulled a chair up to the table and laid his stenographer's shorthand book open. The others pulled up.

Gately said, "You were on tower watch, Stavoli. Suppose you take it from the beginning."

The thin, black-haired boy sipped noisily from his heavy cup.

"I musta noticed it before it broke through the roof. You know how fire looks through a fog at night. First I think it's someone having a hot-dog roast there on the beach. Then the flame gets too big and it's too high and I know it's Miss Harrow's house so I sound the alarm, that's all."

"You, Breckman."

Breckman picked it up. "Stavoli is yelling the house in the dunes is on fire. Cassidy and I grab the big fire extinguisher and run for the jeep. Cassidy is in his shorts. I got my pink pajamas on."

"I don't give a damn about your shorts and pajamas," said Gately. "Don't put that stuff in the record, Cartwright. But wait a minute. Put it all in—shows we didn't waste any time."

"He shouldn't wear his shorts to bed," Breckman said.

"I'll go bare-ass before I wear any pink pajamas," said Cassidy.

"Keep that crap out of the record."

"I was just thinking how funny he looked. And it ain't hygienic. You wear shorts all day, I say it ain't hygienic to wear them to bed at night."

"Oh, for chrissake, shut up." Cassidy's brows were singed and he had a smudged nose and cheek. "You want to tell it, or me?"

"We hurl the extinguisher into the jeep," said Breckman. "We have a little trouble starting, moisture on the plugs from the fog."

"That's it. Louse it up. Make the station look bad."

"Oh, it don't amount to nothing. Goes on the third or fourth try. We roll quick. We're 'way ahead of you guys in the duck. But time we get there, the whole house is ablaze and a part of the roof has caved in. The old dame, the housekeeper, is lying outside on the sand. Some of her clothes is burned but she seems okay except she's yelling for the kid, Donnie."

"And Donnie ain't there," said Cassidy.

"She says Donnie's in the house. We rush the front door and Cassidy has the squirter. He might as well be pissing on the fire."

"Cartwright, use some common sense in taking this stuff. Don't let any unexpected words get in the record."

"Okay," said Yeoman Cartwright.

Cassidy said, "You can't get close enough for the extinguisher to do any good anyway because the heat's too tough. We're moving around to try the back door when the dame comes running up out of the dark, screaming like all hell."

"What dame?"

"Miss Harrow."

"She ain't no dame. Cartwright, you just got to use common sense taking this down. These lugs don't have any savvy in making out a report. Put it, 'Miss Harrow came running up out of the dark, screaming.' You can have her screaming but not like hell. Make it 'screaming loud.'"

"All screams are loud," said Cassidy. "She was screaming like hell."

"Okay then, go on."

"She's yelling where's Donald and we don't know. Anyways, we don't say. Suddenly she yells, 'Where's Maddox? Get Maddox! Maddox is in there, too!' Then she begins yelling, 'Maddox, Maddox, Maddox!'"

"Got that, Cartwright?"

"Yuh, I got all of it. You don't have to ask me."

"I said, 'How do you know the Chief's in there?' and she says, 'I know. Dear God, get them out.' They ain't nobody going to get them out."

"Nobody but Maddox," Breckman said.

"Yuh."

Gately said, "Cartwright, ignore the comparison of Maddox with God. Go on, Cassidy."

"Well, it's about then you guys arrive in the duck with the small pumper and we get some kind of a stream on the

225

house and the Doc is giving the old lady a shock treatment. Doc can tell you that."

"She wasn't bad off," said Pharmacist's Mate Grant. "I gave her a shot and we moved her off to one side in a blanket. She's mumbling about she knocked the kerosene lamp over and she couldn't get to where the boy was."

"That's when the—when Miss Harrow tries to go through the door," Cassidy said.

"I want all of it," said Gately, "because someone will likely catch hell from headquarters."

"You mean me, to hell with it," said Grant.

"I don't mean you; shut up. Spill it, Cassidy."

"Miss Harrow rushes the door and the flames are still leaping out though the stream is on it. Ryan here grabs her and she kicks and breaks loose."

"I got a cut in the shin," Ryan said. "Treat and I grab her and she bites Treat's arm."

"Look," said Treat. He displayed his right forearm. There were teeth punctures, deep.

"I better put something on that," said Grant.

"Wait," said Gately. "Wait'll after we get this in the record."

"She bites Treat. She's yelling she wants to be with Donnie and Maddox. You ever try to hold a panther? So Treat clips her."

"I clip her easy," Treat said. "Tried to, anyway. Just on the side of the chin, a little short one."

"You think it was necessary, Ryan?"

"If he hadn't, she'd have been in the house."

"Okay. Get that, Cartwright. Go on, Treat."

"Then I see Maddox."

"I didn't see him at first," said Ryan.

"I see him coming through that flame towards the door

226

and, Jesus Christ Almighty, I never see the like. He's crouched down with the kid in his arms and he's got his head lowered like a bull, kind of covering the kid's body with it and the top of his head is afire and his clothes are all lit up and he's kind of stumbling and swaying like he's looking for something to lean against."

"Then *I* see him," said Ryan. "He's just about made the door. So help me God, I never see such a sight. The kid's face is all blood and the blood is sizzling little bubbles. I get the stream over Maddox's head and he comes out grinning."

"Now I want what Maddox said and I want it right for the record. Who heard him?"

"I heard him," said Cassidy.

"I heard him," said Ryan. "I heard him first time and I heard him when he repeats it. He says, 'Take this kid and get Doc and rush 'em to the station. I'll go along.'"

"That's right," Cassidy said. "When he repeats it he adds, 'That's an order.' He's dripping some skin from one arm and most of his hair is gone but he doesn't seem too bad. The kid is out and looks in tough shape. I yell for Doc and he comes running and we pile into the jeep and race for the station. Maddox is still holding the kid in his arms."

"Doc, you better pick it up."

"That's okay so far," Grant said. "On the way Maddox says the kid's hurt bad as well as burned, and when we get to the station I see why—got a long cut across his throat. Missed the jugular but he's losing plenty blood. There ain't much chance for him but there ain't no chance at all unless he gets blood but fast. I get a packing and set up for direct transfusion. There ain't no time to lose. He's an O-RH positive or he's a goner anyways because every man on the station is O. That's the big percentage. I can give you the statistics on O and A and B and AB."

"Frig the statistics," said Gately. "Give us what happened."

"Maddox said, 'Take the blood from me.' I said, 'I'll take Cassidy.' Maddox said, 'Goddamn you, Doc, take it from me or I'll cut your heart out.' So I took it from him. It had to be fast. I took his good arm. He didn't look too bad but when I take about a pint he's white under the burns and his pulse is bad. I said I'd take the rest from Cassidy and he said, 'You son of a bitch, you'll take all you need from me.' So I did. I took about a quart, getting some stuff on the kid's burns while I'm doing it. I get a pulse from the kid and the kid looks better and I say so, and then Maddox he looks a little better, too. He's grinning like he's got some secret. How could I know?"

"Who the hell said you *could* know?" said Gately. "Nobody's blaming you. You obeyed an order."

"Maddox asked how the kid was going to do. I said, 'Maybe he will, maybe he won't. We got to get him to the hospital quick,' and Maddox said, 'Well, get him there. What the hell you waiting for? Then come back and fix me up.'"

"So Doc and I took the kid," Treat said. "Cassidy phoned ahead and they were ready for us."

"That leaves me alone with the Chief," said Cassidy. "Rest of you guys is still playing fireman. Doc's given me some stuff for Maddox's burns and I get it on his arm and head and face. He's acting kinda funny and talking funny. Mostly he's talking about the kid, but drowsy-like. He says, 'You know, Cassidy, that's a great kid because his mother is a wonderful woman and he's going to be even better now with Maddox's blood in his veins.' He says, 'That's what I want you to tell his mother, Cassidy. Tell

228

her it's okay now, the kid is a Maddox with my blood in him.' So I say, 'Okay, Chief, take it easy. I'll tell her.' Then he just kind of goes to sleep in the chair. I figure he's pretty well pooped so I don't bother him."

"You didn't try his pulse?"

"I tell you no. Christ, how could I know if Doc didn't? I ain't no pillpusher. Even if I'd thought of it I wouldn'ta known where to feel nor what to count."

"Okay, okay, nobody's blaming you, either. I want it for the record. Go ahead, Doc."

"Maddox is out like that when I get back," Grant said. "I take one look and I know it's bad. Then I find the place in the back of his head and you come back with the duck and we get him to the hospital, too."

"What they tell you?"

"I told them; I knew."

"Told them what?"

"He had a fractured skull."

"So you took a quart of blood from a guy with third-degree burns and a fractured skull?"

There were tears in Grant's gray eyes. "I did," he said. "Under orders."

"Would you have taken it if you'd known his skull was fractured?"

"Of course not."

The door opened and Father O'Meara was there, the weariness and worry heavy on him after the hours in the hospital. He read the question in their faces.

"The little boy is going to be all right thanks to the blood of Maddox. The doctors say Maddox can't possibly pull through, barring a miracle. So it was my duty to administer the last rites. But I am a man who believes in the miracles of God, and to a great degree in Maddox. I think Maddox will live."

"Maybe if we pray for him it will help," said Cassidy.

"No doubt of it," said the priest.

"Will you pray with us?"

"Of course."

"You can put it into better words, Father."

"It's the spirit, not the adjectives, that counts."

"But you will?"

"On my bad knees."

He knelt by a chair and made the sign of the Cross, and one by one each knelt.

"O God of strength and refuge, blessed be Thy name and blessed be Jesus and Mary and St. Joseph. Maddox is a strong man made weak and humble at Thy feet and we're going to lose him unless You prevent it. A woman and a little boy are in great need of him and if it be Thy will to save him for them this crew of his will try harder to live within Thy grace. And so will I. Praise be to God. Amen."

He stood, flexing his knees, great sorrow on him but a smile on his lips. First Riba, now Maddox. His cross was heavy, but he must not let the burden show. He said in a loud, clear voice:

"What's the matter with this crew? Would Maddox put up with the long faces among you? Where is your faith in God and where is your pride in Maddox? Get those glum expressions off! Let's see those grins!"

"Miss Harrow's at the hospital?" It was Cassidy's question.

"Of course."

"Did you give her Maddox's message about the transfusion as I told you?"

"Just as you told me. The very words."

"What did she say, Father?"

He grimaced. The knee pain was sharp. But he must go through with it.

"Barring the miracle, I will tell you. But I don't think I ever will."

AUGUST WANED. Days of intense heat were followed by brief tempests that failed to clear the air. The dawns were red beyond the eye of the sun. Chain lightning, distant, licked the evening sky. There was no thunder. A season was approaching its end and the approach communicated itself to all life.

Man witnessed the quick ripening of his tomatoes, the sudden, overnight toughening of his corn, the withering of his potato vines, the indefinable feeling that a chore so long delayed as tacking a new tin blade on his snow-shovel had better be attended to. There were days and weeks and possibly months before a sterner season claimed the earth, yet the grasp of change was on it.

The terns, their young flown, were hungrier for themselves; the mackerel gulls were less lazy; the fierce-winged gannet dived from greater height. The curlew cried above the moor at night and the plovers called at daybreak. The young of the native black ducks tested their strengthening wings above the guzzles. Sandpipers and swallows flew in clouds, and in the marsh the red-winged blackbird tucked her song beneath her wing.

In the dunes the hares developed a scent the gray fox could follow, and in the marsh the muskrat made a tentative selection of winter quarters. The otter ranged far and in the night his whistle was a distant locomotive.

231

The life of the sea also felt change. Tuna coursed east, the killers in their wake. Cod and haddock began an inshore movement and the whiting went into the surf's first roller. Bluefish followed the whiting into the surf and the scup turned south. Off the beaches the young of the menhaden were nearly four inches long and the adult fish had disappeared; some said the pogy fleet had taken all of them, but they had merely moved into deeper water, a movement which was scarcely more than a drift accomplished on the ebb of a high-course tide.

Off Plum Island and Parker River, off the estuary of North and South Rivers, off the Gurnet, outside Saquish and Clarks Island, off the Cape Cod Canal and Sandwich Harbor Creek and Scorton Harbor Creek, on shoals, the young striped bass began to school, school joining school, for southward migration, a movement wholly depending upon the movement of bait fish, which, in turn, depended completely upon the development of weather.

Roccus, mending slowly, felt a similar urge, though the schooling fish were mostly between five and fifteen pounds. Pods of the larger migrating fish usually formed later. She began to feed on the fugitive small bait, on a few late soft-shelled crabs. She mended slowly.

On the last night of the August moon, while a tempest cloud covered the crescent, Roccus dropped back through the narrows down, down the river and into the pulsing sea. Her wound had not healed completely and never would; she swam with half the strength of her usual tail thrust and only half her eagerness of questing. Otherwise she had the fair health of old age and a sudden desire to be gone to the far waters of her birth. With the tide she dropped back, until she reached the Mashnee Shoals at the western approach of the canal.

232

THE SPOTTER PLANE for Webb Everly's seiner was a fast-crawling fly on the bright pane of the sunset sky. Clifton Hartwell, from his captain's walk, trained his glass on it and followed its course across the bay between Butlers Point and Bassetts Island.

Weeks of watching had taught him much about the operation. For one thing, it wasn't true, as Everly had stated, that the pilot boarded the seiner each evening; and Hartwell told himself he had been a fool, especially in the light of his knowledge of the seiner's infrequent anchorages off the point, not to have realized this before. Everly had sought to bilk him of a larger share for the flier on an excuse of double jeopardy, but he had established the fact that the latter was seldom aboard the boat.

Hartwell observed that there was some contact nearly every evening between vessel and plane. Almost daily, just before darkness fell, the seiner stood in from the general vicinity of Cleveland East Ledge; and the plane, having finished a survey of many square miles of water, circled near her, not too obviously. Through some signal, perhaps radio, the plane communicated to the seiner the location of the largest schools of bass. After contact the plane flew straight for the airport in Wareham and the seiner stood offshore again. Twice in the small hours Hartwell had located the vessel in the moonpath close inshore, in areas where, having marked the plane's actions, the banker knew schools of fish had been located.

His mind sharpened by acute suspicion, the banker was convinced that the air spotter located many more

233

fish than showed in Everly's weekly accounting of profit. He could not be positive that most of these fish were being seined, but he wanted to believe they were and he did so believe, the belief adding fuel to the flames of his resentment. Hartwell was a man whose strongest fear was to be bested in a financial transaction of any kind.

Since his showdown meeting with Everly he had nurtured a plan to cram Everly's deceit down his throat; and this plan, having been born in anger and developed in contained fury, incorporated certain elements of risk which he would not normally have embraced. He recognized this, weighing all the chances, and still was determined to carry it through to a conclusion when the best opportunity arose.

The opportunity, it appeared, as he watched the air spotter, might develop this very night. He watched the plane go through maneuvers that he had come to recognize meant the sighting of stripers. Flying at about five hundred feet beyond the Stony Bar sand spit it climbed sharply and circled over the sandy shoals, throttled down, turned back on its course and made two tight circles at diminishing altitude. There were bass there, under it.

The sun vanished. Hartwell watched the plane climb to about fifteen hundred feet and disappear against purple cloud down the bay, where, though he could not pick her up, he knew the seiner would be waiting. He continued to watch as dusk fell, taking two bearings on the area over which the plane had circled. Then, though he could not see it, he heard the distant drone of the aircraft's return.

He cased his glass and went down the ship's ladder from the captain's walk and leisurely ate a dinner to his taste. His mind was made up but there was no need for hurry. The tide would fill at about two o'clock in the morning and he knew Everly preferred to work after midnight and especially on a flood tide.

When it was full dark the southwest wind died away and the bay ripple died with it. There would be no fog and, until about three o'clock in the morning, no moon. Conditions were ideal for his purpose. He summoned the housekeeper and told her he was going out on a matter of business and might be very late. Then he changed into woolen clothing, filled a thermos with coffee and strode down to his private float.

The cruiser he maintained mostly for appearance's sake lay moored about seventy-five feet off the float. He had no use for her. On the float, overturned, was his ten-foot plywood dinghy. He launched it and tied it up. Then he fetched a five-horsepower outboard from the boathouse and secured it to the dinghy transom. In the bow he placed a cement block as counterbalance for his own weight on the stern seat. Soon after ten o'clock, taking a bearing on the Stony Bar spindle, he set forth.

Hog Island Channel was chunky with the weight of tide but not uncomfortable though he crossed diagonally to the current. Out of the rip, on shoal, he ran parallel with the dike for a mile in smoother water. Then he met the cross-rip at the end of the dike and swung through it to placid water inside. Here he cut his motor and took to the oars. Almost at once he was over bass.

There was a big school or there were several schools of fair-sized fish. They swirled and splashed under his bow; the surface was agitated over acres. He rowed in to the beach, noting the frenzy of thousands of small bait in the very shallow water. Then he carried the outboard motor into the grass above high-tide mark and dragged the light

235

dinghy up beside it. He scuffed the drag track in the sand though this was a precaution not based on the plan in his mind; if the plan was sound the tide would have covered any mark he left. He crunched into the grass and sat down to lonely waiting.

Despite the stars the darkness was a smother, pressing. The only sounds were those of the tide on the beach and an occasional distant engine churning in a canal-bound vessel, and, close by, the bass on the feed, driving the bait that skittered like rain, sometimes landing on the sand. The tail smashes of big fish were like pistol shots.

The night was seasonably warm and Hartwell was comfortable in the grass. Once he dozed. He roused himself with coffee. At one o'clock he took a turn up the beach and stared down the bay from the end of the dike. He could distinguish nothing. The masthead lights of vessels passing east into the canal with the serving tide rode the grass tips like the lights of Nauset mooncussers. Impatience grew in him but he resumed his hide by the dinghy. Was Everly coming? Had the plane located other schools farther out that the seiner might be working? Wouldn't it be better to call quits to an expedition more than a little foolhardy?

His stubborn anger supplied the answers. He stayed. He dozed, roused, dozed again.

It was close to flood peak just before two o'clock when he became aware of the seiner. She was rounding the point of the dike in a soundless drift, showing no lights. Two hundred yards distant he could make out her single mast with the barrel lookout. Her hull was a space which did not reflect the stars. He heard a block squeal, heard subdued voices, heard one voice raised: "It's lousy with fish."

236

He could not see the seine boat put off, but he heard the thuds of the cork buoys payed over the gunwale, and then he made out the shadow of the boat moving under two pairs of oars. It moved with the tide a distance, then turned for the beach quickly and swung parallel with it over two or three feet of water. It passed so close he could have tossed a handful of sand into it. Two men rowed, one still payed seine. They conversed in low voices. One said, "We'll make three fat hauls unless the fish move," and the man in the stern, "The Christly net is heavy already."

Then the boat angled off the beach at a swifter pace toward the shadow of the vessel, and a turmoil began on the surface within the closing circle of the seine. The closing and hauling took the better part of an hour, during which a new school of bass moved into the bait-filled waters already hauled. From the seiner came the steady thump of clubs on bass heads, the sound of bass being tossed into the hold. Then the Diesel came to life with a subdued roar immediately throttled. Hartwell swore softly, fearing he had missed his chance. But Everly was merely holding position against the newly turned tide. His vessel moved forward against the new current for a hundred yards. Her engines died again. Her seine boat began a new sweep.

Hartwell moved quickly then. He lifted the dinghy into the water, leaving the motor behind. He rowed swiftly down the beach, knowing he would not be seen against its shadow, and passed far below Everly's position in order to make an approach from the seaward side.

Hartwell rowed hard and silently. With the seine boat away again, Everly might be the only one aboard; at most there would be one other. Everly would be at the pilothouse. He circled outside the seiner and moved under her stern. He made fast and peered aboard and in the binnacle light saw Everly's capped head in silhouette, saw the glow of his cigarette. He was alone. The banker climbed aboard and stepped softly to the pilothouse.

"Looks as if we're doing better tonight," he said.

Everly jumped and said, "Jesus!" He yanked his visor, turned and peered. "What you want here, Hartwell?"

"Merely to see how you do it and how well you do. That first haul will net me a bigger share than I got for all last week's fishing. And there are a lot more fish in there."

"So what? What are you getting at now?"

"I'll take my rightful share hereafter. I've known all along I was being cheated."

Everly yanked his cap again. "You'll take what you deserve—what we decide to give you. Now you know."

"My third, or else."

"Else what?"

"I'll report to the authorities that I suspect a boat on which the bank holds a mortgage is engaged in illegal seining."

Everly laughed. "By Christ, I think you would! How'd you get here?"

"Ran across in my dinghy after watching your spotter plane this afternoon."

"Who'd you leave a trail to follow?"

"Nobody, naturally."

Everly flipped his butt overside. The shadow of the seine boat ahead was turning toward the beach.

"Hartwell, you ever figure you might not get back?"

A small fear leaped in the banker's pulse. "What do you mean?"

"I mean you're here. Suppose we decide it's best you don't get back? What do you think my crew will do when I've told them what you said?"

Hartwell saw his mistake. "It was a jest—a joke. Of course I couldn't afford to make any report."

"Why not? There's no evidence you're involved."

"I wouldn't. You know it."

"I'm not so goddamned sure! I'm not so sure but the best thing to do with you is to weight you down a little and toss you overside. Better still, just hold your head under water and overturn your boat for someone to find."

All the chances Hartwell had weighed had not included this possibility, any possibility of physical violence, of murder. He didn't think Everly capable of carrying out the threat but he wasn't sure, and he was less sure of Everly's crew. And it was true enough that if he was found drowned, his boat upset, it would look like an accident.

He said quickly, fear rising in him, "There's been talk of seining, as you know, and if anything should happen to me you might be suspected. I'm getting out of here. There'll be no report to authorities but I want it understood I get my rightful share."

"You're not going anywhere right now," said Everly. "That's what I understand best."

Hartwell, his bravado punctured, was indecisive. He weighed his chance in a dash for the dinghy against the likelihood of Everly's violence. It was only a moment or two but time and sound were magnified in it. He seemed to feel the tide falling; he heard a restless tern, the splash of the seine boat's oars, a deep-throated motor in one of the engineers' boats on the other side of the dike. He said, "Listen, Everly . . ."

239

Everly, listening, but not to him, said, "That god-damned boat ain't in the canal and it ain't an engineers' boat! It's rounding the point!"

Even as he spoke a powerful searchlight swept along the inside beach, caught and held the vessel, the distant seine boat. A voice hailed from an onrushing cruiser. The seiner's Diesel roared to life. Hartwell jumped from the pilothouse but Everly's foot sent him sprawling on deck.

"Stay and take it with the rest of us," said Everly. He cut the engines as the other vessel bore down, her searchlight blinding. *Carey's Chicken* leaped alongside as Cal Knight threw her into reverse. Three men wearing badges and sidearms boarded the seiner.

"You're under arrest. Call in your boat."

"To hell with you," snarled Everly. He bellowed, "Drop your seine and run for the beach."

"It doesn't matter," Cal called. "Everly's your man. Who's that with him?"

"Who are you?" a warden demanded of Hartwell.

The banker couldn't answer.

Everly answered for him. "Why, that's Banker Hartwell of Bournham. He's backed this enterprise and worked with us and grabbed all he could of the profit. Your evidence is in the hold if there's none left in the net."

"It's a lie!" Hartwell screamed. "I suspected him and was checking up. You'll find my motor on the beach."

"And my money in his bank account," said Everly.

THE PHLOX blew white and coral and red beside Stormy's house and were dropping their petals.

"I like the white best," said Father O'Meara. "It may revert if you don't watch it."

"I know," Stormy said. "Mr. Sears warned us. He planted it for us."

"Years ago, I've heard, he had a beautiful garden."

"It's only a garden of dreams now."

"That interests me. You asked Clystie to stay with you?"

"Of course. She said she'd prefer the rooms in town, where she could be close to Maddox and Donnie. Donnie seemed good yesterday, Father. How is Maddox?"

"Maddox has a tough skull. I never could get a suggestion through it. I think it is mending, having hardened against all my abuse. I think Maddox will be around again, God willing. We still can't know for sure. Do you see Clystie?"

"As often as I may."

She believed she had seen through the priest for weeks. Cal had admitted he'd confided in him about Pickman Brown, and she suspected Father O'Meara was trying to help her forget by focusing her attention on his own problems, pretending she might share the weight of them. It had helped, yet it was Cal and his undeviating faith in her and his love for her which had saved her. There was only a little of the nightmare left. Someday—she knew when it would be—that time on *Tiderunner* would be, as Cal had promised, erased from all time's computation.

241

"Are you fond of her?"

"Clystie? Very much. Without being able to understand her."

"Someday we'll all understand her—as Maddox, I think, does."

"Maddox did well in his love of her."

"He did. He would. I would not have expected less from Maddox."

"You're fond of him."

"Strong fond of him."

"Will she marry him—will Clystie marry him?"

"If he recovers I hope she will; I cannot know. There are many things here under the surface. Some I still may only guess at. You resemble Clystie somewhat. Had you ever realized? Something about your features—you might be taken for a younger sister."

She snatched a head of phlox in her reaction. She heard a voice saying, as she had many times before: *"You're the one looks like my little girl who went away."*

"Father!"

"Let's go in," he said. "Will there be hotting for the tea?"

September

To THE COURTHOUSE of granite blocks and fluted pillars under the ancient elms of Barnstable, Clifton Hartwell, too emotionally distraught to drive, rode as a passenger in his own car, his attorney at the wheel.

He had experienced a fearful night, knowing it was only the beginning of humiliation and exposure that were likely to destroy his career.

In the beginning he had been locked up in a cell at the Bournham police station, in the same cell with Webb Everly. It adjoined a cell shared by a pair of boisterous town drunkards, one of whom had recognized him and welcomed him with a profane discourse which the banker had feared was audible over half the town.

It had taken him an hour to contact his lawyer and arrange for the release of Everly and himself on their own recognizance, for later arraignment in the district court at Barnstable. Without thanks and without commitment as to his future intent, Everly accepted this gesture. Hartwell whispered all manner of entreaties and promises in an effort to induce his surly co-conspirator to clear him, an argument finally compounded on promise of handsome financial reward. But in the approaching dawn outside the police station they had parted company without an understanding.

The banker went home, showered and shaved and tried to snatch a nap, but he could not sleep. Soon after sunrise he made a pot of coffee, which he drank black, and smoked a cigar that was sour on his tongue. His attorney, who was also the bank's counsel, reappeared at eight-thirty and they discussed various aspects of the case for the first time. Hartwell insisted that he had become suspicious of Everly's activities and, in the interests of the bank's investment, had determined to make a private investigation. He labored the point that his hiding of his outboard motor, in order to approach the seiner undetected, was proof of his innocence of any connection with the enterprise.

"If I'd been in with him I certainly wouldn't have been sneaking up on the vessel. Everly's vengeance is his plot to implicate and destroy me. He suspects I gave him away."

"Did you ever report to any authorities your suspicions regarding Everly, or discuss them with anyone in the bank?"

"No. I considered it more or less a personal matter— a bank matter—and I wanted the evidence first. I'm not given to making loose charges, as everyone knows."

"Then it's Everly's word against your own unless they catch up with the members of his crew. The police recovered your motor, which is evidence supporting your defense."

The banker was nearly led into saying that he didn't think the crew knew of his participation. He barely checked himself in time. How much, he wondered, had Everly told them? And what were the chances they would be caught?

"You realize what this will do to me in this town regardless of the outcome?" Hartwell asked, and answered himself, "There'll always be some to believe. There are plenty here who have been envious of me and unfriendly."

The attorney nodded. He was, though he could never say so, among the number who would believe in Hartwell's guilt.

Driving from Bournham, the banker caught himself slinking in his seat and hastily sat erect to stare out with an air of general hostility, meeting the gaze of several acquaintances whose expressions, his imagination told him, indicated they had heard the news of his humiliation. They had not, but they soon would.

It was a beautiful morning along the old highway with the sun of the new September bright on the dunes of Sandy Neck and a gold-leaf edging for the marshes. He felt no appreciation of beauty. His heart hammered with the approach to the courthouse. He had little knowledge of the interior of the county seat except that here were recorded, in land court, the deeds of property on which his bank held mortgages, upon some of which it had occasionally been to his profit, and pleasure, to foreclose. He had never been inside a criminal courtroom, not even as traffic violator or witness. The palms of his hands were wet and his stomach churned. He wished he had eaten something.

The judge of District Court was an elderly man from an old Provincetown family with which Hartwell was not acquainted, and the banker searched around in vain for a glimpse of someone with whom he had influence.

245

It quickly developed, to his consternation, that the proceedings were a little out of the ordinary. Present were not only the marine wardens who had made the arrest but the law enforcement officer of the State Department of Conservation. Everly sat on a front bench without counsel and talked with one of the wardens. Once he turned and boldly met the banker's eye without sign of recognition.

There was a protracted bench conference during which Hartwell felt forsaken, his apprehension choking him. His fears were realized when his attorney returned.

"There's more trouble than we anticipated. There's a complaint asked for violation of the seining law and there's application for a warrant for conspiracy, one likely to issue with a hold-over for grand jury action and the jurisdiction of Superior Court. Also the Commonwealth is moving in the civil session with a libel for forfeiture of the vessel."

Hartwell mopped the back of his neck.

"The State claims to have Everly's complete confession involving you," the attorney said. "Also it has the identity of one of his crew, an airplane pilot whom, Everly said, you refused to pay his worth."

"They're lying," the banker said. "They're all lying. It's a plot."

"I don't doubt it. But there's something else. Do you know a Calvin Knight?"

"He brought the wardens last night."

"And a priest, Father O'Meara?"

"A meddler. One of the Roman Catholic meddlers."

"The State professes to have them as witnesses to several visits made to your home at night by Everly, though it's not likely the priest will testify."

246

"Everly came once or twice on bank business."

"I have no doubt of that either, but it may be difficult to convince the Court."

The hearing was brief. The complaints issued. The State didn't oppose the request for continuance; it needed a little time to apprehend the pilot of Everly's plane.

The Provincetown judge weighed the status of the defendants.

"Release Mr. Hartwell on his own recognizance. I'm sure he'll be here." He smiled. "The bond for Mr. Everly is five thousand dollars."

Hartwell knew that ruling would hurt, increasing Everly's resentment.

His knees were too loose as he moved down the corridor. He rested a hand on the arm of his attorney.

Near the main door he saw a youth of dark complexion being hustled along, handcuffed to a deputy sheriff. The prisoner seemed dazed. His eyes were shadowed mirrors reflecting the fear in Hartwell's eyes and the banker turned his head for a quick second glance at Manuel Riba.

ORDINARILY LABOR DAY would have found Judge Wickett back in Boston inspecting his judicial robes for the ravages of moths and studying the annual grist of the legislative mill that ground through most of the summer. But that was before he angled.

"Would you mind very much if I stayed on here a week or so while you return home?" he asked his daughter.

"Of course not, Dad. But aren't you overdoing it—this fishing business? It's supposed to provide relaxation, but

247

you don't even look as if you'd had a vacation except
for your tan. You're thinner and your eyes are tired. Ever
since you saw that big one you've been on the go night
and day."

"I'll take it easier," he promised, knowing he wouldn't.
"Besides, the Chief Justice isn't back from Honolulu and
the assignments haven't been made up for the fall sitting. There are enough judges available for the grand
jury reports."

He saw them off eventually and went down to the
locker for his rods. He'd keep them handy in the kitchen
and work on his lures. He was rigging his plugs with
heavier hooks and he was using 8/0's behind double spinners for trolling. He sought only big fish, one big fish in
particular.

UNDER THE stars of midnight Clystie Harrow walked to
the rectory where Rosie Carmody, gray-pigtailed, resent-
ful, opened the door.

"Perhaps Father O'Meara will see me."

"In his dreams, though I doubt it," said the housekeeper. "He's asleep these two hours and it's time all
decent people were abed. What is it? Unless it's a matter of life or death I'll not be waking him. Is it the last
rites?"

"No," said Clystie, "and there's no matter of life or
death involved. I guess it is urgent only to me."

"He's an old man and lately he's not been well at all."

"I'll come tomorrow then."

"Very well. Who are you? You're not of the parish?"

248

"Miss Harrow. I was of the parish."

"Wait now. Miss Harrow? I mind he spoke of you recently and said you might be coming. I'd best wake him. Come in."

Clystie followed into the study, where the housekeeper lit a second lamp. Rosie climbed a steep stairway and her knocking resounded through the house. Clystie heard the priest's sleepy response, heard Rosie call, "It's Miss Harrow. She's come," heard a mumbled response. When Rosie returned she said, "He'll be down in a bit. I will pour you some tea."

"Thank you. I wouldn't think of troubling you."

"The trouble is only an extra cup. I just brewed a pot. It may be stronger than you like but there's hot water." She started from the room but turned abruptly. "You wear no hat," she said.

"No. I'd forgotten."

"I'll get you a hat; you should have a hat." She vanished for a minute and reappeared with a green velvet creation of her own. "It's not new; it's ten years old, in fact, but it will serve the purpose. It's my best."

"Thank you," Clystie said. She tried it on, adjusted it. "So?" she asked.

"It becomes you," Rosie said. "If it looks half as good on me as it does on you I shall cherish it another ten years. Now I'll fetch the tea."

It was a quarter-hour before Father O'Meara descended, the sleep rinsed from his eyes, the white tufts of his poll fringe standing stiff. He greeted her with a warm and hopeful smile and interrupted her apology. "I thought you might come and left word I wanted to see you whatever the time."

"I should have come long ago. As you know, I told Mad-

249

dox some of it. It was not in contrition. That was emotional. It was an attempt at justification. I was trying to excuse myself."

"Yet it was good that you told him. It is better that you come here."

"If you will hear me."

"I will hear you if you come for the sacrament of penance, repenting of mortal sin. I believe you would not have come otherwise."

"I have had long days and nights with the problem of extenuation. There is no self-justification. I know the sin and I regret it, and I am ready to accuse myself."

"In complete faith?"

"In the faith that I tried to lose and could not."

"Come," he said. "Follow me. The church is through this way. 'Whose sins ye shall forgive, they are forgiven them.' . . ."

He snapped on the altar lights, knelt stiffly in their general direction. She was on both knees.

"The church is never locked and never empty, Clystie Harrow," said Father O'Meara. "I come here in the darkness and I feel His Presence. The confessional is over here. You have not forgotten?"

"I remember," she said. "I've always remembered. There is the prayer of 'Now I beseech Thee to accept me,' and there is the prayer that is supposed to follow Holy Communion. May I say some of it now?"

"Of course," he said.

She bowed her head.

" 'I give Thee my body that it may be chaste and pure. I give Thee my soul that it may be free from sin.' Those are the two lines, Father."

His knees ached and he expected this would be a long

250

one. Yet he felt fiercely uplifted entering the confessional. "Come home," he said. And suddenly there was no weariness in him.

When they had finished she said, "I'll stay here awhile alone."

"You will. Snap the lights off when you go. Here is my rosary. I'll see you tomorrow. God bless you."

He left her alone, and she was not lonely. She lit a candle and walked to the altar rail and knelt there. When she left the day was tiptoeing in, peaceful and radiant. She felt at ease for the first time in years; she knew a peace disturbed only by the exultation of realization that she was at peace.

In the half-light she walked to the hospital. The night superintendent, going off duty, said, "Your son is improving so swiftly he's getting to be a problem to keep in bed."

"And Chief Maddox?"

"He had another good night. I wouldn't be surprised if his name came off the danger list in the morning."

To THE submerged granite boulder on the Bird Island ledge, where she had paused in her migrations of many years, Roccus made her way driven by the urge to begin her southward journey. For three days of early September she occupied this hold. She gained strength as the wound at the wrist of her caudal healed despite its fouling, and her appetite returned. Here in May she had fed upon Anguilla, and here now the eels dropping back from the rivers to spawn swam in abundance and were tasty and nourishing.

251

These were bright days of mistrals at dawn, warming surface water through the hours of sun, and cool nights when the pattern of the universe beyond earth was mirrored on the frosty tides.

No striped bass joined her on the Bird Island ledge and on the night of the third day of her lie there she returned to the Mashnee shore. The instinct of early migration remained strong within her, but she was possessed by a stronger urge to seek the company of her kind.

Off Mashnee smaller bass were beginning to school. Some had passed through the canal from Cape Cod Bay, others were from the rivers and harbors adjacent to the canal's west end. These fish were restless, undetermined in their movements, uncertain, wavering with the tidal changes, held in the gathering place by the flow of feed on the canal edge, waiting on the weather.

Roccus joined a school of bass in the fifteen- to twenty-pound class. She was neither welcomed nor made unwelcome. She swam in a flanking position like an outrider edging a herd of cattle.

THE NURSE asked, "Do you feel well enough for company, Chief Maddox?" She had been in and out and he had pretended to sleep and she knew it. "Maybe," he said. "It depends upon the company, nurse."

"There's someone down the hall who's been badgering us for days to let him in—a fellow who says he knows you. Claims he's been fishing with you."

Maddox lifted his head too quickly and felt the ache stab through it. "Youngster named Harrow?"

252

"Yes."

"Bring him in."

She opened the door and pulled in the wheelchair bearing Donnie Harrow. The boy's eyes, throat and right arm were swathed in bandages.

"Hi, son," Maddox said. "Over here, Donnie. Wheel him over, nurse."

"Jeff, my eyes are okay. I can see good. We tried yesterday and this morning."

"That's something, Donnie, isn't it? A fellow needs his eyes to appreciate a good-looking woman like your mother."

"Yes. Jeff, there was a big fire. I remember you taking me out when I was hurt."

"Well, you better get well fast now for the fall fishing. We both got to be out of here mighty quick."

"You bet we will, too," Donnie said. "Will you take me fishing again, Jeff?"

"Just as soon as we can get going, boy."

"We can maybe catch a big one, Jeff, the biggest striped bass ever caught."

"We'll try, and be satisfied with smaller," Maddox said.

He watched the boy turning this over in his thoughts.

"Jeff?"

"Yuh?"

"Will you be my father?"

"I sure will," said Maddox.

The nurse came in. "Time to go, Donnie. Back to your bed now."

"I want to sleep here with my father," Donnie said.

"Not now, Donnie. Chief Maddox isn't all mended yet and you have to get your rest."

253

"I want to sleep with my father," the boy persisted.

"Bring him over and tuck him in, nurse," Maddox said.

"I shouldn't, sir."

"You should. Bring him over."

She wheeled the chair close to the bed.

"Can you lift him in?"

"I think so."

"I can climb it. I'm a good climber, Jeff."

"Climb it, son," said Maddox. He reached out a bandaged arm to give the boy a lift. The exertion was painful but Donnie came aboard.

"Take out the wheelchair and let him rest awhile with me."

Nurse and wheelchair disappeared. Maddox felt the warm buttocks tucked into his belly. He heard beside him the suddenly relaxed deep breath, then the slow, steady breathing of a child who sleeps, reassured against all fears.

He laid an arm across the blanket covering his companion. His hand felt the small head, brushed the temple hair. He leaned over, tempted to kiss the space where a cowlick swirled, but he did not.

The twilight fell and the boy slept on while the man remained awake.

"I'm glad you're both in the hospital," Clystie said.

The statement, Maddox thought, needed a bit of analyzing. He and Donnie, the boy's eyes unbandaged, lay in the elm-cooled shade of the hospital porch, Clystie Harrow's chair between their beds. Stormy Force and the professor had just left.

"So we can get out?" asked Maddox.

"So you'll not be going to the Bournham Theater next

week. They've been running old B pictures for the first half of double features and next week it's *The Vagrant Wind*. That's the first picture I was ever in."

"Mother, you in a movie?"

"For about two minutes, as I remember, and it was a long time ago."

"I want to see it, Mother."

"Me, too, son," said Maddox.

"I was pretty awful and the film wasn't much better than my small part."

"I'll tell Stormy and she can report to Donnie and me."

"Don't you do it. . . . Maddox, my son's sight is un-impaired."

"Yuh. I thanked God for it."

"I slept with my father. Didn't I, Jeff?"

"You did," said Maddox.

"Thank you, Jeff," said Clystie. "In a while, a little while, I guess, if you still feel the same. . . ."

"And not because of the fire."

"I showed you before the fire."

"Guess you did at that. Okay, I can wait. You look nicer than I've ever known."

"I'm at peace, Jeff. There's only one small worry left and when the time comes I will tell you."

Donnie climbed into Maddox's bed and snuggled up. Clystie kissed him on the cheek and then her hair was around Maddox's broken head and her lips on his, quick and warm.

"So long, you guys," she said.

THREE PODS of bull bass which had summered in Cape Cod Canal, one group of fish individually approaching half the size of Roccus, joined the school to which Roccus had attached herself. Two days later more than one hundred striped bass from six to twelve pounds each joined up. All acted in response to the same urging that moved the matriarch for company of her species in a journey of varying lengths, none short, to the warmer waters of early life.

In the rips and backwaters the young menhaden and herring and the silver eels were plentiful. The nights were noisy as the bass fed and fattened on them. Only Roccus fed and strengthened yet did not grow in size. Despite her healing, her feeding, her strengthening, she continued to waste away.

Now the nights were cold, and the surface water, from the night air, was sometimes colder than the depths, and in the limitless element above the sea migrating birds were a-wing to lesser latitudes, quiet in their passage.

MADDOX LAY on his side with his back to the door and heard the step on the bare floor.

"How are you, Father?" he asked.

"The extra eyes will be behind the devil's ears," said Father O'Meara. "You are a laggard pretending if you can name your visitor without seeing him."

"I always see better when I'm not looking. For instance, you're tired—pretty close to being pooped out."

"Weary enough in the flesh, Maddox, but the spirit is rosy-cheeked. Why do you say it?"

"Your game leg is a bit gamer from the sound of your tread."

"Then 'tis the devil's ears alone."

"Wading the midnight surf—fishing, no doubt."

"Well, you are not far from being right. It was an incoming tide and the stars were bright upon it."

"Did you catch anything?"

"God did. I merely handled the leader at the last moment."

"Then Clystie visited you. She did not tell me, but I guessed."

"She did, she did."

"I'm glad, Father. For her, for you and for God."

He turned over slowly so as not to set his head pounding.

"Hi!" he exclaimed. "Damned if you don't look bushed! How old are you, old man?"

"Of an age sufficient to have grown armor for repulsing the shafts of impertinence. How are you coming?"

"Well enough, they say. There was no depression of the fracture and Nature merely has to take her plodding course. I'm a thick-skulled son of a bitch anyway."

"I'll accept the adjective, having used it in my own description of you. The noun you may ask forgiveness for."

"So I may. But drag up a chair and give me all the news. What about Manuel?"

"I saw him this morning. He was indicted for homicide. I told him you'd been injured, and how. He sent his very

257

best wishes to you and asked me to give you a blessing."

"Will you?"

"I've always asked God's blessing on you in my prayers."

"I know. Has Clystie found her peace? She says so."

"I think she has."

"It was not to have been found through me, though she tried."

"As I expected her to. Her faith was always there, Maddox. What of yours?"

"You're trying to catch a double now, Father."

The quickly-assumed aggrieved expression was an old trick of the priest's in his dealings with recalcitrants. Maddox, early in their relationship, had analyzed it and considered himself immune to it. Yet now he felt himself under its influence.

"In the fire, when the beam fell, I prayed a second time. That will not have any particular significance for you because it was in desperation. I needed help and I was terribly afraid. Yet the other night was another matter."

"Tell me of the other night."

"It was like a big wave with the long swell of the ocean behind it, smothering over me. I had my arm around a child."

"Do you still feel the same?"

"I do. So when I get out of here, as they tell me I will, I'll come to you, too. Will you shake my hand, old man of the Church?"

Their hands met in a long grip, that of the priest as strong as that of Maddox.

"Is that woman going to marry me, Father?"

"I hope she will. I'll tell you this, Maddox: there is an

apprehension in Clystie Harrow not based now on any fear for herself. I have tried to guide her in the acceptance of something she must do. If she does not do it, then I must do it myself—a duty unpleasant but necessary. Someday very soon it must clear up and then I think she will marry you."

Maddox punched his pillow. "Then everything will be all right."

Father O'Meara pushed back his chair. "I must be along. Next visit I'll bring delicacies for your long gut."

"A man idle abed puts on belly without eating. I feel well fed and drowsy. Take the delicacies to Riba and the money for them you'll find in my trousers unless somebody thieved it. Tell Manuel that Maddox sends his best. I didn't think highly of him but I thought of him. Wait, Father; come here."

The priest stood beside the bed.

"You're still blaming yourself."

"I am. I always will. I am forgiven but I will not forget."

"God knows how you worked with Riba and so does everyone else. Old friend, I love your bones. They and your soul are almost all of you. . . . Give me your hand again."

SURF WAS a daily, changing pattern like Brussels lace spread on the golden beaches. This was summer's end.

Soon after noon of this day, Stormy Force saw Mr. Sears pass her home on his way to the movies. He walked his usual quick step, his head bent slightly forward.

"There goes Mr. Sears to the movies," Stormy remarked

259

to her father. "There's an old one in there you might like to see tonight—*The Vagrant Wind*."

The professor's response was unexpected. "I don't recall it but I'll take a night off and go with you." He'd been accumulating dust at his typewriter and she knew he realized that a change of any kind would be beneficial.

Stormy didn't notice Mr. Sears' return from the pictures that afternoon, but along about six o'clock she saw him heading back down the road from his house again, and he was moving with a sort of jog trot, faster than she had ever seen him before, glancing neither to right nor left. Now and then, for a few steps, he would slow to his accustomed walk.

She called her father's attention to him and Professor Force said, "Why, he actually seems possessed! If he's going to the motion pictures he'll be an hour before the evening show."

"Let's drive along in and we can pick him up," Stormy suggested.

"We can have a frappé before the movies and kill some time at the bookshop."

The bookshop settled it so far as the professor was concerned. They picked up Mr. Sears before he was far along on his walk-trot journey. When they pulled up beside him he climbed right in without saying a word. He didn't start his usual humming.

"You're early for the performance, Mr. Sears," the professor said.

"Oh, no," said Mr. Sears. "Got to hurry some. Fine performance there this week."

He lapsed into silence. He didn't mention any big fat hens, nor the state of the weather or the garden. He didn't comment on the old apple tree. He seemed com-

260

pletely occupied with the need of getting to the theater in short order. The only comment he ventured was "Car goes slow, don't it?" Professor Force was driving, for him, unusually fast.

When they swung into the main street of Bournham, Stormy invited Mr. Sears to join them in an ice cream. "No, no, can't do that, girl," he said. "I got to hurry for the picture. Let me out at the picture house."

"The box office won't be open yet," the professor said.

"That's good," said Mr. Sears. "I'll be first in line."

Professor Force stopped the car across the street from the theater. The marquee lights weren't yet on. Mr. Sears scrambled out on the off side, not bothering to close the door behind him. He didn't voice his thanks as, always before, he had done. He rushed around in front of the car and fell there and did not move. Stormy screamed. The professor swore.

Mr. Sears had suffered a stroke they saw when they reached his side. He was partially paralyzed but his tongue was clear.

Professor Force and Stormy attempted to impress upon him the need for lying quiet until a doctor arrived. A policeman joined them. Mr. Sears refused to be quiet. He recognized Stormy and said, "You look like her, girl." He got to his hands and knees, weaving, and said, "Got to get to the pictures. What time is it? Have the pictures begun?"

The professor was trying to convince him that a half-hour still remained before the box office would open when the small crowd parted to admit Father O'Meara. The priest, accustomed to such situations, made a quick appraisal.

"Stormy."

"Yes, Father O'Meara."

"You know where Clystie Harrow is rooming?"

"Of course."

"Go to her there. Tell her that her father is dying."

Mr. Sears had collapsed on the black top. The priest began the office of the last rites.

Mr. Sears died at the hospital that night.

"I'm convinced his physical hurts didn't amount to much." It was Professor Force in his analysis to Stormy. "He kept leaving his bed. Twice they caught him at the door of his room in his johnny, trying to get away."

The news left her bereft but without sorrow. "He wanted to go to the movies," Stormy said.

"To the movies and his cranberry bog," said her father. "He mumbled about them constantly before he died."

"And he was Clystie Harrow's father. Father O'Meara knew it some time ago."

"So he may have. I didn't. Did you, Stormy?" She was leaving the room to replenish his tea. "Did you, Stormy?"

"You were the little girl who went away," Stormy Force said.

"Yes," said Clystie Harrow. "It's true I went away—ran away."

"You're the reason he went to the movies every day without knowing the name or plot of a picture. He was just searching for your face."

"Yes, Stormy."

Cal Knight said, "One time he must have seen you in

the movies and ever after he went in the hope of seeing you again."

"That would have been years ago," Clystie said.

They stood on the slope outside Mr. Sears' home. Clystie had seen the inside; Stormy had taken her through the rooms as Mr. Sears had left them since her mother's death. She held in her hand the fragile stems of the long-dead old-fashioned pinks from the bedside vase of her mother's room.

"Didn't you ever correspond?" Stormy asked. "Didn't you know he loved you?" She succeeded, she thought, in keeping accusation from her voice.

"Oh, yes. I wrote many times after I went away. From Boston, from New York, from Hollywood and London and Paris. I never heard from him."

"But he must have written."

"No," she said. "He never did. For a time, when I could, I sent checks to him. He never cashed them. He didn't need them. All he ever wanted of me was a memory. He never left the Cape in his lifetime. It was only when I went into pictures that I could return to him."

"He adored you. I know from things he said."

"I loved him deeply," said Clystie. "These last months, living a few miles from him, loving him, were a horrid torture. Yet I knew he would have wanted it that way. You see, there was a condition that caused me to leave and prevented me from returning, a problem that could not be resolved."

Cal thought she shouldn't but Stormy plunged on. "Is your mother alive then? Most folks think she ran away with you."

"That's what I hoped," said Clystie. "I had to go. You see, I didn't admire my mother, nor respect her."

263

Cal cleared his throat noisily.

"All his life," Stormy said, "all his life after you went away he lived on dreams. There was never anything of the present for him except that daily search of a movie screen for your face; he recognized you in that picture just before he died."

"There was something else," Cal said. "His cranberry bog."

"And that, too, I suspect, was of the past, of his dreams." She turned to Stormy. "Will you go there with me now?"

"Of course."

"I'll go, too," Cal said.

They walked across the road to the woodland and Cal led the way on the downhill path that Stormy once had taken. Clystie followed him and Stormy, her. There was again there, under the sun, a sense of cool, damp shadow. There was the same eerie stillness. The leaves of the scrub oak, browning, did not stir. There was no whisper, rustle, or whimper in the pines. The brush was voiceless. Underfoot the scarlet pimpernel and the St. John's wort still flourished in ragged patches and Queen Anne's lace was cupped into nests. The goldenrod and the thistle still bloomed.

"My father," said Clystie Sears, "was a wonderful man. He was the last of a family prominent on the Cape since the colonists settled the land—an only child, early orphaned by storm at sea, with a sufficient inheritance to maintain him in the only manner of living he ever could comprehend. The old house on the bay was his birthplace. That and these many acres were his. He had a foodstore in bay and garden, sufficient fuel in the woodland. He had no ambition but to live in peace and contentment in the midst of beauty for all his days."

Her voice, low and throaty, was unshaken, Stormy thought.

"It may have been said he lived a solitary, purposeless existence. Purposeless in the sense that he never felt a need of anything beyond his reach. Yet I sometimes think that is a state of mind we all are striving for. For whatever artistic sense he possessed there was a magnificent collection of pottery which had been in the family since the days of the Wellfleet clippers. He had that, and always the tranquil beauty of the bay. He was content."

"Best view on the Cape," Stormy heard Mr. Sears say.

The path now wove downhill gradually. Stormy checked a question; she had asked too many.

"My mother," said Clystie Sears, "was a beautiful woman. She was a great deal younger than my father. The only time in all his life, I've heard, that he ever paid any attention to a woman was when he courted my mother. Why she married him, God only knows. She was a Bournham girl, an orphan of French parentage, and she had been a state ward. I think she was the most beautiful woman I ever saw, bold-featured with molded cheekbones, straight strong nose and sensual mouth. Her hair was as black as an old squaw's dark winter plumage. She had eyes that smoldered. She was lithe, quick, tireless, forever wearing an expression of desire. Her beauty trapped him."

There was a small scampering in the brush ahead of Cal, not close. It could have been a rabbit. It ceased abruptly but Stormy's heart beat faster for it.

"Her beauty consumed him in its fire. I can guess that as early as he married her he was afraid of losing her. As a child I could sense a distance between them and came close to measuring it and to guessing, as I grew

265

older, at its cause. She was too young, too gay, too thoughtless—a vain and selfish and passionate woman as restless as the wind. She wanted to be ever on the go, to dances, to the movies, to socials—with him or without him. She was too young and he was too old to hold her. He was too old, and knew it."

Cal called back, "It's cool but close in here."

Clystie would not stop; Stormy was sure Cal hoped she would. The dam of her reticence had collapsed.

"My mother's mind was as shallow as a rain puddle. She had no capacity to appreciate my father's fineness. Yet he admitted to no lack in her. He never blamed her. He pretended she was not responsible for what she was. He was set in his ways and could not change them even if he would. He blinded himself to her misbehavior, and the more flagrant it became the more exalted she became in his professed misconception of her. He built around her, during their unhappy life together, a dream of the happiness he had hoped their life together would become."

She turned, smiling. "Are you tired, Stormy?"

"No. Let's go on."

"He gave her many beautiful things which had been in his family for years. He deeded house and land to her. They meant no more to her than the worthless bric-a-brac, the cheap pretentious knickknacks to be found in any dime store—the things she bought of glitter and tinsel. She made no effort even to pretend to understand him. She contacted a real estate broker to sell the land and his home. She wanted a place in town. All she ever desired she demanded. What he could he gave. He sold some antiques. When she had an offer for the property, far under its worth, and would have accepted, she discovered there was a clause requiring his permission for sale. He wouldn't give it. This was his home. I was old enough then to know her bitterness, her hatred. For money she nagged him into starting a cranberry bog. The land below here was well suited, swampy, with a flow of brook, and a sandbank. At her insistence he built the bog. He hated it. Do you know why?"

It was Cal who asked why.

"Because the attention it required kept him from her presence. He still adored her as much as she detested him."

Cal moved slower in the lead. The brush was dense on each hand—blueberry in high-bush with wasted, shriveled berries; black alder and gray beech among the sparse evergreen. The silence, during the little pause of Clystie's voice, seemed an ominous silence.

"Toward the end she forced him to know what he did not want to believe, the truth he had tried to avoid. That she had never loved him. She told him. I heard her tell him—lying in my own room across from theirs, beyond those closed doors a cat could chase a mouse beneath. It was that year she died, the year his bog was to have borne its first harvest. I was sixteen then and I loved him and I knew enough of her and life to . . . Well, I said I didn't admire her. She was not a discreet woman. No part of her in reality was a reflection of the dream he clung to. I knew why, each Saturday, she would send me to town on errands when he was leaving for the bog. Many in Bournham knew why."

Cal stopped and uttered an exclamation. He had reached the foot of the hollow and ahead was an expanse, flat, of more than an acre. Here once, long years before, there had been a cranberry bog, or the start of one. Likely it had never borne more than a few berries before the

267

wilderness encroached. Pines, now taller than a man, had rooted in the bog; brush in rank growth filled the squares of the irrigation ditches, with alder saplings along them. Dark woods frowned from the slopes. It was as desolate as a Ulalume landscape but Clystie said matter-of-factly, "He just let it go to ruin. You can tell he never harvested a crop."

Stormy heard Mr. Sears' voice: *Mighty struggle with the worms. Expect a good crop though.*

"The path goes off across the bog," Cal said. "Shall we go on?"

"Now that we're here," said Clystie. And, as Cal straddled an overgrown ditch: "That day—that morning—she sent me to town as usual after my father had gone to the bog, I knew she was getting ready to clear out. I hoped she would go. That was a terrible thought, something I've dwelt on for many years. I knew what it would mean to him, but still I hoped she would go, that she would leave us."

"You just be sure you can manage her, boy," Mr. Sears said. *"My wife was a great hand for pretties . . . My wife used sit for time on end just looking at the view."*

The path came to a small clearing near the center of the bog. Here the brush had been carefully cut away but instead of cranberry plants there was a great mound of old-fashioned pinks, a few in second bloom. Seed pods emptied by the sun stood as brittle as the stalks in Clystie's hand. Here, Stormy thought, as in that room of the faïence vase and dust and dreams, there was no motion of life. Death lies dead, she thought, in a phrase of Swinburne.

There leaned, in the center of the pinks, an ancient Salem rocker, one arm gone, its finish completely eroded.

"I missed that chair from the house," said Clystie Har-

268

row. "My father gave it to her. She used it only because she despised it least of all the furniture. He told her it was hers because he enjoyed watching her in it. She hated him watching her and eventually came to hate the chair."

She was crying, Stormy thought, though her voice was unshaken.

"That day I returned early from town. I caught a lift both ways. All my life since, I've wished I'd walked.

"Father, too, had returned early from the bog that day. My mother was dressed in her best. She lay beside her packed bag just inside the front door. The shotgun blast had not touched her face. Her expression, in death, was that of the woman his hopes and mind had remembered. She seemed sweet and devoted and gentle and thoughtful and kind, with a new beauty on her face I cannot describe—a beauty of release and peace, perhaps.

"And when he lifted her and carried her from the house across the road and down the path toward this bog I experienced a feeling I have never since been able to shake off—that for the first time she was returning an embrace to which, in life, she never had responded.

"My father saw me and said no word. I did not speak to him. And that was the last we ever saw of one another until last night."

Though the sun was high its light shone dimly. This was the hour when Whitcomb Sears would have completed his morning vigil at the grave of the woman he could not keep except through death. It was the time when he would have been starting up from the dank tarn to resume his daily search of a movie screen for a glimpse of the daughter who had gone away.

They stood there only a brief time. Clystie Sears said,

"Let's leave it now. Father O'Meara says I must go to the district attorney as a formality. Then I will go to Maddox."

JUDGE WICKETT needed those extra weeks after departure of his family and the regular summer colony to attempt the readjustment of his mental processes. His equilibrium had been violently upset by his unfortunate encounter with Roccus. His ideals as well as his sound common sense had suffered. For the first time since the death of his wife he was involved in an emotional reflex that influenced his every thought and action. The first had been grief—sorrow deeply rooted in a great love that had ceased to be. This, the second, was an anger, first smoldering, then aflame, resulting from the obvious disbelief of even those who had been closest to him.

He was frustrated and bitter to a degree that, in a man of lesser character, would have led to violence on one or another provocation. His leadership of the colony had been undermined by his story of the huge fish; his position as a solid member of the community was threatened. The experience he had widely related, his phobia for fishing, which was a result of that experience, made him a laughingstock among some groups and among others the object of a sympathetic attitude more galling than open disbelief.

So he needed those extra weeks for attempted readjustment. But he also needed them for a final attempt to catch Roccus, the only means by which, his lately twisted mental processes decreed, he could establish again his old reputation for unquestioned integrity and judgment.

He fished.

He fished and caught several bass which, to his annoyance, were progressively smaller; and he had many strikes from small bass that were not caught on the big hooks he was using. Some of these missed strikes from small fish, he imagined, might have been from Roccus. He tired, aged, began in some strange fashion to resent himself.

One day in late September, on returning to the huge emptiness of his summer home after another long and unsuccessful trolling trip near the ledge where he had seen Roccus, he found awaiting him a letter forwarded by his daughter from the Chief Justice of the Superior Court, an old, admiring friend who wrote informally that he had just returned from Hawaii and had been delayed in making out the fall assignments. He wrote:

> After conference with the chief clerk and every consideration of the dockets, it is impressed upon me that your experience and talent are most demanded in the sitting at Barnstable County not far removed from your own summer place. I sincerely hope this will not be at conflict with anything you may have in mind. There is a heavy docket of important cases, the list enclosed.

Judge Wickett experienced a pleasurable reaction. Sitting in Barnstable meant that he could remain here, with a considerable time for fishing, at least until the cold weather set in. He must write his daughter to ship his things down. He didn't mind getting his own meals.

He scanned the separate sheet, the docket, listing the cases scheduled for his jurisdiction. There were a burglary, three cases of armed robbery, a conspiracy to extort, a violation of seining law on appeal from lower court. There was one capital case, he noted. His eye ran along the line:

Commonwealth versus Manuel Riba, homicide.

271

He laid the list on his desk and went out to his workshop where he was turning a new bass plug, a plug for big fish.

Roccus FELT the change of pressure on the weight of waters at the Mashnee gathering place of the tides. Of the great and growing school of bass she alone felt it, being wiser in age and experience. It was a subtle change, not marked, telling her that heavy weather was definitely approaching, though not yet close. Only five barometers hinted this change; most did not. Yet next day all the school felt it, the larger fish first.

It was a signal for application to appetite, for satiation beyond appetite, for gorging against the needs of a journey that would begin at the height of the storm and allow no interval for seeking food. With the storm the school might move along to Cuttyhunk or to Sakonnet area, or even as far as Montauk Point; it would positively move from Mashnee and during passage it would not feed.

Roccus fed almost exclusively on the migrating eels, whose oily flavor, more pronounced now than that of young menhaden, she somehow needed. These she pursued at leisurely pace, approaching them from behind, accelerating to seize them broadside at the head. Some she bit in two, others she swallowed whole. Her best hunting was at night when the eels were most active, emerging from their hiding places.

Because a high-pressure area from Canada slowed the storm's progress up the coast from Hatteras, the weather held fair beyond the time Roccus' instinct told her it would foul. The barometer even showed a slightly upward trend.

So came a cloudless night of thin moon, nearly dark o' the moon, a windless night, the sea flat, cold flat except for a distinguishable offshore ground swell. In the marshes, gathering, black ducks were raucous. A flight of geese went over.

IT HAD been a good summer, Bobby Meade thought, and there was still a month or more of fishing if the weather held as it promised to do. True, the tuna hadn't lingered, but the bluefish run had been spectacular and there was a sufficiency of big bass to keep the striper addicts on edge. *Carey's Chicken* had done well but charters were tapering off as they always did after Labor Day. And he knew Cal was wanting back on the Vineyard. Cal was going to get himself hitched up to a wife and things wouldn't ever be the same again. Not that Bobby didn't like Stormy, he told himself; he did. But what's a guy want to go get himself tied up to any dame for?

"Hey, Cal?"

Cal Knight thrust his head from the cabin and winked up at where Bobby sprawled on the dock. "What's bothering you, mate?"

"You reckon on fishing next year?"

"Sure do. Why not?"

"Just wondered. Who you going to take along for mate?"

"Well, I don't know. You quitting me?"

"Thought you might be making a change."

"Hadn't thought about it. You've learned and you've

saved and Father O'Meara and I've been able to keep you in hand. Good report for your ma."

"When you getting yourself hitched up?"

"The man doesn't set the date, mate. It's up to the lady and she hasn't said. First off, I'm taking her back to the island to visit my mother."

"Figured so. When you going?"

"Oh, end of the month, likely. Charters'll be about done and the weather gets moody-like. You wanting to get back?"

"Naw. Let's fish through October. It's bound to be hot fishing."

"Next year we might."

So, he could tell, things wouldn't be the same. Cal'd always fished October other years. A woman changed a guy.

"You never made another plug like I lost on the big fish."

"Haven't had time to turn it out." He grinned. "Maybe I mean I had other things to do. Look here, squirt. Come down and turn on the bilge pump and get this cabin squared away. We got a special guest tomorrow."

"Stormy Force, I bet."

"No. Father O'Meara. It may be our last chance to fish him."

"He made up his mind to go to Worcester?"

"I think he has but he doesn't know it himself."

"There's more striped-bass bugs come out of Worcester than off the Cape."

"I know. Maybe he's going to reform 'em."

Bobby jumped aboard and switched on the bilge pump. It hummed and went *squirt, squirt, squirt.*

"I'm no squirt," Bobby said and Cal laughed.

274

"You know it's coming on to storm, skipper?"

Cal studied the late afternoon sky, the cirrus, the edge of cumulus distantly visible on the western horizon. "Guess you're right, at that."

More proof, thought Bobby. You let a guy get his mind on a dame and he goes around in a daze, even unconscious of the weather signs.

"You're not going fishing this day," said Rosie Carmody.

"I am that," said Father O'Meara. He sat at the breakfast table, having changed from his vestments after early mass. A heavy mist washed the windows of the rectory kitchen and the wind driving it came from the northeast.

"I'll not be letting you."

"You'll what?" he thundered in mock anger.

"Wisdom comes with age. Which is an old and trite saying having no foundation in fact. No sane person would be out in the weather of this day and it blowing up. You hear it?"

"I hear it. See that your ears are as quick when I tell you of a button off or a hole in my sock. We'll be fishing in the lee of shore, Knight said, and I can stay in the cabin if it gets bad."

"You can but you won't. You'll come home wet to the skin like a little boy and sniveling with a cold. And you know what the dampness does to your knees."

"Have on the eggs," he said. "I'm having one more go of it."

"You'll be taking Worcester then?"

"It may be."

275

"You'll not. You'll not give up the fishing!"

She knew that was iron in his soul, and he forbore an answer. He had felt more at ease mentally after a long talk with Thomas Salter and a good night's sleep. Certainly, in accordance with his faith and high hopes, the problem of Clystie Harrow and her son was working out, and the conflict within Maddox was being resolved as God would have it. Riba, and his own personal lapse in Riba's case, remained a concern he could not put aside.

He left Rosie grumbling. He was glad of his foul-weather gear before he reached the dock where *Carey's Chicken* bobbed in her bridle, all bumpers outboard. The rain—it was no longer mist—drove on the rising wind.

Cal hailed him. "Come aboard, Father. We'll find a lee and I'll almost guarantee you a fish."

"God's blessing on the boat and those aboard."

Bobby gave him a strong hand down the ladder.

"There's coffee, Father," the boy said. "Too strong from Cal's heavy hand but hot for your insides." He poured a cupful for the priest and, as Cal warmed the engines, climbed to the wharf and cast off.

The priest sipped his hotting and decided, regardless of Bobby's criticism, it was better than Rosie's brewing.

"There'll be some protection off Mashnee and Hog Island and in Phinney's harbor," Cal said. "I'd hoped we could fish Scorton because the bass are schooling there, but it's tough shore in a northeaster and this will be getting worse. But there are plenty fish where we're going and they'll be larger."

Father O'Meara heard Rosie's voice again. He said, "I don't care whether we take a fish, Cal. It's just wanting to be out and I'm grateful for the storm. Maybe it will blow the cobwebs from my brains."

"I guess there's no dust on them, Father."

No dust? He wondered. Old things were apt to gather dust and he was beginning to feel very old.

They ran through a heavy chop across the canal, but the water off the windward shore was comparatively calm.

"What'll it be, Father, casting or trolling?"

"I'd rather troll, Cal; I'm a bit weary."

"Eelskin or spinner and worms?"

"Whatever you recommend."

"I heard geese last night, southing. On the island and down on Cuttyhunk when the storms begin and the geese start moving we like a whole rigged eel."

"Have you one aboard then?"

"A half-dozen in brine, all rigged. Break one out, Bobby."

From a wooden pail of brine Bobby drew a twenty-inch eel rigged with three 9/0 hooks secured to forty-five-thread tuna line threaded nearly the length of the eel alongside the backbone.

"Scrape it, Bobby."

Bobby used a knife blade to scrape the black skin. The resulting color was silvery-blue.

"Looks good," Cal said. "Almost eat it myself. Take the heavy copper rod, or the heavy glass; both have forty-five-pound test line. Better make it the glass; it will be lighter for Father. Fish the eel long and deep, Father, and, Bobby, you pop a plug over it. That sometimes works."

"How's your lady, Cal?" the priest inquired. He fought down a rising interest in the fishing.

"The best, Father. She's going home with me end of the month. I'm hoping we'll be married around Christmas. I almost wish we were Catholics so you might marry us, but you'll have Bobby when he's met his match."

277

"I ain't getting married, not ever," the mate said.

The priest laughed. "I've celebrated many a nuptial mass for those who have said the same."

He stood with his back inside the cabin, most of his body sheltered, but the hood he had pulled over his poll was soaked from the drive of the storm.

Cal cut the throttle and Bobby dropped the eel astern and passed the rod to Father O'Meara. The priest stripped line against a drag set too tight. Bobby put a popping plug overboard.

"You getting out, Father?"

"Oh, yes." The priest seemed preoccupied.

"About one hundred fifty feet with that rig."

"Very well." He really was preoccupied. He stripped mechanically, but his thoughts were jumping between the rectory and Barnstable jail and Worcester; and they were in Worcester when, as he still stripped line, a fish struck with tremendous force, yanking him from the cabin doorway and arcing the heavy glass.

"Hold on!" he gasped.

Cal laughed. "You hold on, Father. That's a mighty big fish. Ease up the drag. How's he feel?"

"Heavy, lad—and heavy on my soul."

"You in, Bobby?"

"All clear, skipper."

"Go to work, Father."

The fish tore line against the drag, the priest struggling. The wind whipped back the hood of his rubber parka and the storm beat on his dome. He backed up to the cabin bulkhead.

"Bobby," he called, "pass me the knife. . . . Where's the knife?"

"What's wrong, Father?"

278

"There's nothing wrong, now. It's just come right. The knife, lad, and quick now."

Bobby passed him the knife and the priest held the blade of it against the line above the reel. The line *twanged* and the freed end snaked through the guides and disappeared across the stern into the gray chop.

"Cal."

"Yes, sir—yes, Father."

"Will you head in now? You don't mind?"

"No. Are you all right?"

Father O'Meara smiled. "All right," he said. "A penance only. This is mine, self-imposed. I shall not fish again."

"Not ever you mean?"

"Never again."

"You'll be missing it."

"So I will."

"You'll be going to Worcester then?"

"I will not," said Father O'Meara. "I'll be staying on. I'll not be running from the temptation. The greater the temptation . . ." He stopped. "I will tell you what I never told anyone but God. That evening before he killed in the tavern, Manuel Riba came to the rectory looking for me, seeking my guidance. I wasn't there. I was off on the beach, fishing. . . ."

DOWNTIDE, sounding, Roccus fought her doom with the utmost of her half-mended strength. Her savage strike had driven the head hook of the rigged eel through the roof of her mouth, and the barb of the middle ·hook had pierced her tongue and lower jaw. As pain stabbed her

279

and she swirled, the tail hook of the false Anguilla slapped under her open gill cover and secured itself in her rakers.

A resistance which sought to turn her course, a sensation she had experienced in other misadventures, quickly ended. But one hook bled her gills, and the others, like a chain bolt on a door, secured her jaws, nearly locking them. Her breathing became labored. She was in a state of slow suffocation.

She surfaced in a flurry of panic, violently shaking her head, circling, creating a disturbance which in decent weather would have attracted the gulls from afar. This day the gulls were on the beaches or the pierheads or the rocks, or riding the updrafts of the wind above the faces of the dunes. None observed her.

She drove for bottom again, but not to rest. Although the pain of the hooks, a sudden reflex of her nervous system, subsided, there grew within her a feeling of bursting and a terror of the unknown that gripped her jaws. Without sense of direction or purpose, regardless of changing pressures, she swam swiftly about, often striking the rocks.

This phase of her struggle lasted for hours, but her strength waned as the day waned and the storm gathered itself for night assault. Finally her terror vanished and her aimless movements ceased; and in the late afternoon, the ebb tide nearly spent, herself spent, she gave herself to the tide, unconscious, drifting with it, her fins moving only from the turbulence of the water, and an uncontrolled trembling in all her muscles. Her tail was completely paralyzed.

Through the quickfall of night, into the first of the tide's resurgence, life clung to Roccus rather than she to life.

Then it was full dark and, though the heavy clouds

completely obscured the new moon and the constellations, there came a moment when it seemed as if Roccus had entered again the spangled shallows of her youth. The golden burst of Capella in Auriga fired the sea. Bright were Deneb and Altair and Algol, and bright was Jupiter below the Great Square of Pegasus. And suddenly all of the planets and their moons, every one of the myriad stars, were pouring down the tide, streaming down the tide that had turned for home.

Author's Note

In the somewhat intricate construction of *The Shining Tides,* I have taken certain liberties which will be recognized by all familiar with Cape Cod. These include the founding of a new town, creation of a new river, recommissioning of the Wings Neck Light, others of a minor nature. Like the town and the river, all principal characters are wholly imaginary and any resemblance to persons living or dead is entirely coincidental.

The size of Roccus is roughly based on an estimate provided by Dan Merriman of The Bingham Oceanographic Laboratory, Yale University. Though some may challenge her leaping in the strict sense of the word, she leaps because many years ago in the Weweantic I saw her leave her natural element.

For the inspiration to complete what proved to be for me a formidable assignment, for suggestions and assistance far beyond the scope of their ordinary professional duties, I express my gratitude to Frances Phillips, John Willey and Thayer Hobson, all of William Morrow & Co., Inc., and to Helen Strauss of William Morris Agency, Inc.

WIN BROOKS